Chelsea st ▮▮▮▮▮▮▮▮
at what sh D0283181

The fat, laughing baby slapping his ▮▮▮▮ against the water in the tub so that showers of droplets exploded all over the place. And the big man kneeling on the floor beside the tub, one hand firmly around the baby so he wouldn't fall, while the other ran a washcloth over a round little belly.

Garrett had stripped off his T-shirt. And he was laughing as much as the baby. A deep, rich sound that made her shiver.

Suddenly he scooped the baby out of the tub and wrapped him in a big, fluffy towel. "Do me a favor and take it from here, Chelsea?"

Her eyes burned and her throat closed too tightly for words to emerge as Garrett gently placed her sister's child into her arms.

Dear Reader,

We've got some great reading for you this month, but I'll bet you already knew that. Suzanne Carey is back with *Whose Baby?* The title already tells you that a custody battle is at the heart of this story, but it's Suzanne's name that guarantees all the emotional intensity you want to find between the covers.

Maggie Shayne's *The Littlest Cowboy* launches a new miniseries this month, THE TEXAS BRAND. These rough, tough, ranchin' Texans will win your heart, just as Sheriff Garrett Brand wins the hearts of lovely Chelsea Brennan and her tiny nephew. If you like mysterious and somewhat spooky goings-on, you'll love Marcia Evanick's *His Chosen Bride*, a marriage-of-convenience story with a paranormal twist. Clara Wimberly's hero in *You Must Remember This* is a mysterious stranger—mysterious even to himself, because his memory is gone and he has no idea who he is or what has brought him to Sarah James's door. One thing's for certain, though: it's love that keeps him there. In *Undercover Husband*, Leann Harris creates a heroine who thinks she's a widow, then finds out she might not be when a handsome—and somehow familiar—stranger walks through her door. Finally, I know you'll love *Prince Joe*, the hero of Suzanne Brockmann's new book, part of her TALL, DARK AND DANGEROUS miniseries. This is a royal impostor story, with a rough-around-the-edges hero who suddenly has to wear the crown.

Don't miss a single one of these exciting books, and come back next month for more of the best romance around—only in Silhouette Intimate Moments.

Yours,

Leslie Wainger
Senior Editor and Editorial Coordinator

Please address questions and book requests to:
Silhouette Reader Service
U.S.: 3010 Walden Ave., P.O. Box 1325, Buffalo, NY 14269
Canadian: P.O. Box 609, Fort Erie, Ont. L2A 5X3

THE LITTLEST COWBOY

MAGGIE SHAYNE

Silhouette

INTIMATE MOMENTS®

Published by Silhouette Books

America's Publisher of Contemporary Romance

To the Otselic Valley Lady Vikings soccer team of 1995.
You're #1 in my book!

SILHOUETTE BOOKS

ISBN 0-373-07716-5

THE LITTLEST COWBOY

Copyright © 1996 by Margaret Benson

This edition published by arrangement with Harlequin Books S.A.

® and TM are trademarks of Harlequin Books S.A., used under license.
Trademarks indicated with ® are registered in the United States Patent
and Trademark Office, the Canadian Trade Marks Office and in other
countries.

Printed in U.S.A.

MAGGIE SHAYNE

lives in a rural community in central New York with her husband and five daughters. She's currently serving as president of the Central New York chapter of the Romance Writers of America and has been invited to join the National League of American Pen Women. In her spare time Maggie enjoys speaking about writing at local schools and conducting a romance writing workshop at a local community college.

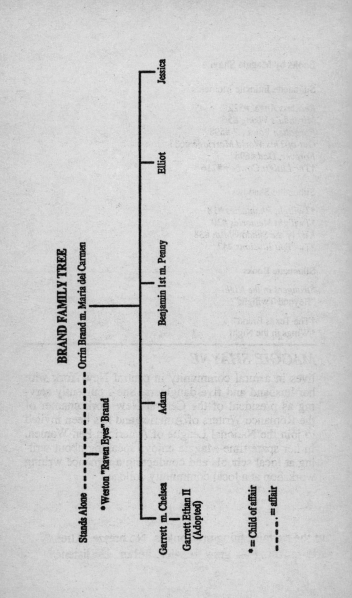

BRAND FAMILY TREE

Stands Alone ---- Orrin Brand m. Maria del Carmen

* Weston "Raven Eyes" Brand

Garrett m. Chelsea   Adam   Benjamin 1st m. Penny   Elliot   Jessica

Garrett Ethan II
(Adopted)

* = Child of affair

- - - - = affair

Chapter 1

Garrett Brand awoke in a cold sweat, some foreign kind of dread gnawing at his stomach. Heart pounding, he sat up fast and wide-eyed, his fists clenching defensively before he got hold of himself. Blinking the sleep haze from his eyes and taking a few deep breaths, he let his tense muscles relax and unclenched his fists. There was nothing wrong. There was no reason for that panicky feeling that had slipped through him like a ghost slipping through a wall. No reason at all.

And still he couldn't shake it. It hadn't been a bad dream. Far as Garrett could recall, he'd been sleeping like a bear in January until that odd feeling had jerked him awake.

Okay, he'd just take stock.

He sat in the middle of his king-size bed and scanned the room. Red sunlight spilled through the open window, but the curtains hung motionless. No breeze. Already the early-morning air grew heavier, hotter. He listened, but didn't hear anything he hadn't ought to. A horse blowing now and then. A handful of songbirds.

Still, the feeling that something was wrong remained. Garrett had never been much for ESP or any of that nonsense. But stories he'd heard about mothers knowing instinctively when something was wrong with their kids floated through his mind now. He was no mother to Wes, Elliot and Jessi. No father to them, either. But he was as close to a parent as they'd had in almost twenty years. He'd only been seventeen when Orrin and Maria Brand had been killed in that car accident, leaving him as sole caretaker to his five younger siblings. And when he thought about anything happening to any of them...

An odd sound reached him then, a sound that made the hairs on his nape prickle. Soft and faint, but out of place, whatever it was.

Garrett pulled on his jeans, socks and boots in the space of a couple of seconds. He didn't bother with a shirt. But he did yank the revolver out of his top dresser drawer and gave the cylinder a quick spin to be sure it was loaded. On the way out, he snatched the black Stetson from the bedpost and dropped it on his head. It was a gesture so automatic it was done without forethought. Like breathing.

Softly, Garrett moved along the hallway to the next bedroom. He was glad of the braided runner covering the hardwood floor. It cushioned and muffled his steps. He stopped outside the door. Elliot's room, though if you looked inside, you'd think it belonged to a ten-year-old boy, not a man of twenty-five. Lariats and spurs decorated the walls, along with a collection of hats and framed photos of champion cowboys. His closet was an explosion of fringed chaps and hand-tooled boots. Only the sizes had changed over the years. Elliot's dreams never had. He'd lived for the rodeo since he'd been old enough to say the word.

Garrett held his Colt, barrel up in his right hand, and pushed the door open with his left.

The hinges creaked loudly when Garrett stepped through, and Elliot's sleeping face twisted into a grimace. "Whaddya want?" he muttered, still half-asleep.

Relieved, Garrett stifled his sigh. "I thought I heard something is all. Go back to sleep." He backed toward the door.

Elliot sat up, his rusty hair so tousled he looked like an angry rooster. "What the hell you doing with the gun, Garrett?"

"I told you, I thought I heard something."

"So you're gonna *shoot* it?" This as he climbed out of bed in a pair of baggy pajama bottoms with rearing mustangs all over them.

Garrett shook his head, not ready to discuss the odd feeling that had awakened him. "I'm going to check on the others."

"I'm coming with you," Elliot said with a pointed look at Garrett's gun. "Just in case you've been so responsible and levelheaded for so long that it's finally driven you over the edge."

Garrett sent him a glare, but Elliot only returned a wink and a crooked grin as he grabbed his hat off the dresser and plunked it on top of his unruly red hair.

They slipped into the hall, and Garrett moved past the next two doors. Adam and Ben had gone their own way last year. Adam had hightailed it to New York City, ostensibly because of a job offer in some bigwig corporation. But everyone knew he'd really moved away because Kirsten Armstrong had left him at the altar to marry an older, richer man, and Adam couldn't stand being in the same town with her anymore. Ben, of course, was trying to find some peace. The hills of Tennessee, where he was living like a hermit, wouldn't heal him, though. Only time could do that, Garrett thought. Ben's young wife had died just about a year ago, and even though they'd both known she was terminal before they'd married, the blow of finally losing her had almost done Ben in.

Garrett and Elliot reached the next room. Wes's. If there were trouble, Wes was likely to be involved. Oh, he'd calmed down a lot since prison. But he still wasn't over the anger of being sent there unjustly. It was a rage Garrett supposed would eat at a man for a long time. And with Wes's temper...well, an explosion always seemed within shouting distance.

He tapped on the door, didn't walk in the way he'd done with Elliot. Wes was still pretty riled up over returning home to find his half brother wearing a badge. And he'd developed a real touchy attitude about privacy, too, while he'd been away. No sense pushing his buttons by walking in unannounced, gun in hand.

The door opened and Wes stood there looking more like a Comanche warrior than a Brand at that moment, despite the jeans and pale denim shirt. His dark hair hung to his shoulders—longer than a man of thirty ought to be wearing it, Garrett thought—and his eyes gleamed like onyx. His Comanche mother had named him Raven Eyes, and Garrett had always thought it incredibly appropriate.

"What is it?"

Garrett shrugged. "I'm not sure. Did you hear anything unusual just now?"

"No, but I was—"

A high, soft sound interrupted Wes, and he went rigid. It seemed to come from farther down the hall, and all three heads turned in that direction. Jessi's room. A second later, the three of them stampeded for their twenty-two-year-old baby sister's door. Garrett saw Wes pull that damn bowie knife of his from his boot with a move so quick and smooth and practiced, it seemed to have just materialized in his hand.

They stopped outside Jessi's door, and the sound came again. Not a normal cry. But obviously one of distress. Garrett's blood ran cold when he tried the knob and found the door locked. He didn't even think about it first. He just stepped back and kicked it open. Three Brand men exploded into Jessi's bedroom at once, one holding a Colt, one wielding a bowie and the other poised with fists raised in a boxer's stance, though the effect was probably ruined by the horsey pajamas.

Jessi screeched as she whirled to face them. Then she just rolled her eyes and shook her head. "You idiots! You almost scared me right outta my slippers!"

"Sorry, Jes," Garrett told her, feeling more foolish by the minute. "I thought I heard—"

"Me, too," Jessi said. "But it's coming from outside." She jerked her head in the direction of her open bedroom window.

Garrett lowered his revolver, sighing in relief. "You okay, Jessi?"

She only smiled and shook her short-cropped head in vexation. "How could I not be with you three on duty?" Giving her bathrobe sash a tug for good measure, she shouldered past them, apparently on her way downstairs to investigate the noise.

It was Wes who gripped her shoulder and gently stepped in front of her without a word. She made a face at him, but stayed behind him as they headed through the hall to the wide staircase and started down it. Wes and Garrett in the lead, Jessi and Elliot behind them.

"I think you guys are overreacting. Sounds like a lost calf or something."

"Shh," Elliot warned, but Jessi had never really known when to shut up.

"Garrett, you haven't got the sense God gave a goat if you think anyone up to no-good would be lurking around the Texas Brand. Everyone knows you're sheriff of Quinn."

"Be quiet, Jessi," Garrett ordered. They'd reached the bottom of the staircase. The parlor spread out before them, but there was nothing out of place. The huge fireplace they used only rarely. A wide picture window on the far left side that looked out over the lawn and the driveway, and the one on the back wall that faced the barns and unending, flat green fields beyond. They gave no clue. The knotty hardwood walls had nothing to say. The golden oak gun cabinet stood silent, its glass doors still locked up tight.

Blue wasn't in his usual spot in front of the window, though. That alone signaled something wrong. That dog barely moved enough to breathe.

They continued on through the wide archway into the dining room and through that to the kitchen.

The front door loomed at the far end, and there was ol' Blue, poised beside it. Not growling, though. His tail was wagging. *Wagging!* Hell, he was about twenty dog years past his wagging days. He stared at the door, tilting his big head from one side to another. His ears as perked as ears that long and floppy could perk. The two black spots above his eyes rose in question as if they were eyebrows.

Garrett tried to swallow, but it felt as if his throat were full of sand. He knew his family—and apparently his dog—thought he was overreacting, but he couldn't shake this feeling, this ominous certainty that something *drastic* was about to happen. Something *horrible* must be awaiting him on the other side of that door.

"Stay here," he said. "Until I make sure it's safe."

"Always the hero," Jessi muttered.

Garrett ignored her and moved forward as his stomach tied itself up in knots. He unlocked the front door and opened it to step out onto the porch.

And then he just stood there, gaping.

A basket sat at his feet. A big basket. And inside the basket, rapidly kicking free of the thin blankets tucked around it, was a fat, smiling baby.

Garrett's gun clattered to the porch's floorboards. He stared down at the infant, too stunned to do much more than push his Stetson farther back on his head.

From behind him, he heard, "Well, I'll be..." and "Who do you suppose..." and "What in the world..."

The baby, though, only had eyes for Garrett. Blue eyes, so blue their whites seemed to have a slight blue tint. It stared at him hard, and then it smiled again, a small trickle of drool running from one corner of its mouth to its double—no, triple—chin.

Blue pushed past the crowd in the doorway and stood two feet from the baby. He looked from it, to Garrett and back again.

"Gaa!" the baby announced.

Blue jumped out of his skin and retreated a few steps.

"Ooohh," Jessi sang, and then she was passing Garrett, scooping that baby up into her arms and snuggling it close to her.

"Garrett, there's a bag over there, and it looks like a note's attached," Elliot said, pointing.

Garrett saw a little satchel with blue and yellow bunnies all over it. A thin red haze of anger clouded his vision, and with his hands on his hips, he turned to face his two brothers, ready to knock their teeth out. "So, which one of you is responsible for this?"

They just looked at him, then at each other.

"How many times have I talked to you about responsibility? Huh? How many times have I told you what it means to father a child? It means you take care of it, dammit. It means you marry the woman and you—"

"Um, Garrett?"

"Not now, Jes. But pay attention. You need to hear this, too. Don't ever let any sweet-talking cowboy with no sense of honor, like either one of these two fine examples right here, talk you into—"

"Garrett, you better read this."

Something in her voice made him clamp his jaw shut. Wes and Elliot, though, both looked decidedly uncomfortable, and he could tell they were mentally going through their list of one-night stands to determine which of them might have resulted in this mess! Garrett wanted to scream and rant and shake them. He'd tried so hard to instill some ethics into them, to be a good example. He never drank, never whored around town the way some did. Hell, he'd been working so hard at showing them how to be men, he'd become known as the most morally upright, impeccably mannered, responsible, reliable, stand-up guy in the state of Texas. To think that one of his own brothers...

"'You were more kind to me than anyone I'd ever known,'" Jessi began, and Garrett came to attention when he realized she was reading from the note. "'Though it was only for one night, I never forgot you.

And I knew I could count on you to take care of our son when I realized I no longer could.'"

"You ought to be pretty damned proud of yourselves," Garrett muttered. Blue sat down close beside him, staring at Wes and Elliot, as well.

Jessi read on. "'He's six months old this week. He hates strained peas, but will eat most anything else.'"

"Well, now, that much is obvious," Elliot joked. But no one laughed.

"'I named him after his father. I only hope he'll grow up to be half the man you are.'"

Garrett felt his two brothers tense beside him when Jessi looked up, her eyes round and dark brown.

"Go on, Jessi," he urged. "Read the name."

She blinked at him, eyes wider than a startled doe's before she lowered them to the page once more. "'His name is Garrett Ethan. But I call him Ethan. Please, Garrett, love him. Just love him, and I'll be at peace.'"

He'd been poleaxed right between the eyes. For a second, he didn't move, and nobody else did, either, except that Wes and Elliot seemed to sag just a bit. Relief would do that to a man. Then Garrett shook his head at the absurdity of it all and snatched the letter from his little sister's hand. His eyes sped over the lines.

"Hell, this thing isn't even signed!"

"What's the matter, big brother," Elliot chirped, thumbs hooked in the waistband of his baggy pajama bottoms, a lopsided grin pulling at his lips. "Been so many you can't remember her name?"

Garrett grated his teeth and drew a breath. Calm. He needed calm here. "This is bull. I didn't father that kid any more than Sam Houston did. It's bull."

"Sure it is, Garrett." Elliot shrugged and glanced at the squirming baby anchored on Jessi's slender hip. "Well, I'll be damned...."

"What?"

"He has your nose!"

Jessi joined Elliot in laughing out loud.

"Dammit, Elliot—"

"Maybe the sainted Garrett Brand has more of his father's genes in him than we realized," Wes broke in, but there wasn't an ounce of humor in *his* voice.

Garrett flinched at the barb, and turned to his sloe-eyed brother. "Wes, I didn't speak to Pa for six months after I found out about his affair with your mother, and that was *before* I realized he'd fathered you and left you behind to come back to us. I wouldn't do something like that."

Wes didn't answer, only lifted his black brows and slanted a glance at the baby as if its very presence proved otherwise.

Garrett groaned. "I can't believe you guys don't believe me."

"Oh, sure, Garrett! The way you'd have believed us if the little lady had scrawled one of our names on that note, right?"

Elliot had a point, the little bastard.

"Stop all this caterwaulin'. You're scaring the baby!" Jessi rocked the wide-eyed child in her arms and cooed at him. "Doesn't matter who fathered him, does it? He's here now and we'll just have to deal with it. Wes, that old wooden cradle is still stored up overhead in the toolshed, isn't it? Go on out there and bring it in, get it cleaned up. And Elliot, the baby quilt Mamma made for me is upstairs in my cedar chest. Bring it out here and hang it over the railing so it can air out some. Garrett, bring the bag and follow me. This son of yours could use a fresh diaper, and you can bet the ranch I'm not doin' it."

Wes and Elliot turned in opposite directions to do her bidding. Jessi reached for the screen door.

"Hold up a second, all of you."

Three pairs of eyes turned to stare at him—no, four pairs. One pair of baby blues fixed on him like laser beams.

Garrett swallowed the bile in his throat, cleared it and said what he had to. "We're not keeping this baby."

Jessi blinked. Elliot shook his head. And Wes just stared at him, condemnation in those black eyes of his.

"Look, I don't know whose child he is, but I do know this. He ain't mine."

"But, Garrett—"

"No buts, Jessi. Somewhere, his real family is out there waiting for him. It wouldn't be fair for us to keep him here. Now, I'm going inside and calling Social Services, and then—"

"Not on a Saturday morning, you aren't," Elliot observed. He lifted his hat and replaced it at a more comfortable angle with just the right amount of smugness. The horsey pajamas ruined the effort, though.

Again, the little bastard had a point. Quinn, Texas was a speck-on-the-map town in a county that wasn't much bigger. There wasn't a thing Garrett could do about this until Monday. Ah, hell, make that Tuesday. Monday was Memorial Day.

"I'll just go get that quilt," Elliot said, and he let the screen door bang closed behind him.

"I'll change little Ethan," Jessi offered, *"this time.* But don't you start thinkin' this is gonna become a habit." She bent to pick up the bunny bag with her free hand.

Garrett held the door for her. "He won't be here long enough for it to become a habit, Jes."

Blue jumped up and trotted into the house beside Jessi. His sister shot Garrett a few daggers as she passed. But

they were nothing compared to the glare of Wes's eyes on
his back. He felt as if his skin were being seared. He stiffened his shoulders and turned to face his silent accuser.

Wes leaned against the porch railing, eyeing him.

"It's not my kid," Garrett said, and the fact that he
sounded so defensive made him as angry as the look in his
brother's eyes.

"At least our father owned up to his mistakes, Garrett. When my mother died and he found out about
me—"

"When Stands Alone died, Wes, it was *my* mother who
found out about you, not Pa. She was the one who went
to the reservation to find out if her suspicions were true,
and once she knew, there was no question about your
coming to live with us. If our father hadn't done right by
you, she'd have skinned him."

Wes straightened as Garrett spoke. "You saying Orrin
wouldn't have acknowledged me if Maria hadn't forced
him?"

"I'm saying who the hell knows *what* he would have
done. He was no saint, Wes."

"And neither is his firstborn," Wes said in a dangerously soft voice.

"No, I'm no saint. I never claimed to be. But I didn't
father that kid in there, and—"

"And you don't want him." Wes turned away suddenly, an act that made his careless shrug a second later
seem false. "What the hell do I care? I don't even like
kids." He banged down the three porch steps and started
along the well-worn path to the barn.

Garrett would have gone after him, but changed his
mind at Jessi's shrill squawk—at least he thought it was
Jessi's. It might also have been a bald eagle caught in a
blender, but he didn't think that very likely. Ah, hell.

He headed inside.

Jessi had one hand at her stomach and the other over her mouth. Behind her, the baby lay on the parlor floor, his diaper undone, his legs in the air. Garrett took another step forward before the aroma hit him full in the face and made his eyes water.

"I can't do it, Garrett," Jessi gasped, "and there's nothing you can say to make me. Gawd!" She headed up the stairs at light speed.

"Jessi!"

No use. She was long gone. He heard the bedroom door slam, then refocused his gaze on the kid. Damn shame Jessi hadn't laid some newspapers or something underneath him.

Grimacing, he squared his shoulders and strode the rest of the way into the parlor. Blue whimpered from his spot on the floor in front of the window, where he tended to bask in the morning sunlight. Then he lowered his head and put both paws over his nose.

"I know the feeling, Blue." Garrett snatched up the bunny bag and dug into it. Clean diapers, that horrible disposable kind that lived for ten thousand years in the dump. If he ever had a kid, he'd use cloth. Good ol' cotton, and...

Taking another look at the condition of little Ethan's diaper, he frowned again, seriously rethinking that position. Who'd wanna try to clean something like that? Hell, he'd swabbed out drunk tanks that had been more appealing than...*that.*

He took a diaper from the bag, and a box of premoistened baby wipes, which made him raise his eyebrows.

"Baby wipes, hell," he muttered. "I think you need a high-pressure hose, kid."

"Dababa," Ethan chirped. He wasn't looking at Garrett. Instead, he held one foot in his hand and eyed his own toes with fascination.

Garrett caught himself smiling like an idiot, checked it and dived into the bag again. This time, he emerged with a half-dozen mysterious items. Oil, ointment, powder. He wasn't sure what to use, but figured he could safely rule out the teething lotion.

"Baa!"

"Yeah, I'm coming." He dumped his plunder on the floor, snagged himself about thirty or so baby wipes and wished to God he had a clothespin for his nose and a pair of rubber gloves for his hands. As he hunkered down beside the kid, he revised that wish. What he needed was a full-fledged space suit.

Despite the unpleasantness of it, though, the job didn't take all that long. Snatch the dirty diaper off, clean him up, dust him with powder, tape a fresh diaper firmly in place. Now the question was, what the hell did he do with the, uh, used one? The trash pail in the kitchen was out of the question. He finally decided on the big can out behind the house, though he'd rather incinerate the thing than can it. If this kid ended up sticking around the Texas Brand, they were going to have to invest in an asbestos tank and a flamethrower. Gathering up the diaper and the used baby wipes, he glanced down at Ethan. The baby had managed to pull his foot all the way up to his face and was gnawing on one of his own toes.

"Stunning good looks and talent, too," Garrett told him. "Will wonders never cease? Stay where you are, Ethan."

"Buhbuhbuh," the baby responded, a serious expression on his face.

"Okay. Bubba it is. I'll be right back, Bubba." And he turned to carry the toxic bundle down the hall and out the back door to the trash can. When he came back inside, he stopped in the downstairs bathroom and scrubbed his hands almost raw. Then he sauntered back into the parlor.

Only little Ethan wasn't where he'd been.

"Hey, Bubba," Garrett called. "Where'd you go?"

No answer. What did he expect, an announcement?

Then he spotted the little pudge. He'd crawled over to where ol' Blue lay in that pool of sunlight and was sitting close beside him. Ethan grinned, lifted the prize he'd captured in his little hands and prepared to take his very first bite of hound-dog ear.

"Ethan, *no!*" Garrett dived in a way he hadn't done since high school football and managed to pull a fat little hand away from a drippy little mouth just in time.

Ethan just stared at him, big eyes all innocence.

Blue lifted his head and laid it down again across the baby's legs. This was nothing less than amazing to Garrett. This morning's activities added up to the most that lazy hound had moved in six months! And he was *never* this friendly. Meanwhile, little hands began smacking down on Blue's head as if it were a bongo drum. Ethan even tried to sing along.

"Gawgawgawgawgagaw..."

Blue's head lifted again. He gave Ethan's chubby cheek a big swipe of dog tongue, then sighed in contentment, closed his droopy eyes and lay his head down in the baby's lap once more.

Garrett swept his hat off with one hand and rumpled his hair with the other. "Well, I'll be..."

Chapter 2

Chelsea Brennan resisted the urge to hug herself against the chill of this room as much as she resisted the urge to grimace at the sickeningly sweet odor of it. The lights were too bright. It ought to be dim in a room like this. Bright lights didn't belong in here. Neither did all the chrome or the shiny white floor tiles.

The cold did, though. The cold was at home here.

The drawer squealed when he pulled it open. Chelsea grated her teeth at the sound. Beneath a stark white sheet, the body jiggled like gelatin when its bed came to a halt. And then an ash gray hand fell to one side and dangled there. Still. Perfect nails, painted pink.

Chelsea didn't move. Couldn't move. Her eyes fixed on the small hand. On every sharply delineated bone and a wrist so narrow it made her wince. Not Michele. Not like this.

"Are you ready, Ms. Brennan?"

She nodded to the white-coated medical examiner, stiffened her spine and lifted her gaze from that limp hand. He pulled the sheet away from a lifeless face. A face as emaciated as the hand, with sharpened cheekbones and hollowed eyes.

A face she'd never seen before, and yet so dear... so familiar. *Michele.*

A great suction drew all the air from her lungs, and Chelsea couldn't seem to inhale any to replace it. Her jaw worked like the gaping gills of a fish when it's suffocating on dry land. For just an instant, Michele's features swam and re-formed again. Only this time, it was their mother's face Chelsea saw. The circles under Michele's eyes became bruises. Her lips swelled and split.

Chelsea tried harder to draw a breath, but the constriction in her chest wouldn't allow it. Her mouth gaped wider, and she blinked the image of her mother away. Michele. It was Michele lying on the table. Not Mom. Ironic that the resemblance Chelsea saw so clearly now hadn't been apparent before. In death, they could have been twins. And that's when the other similarity became blatantly clear.

The young Texas Ranger who'd been standing in the doorway, as if he couldn't bring himself to move further into the stench of death and disinfectant, came forward now. He stepped in front of her, blocking the body from her sight. And she breathed at last.

"I'm sorry you had to go through this, ma'am."

Sweet, the way he called her "ma'am" all the time. She wondered briefly what vices he kept hidden beneath his compassionate facade.

"Is it her?" he asked, fingers twisting the brim of the hat he held in his hands. "Is it your sister?"

She couldn't meet his eyes as she nodded. Instead, she focused on the way his hands worked the hat, and she managed to find her voice again. "She's so thin," Chelsea whispered. "Gaunt."

"Drugs will do that to a person, ma'am."

Chelsea's head rose slowly, and she did meet those clear blue eyes this time. "Drugs didn't do this to my sister. A man did."

It was the ranger's turn to avert his eyes. "I'm sorry, ma'am, but she did this to herself. Injected herself with enough heroin to kill a horse."

Chelsea's knees wobbled just a little, but she snapped them into place again by sheer will. "You're saying... suicide?"

"You did say it had been nearly a year since you'd seen her," he reminded her.

"But I talked with her...just last week. We were making plans. I told her I'd fly down here at the end of the month and..."

And she asked if I could come sooner, right away. And there was something in her voice, even though she said she was all right. I should have known....

"No," Chelsea said at last. "No, my sister didn't kill herself."

"It could have been an accidental overdose, ma'am. Maybe she didn't realize how much—"

"She wasn't suicidal, Ranger. And she wasn't stupid, either."

He nodded to the medical examiner, who slid the noisy drawer closed again. Then he touched Chelsea's elbow as if to ease her out of the room, but she jerked away from the contact. She didn't want any man laying a finger on her. Not now. Not ever.

"You'll want these." When she looked his way again, he was holding out a plastic zipper bag, with a few items inside. "Her personal effects, ma'am."

She blinked, not reaching for the bag. "Don't you need to hold on to them ... until the case is closed or—"

"The case *is* closed."

For some reason, her gaze shifted to that drawer again. The one that held her sister on a cold metal table. God, how the hell had the Brennan women come to this? One left. Just one left.

"I want to make it perfectly clear," he said slowly, as if speaking to someone who barely understood the language. He pushed the plastic bag into her hand and turned to start up the stairway, leaving Chelsea no choice but to follow. "There is absolutely no evidence that anyone else stuck that hypodermic into your sister's belly."

Her steps faltered, but she forced herself to continue up the stairs and outside through heavy metal doors. The rain fell harder now, ricocheting off the blacktopped parking lot and the shiny cars. The ranger's black umbrella popped open and tilted over her head. No colors here, she thought dully. She'd stepped into a world of black and white. Night, and rain, and heat, and mist hovering low as a result of the other three. She smelled rain and exhaust. Cars passed on the streets of El Paso, their white headlights illuminating the gray building, then leaving it in darkness once more.

She didn't have the strength to argue with the ranger. Not now. Not tonight. Seemed he wasn't open to her input anyway. For now ... for now, she only wanted one thing.

She turned to him beneath the sheltering dome of the umbrella, saw the rainwater streaming from its edges. "Where is the baby?"

The ranger blinked, his eyes going wider.

"When my sister ran off with that oversize cowboy a year ago, she was pregnant. Last week, when we talked, she told me she had a son. A six-month-old son. Ethan." Her throat tightened a little when she said the name. But there were still no tears. There hadn't been tears for Chelsea Brennan in twenty years. "Where is he?"

The ranger shook his head. "Ma'am, she was found in an alley outside town. No purse, no ID, and no sign of any baby."

Chelsea's heart pumped a little faster, a swell of panic rising from the pit of her stomach to engulf it.

"We only knew to call you because we found your name and address on a note in her pocket. We haven't even been able to find out where she was living before she . . ." He lowered his head, shook it slowly.

"I don't know where she was living, either. She didn't say, when she called." Chelsea pushed her hair off her forehead, closed her eyes. "I didn't even know she was in Texas before that."

"Do you know the name of the man she left New York with?"

Chelsea frowned at the mention of the bastard. "I saw him once, from the window of my apartment. A big guy in a cowboy hat. Michele never talked about him. I imagine she thought I'd disapprove."

"Why would she think that?"

She lifted her chin, met the younger man's eyes. "Because I probably would have. My sister had a habit of taking up with losers, Ranger. This one was just the last in a long line of men who treated her like dirt."

"But you don't know that for sure."

"I'm as sure as I have to be."

For just a moment, he searched her face, then he sighed as if at a loss and started walking again toward her rental car. She kept pace.

"I imagine the child is with his father," he said after a moment.

"With his mother's killer, you mean."

"Ma'am, there's no—"

"Evidence. I know." Chelsea took the keys from her pocket, but then forgot what it was she was supposed to be doing with them and just stared at them in her open palm. "If he didn't have anything to do with this," she said softly, maybe more to herself than to the ranger beside her, "then where is he? Why hasn't he reported her missing? Why isn't *he* the one here identifying her body?"

He took the keys from her hand, unlocked the car and opened the door, all the while keeping that damned funereal umbrella over her head. "Could be they parted on bad terms," he said as he straightened away from the door to let her in. "Could be any number of things besides murder."

"Could be," she said. "But isn't."

"Why are you so sure?"

Chelsea slid behind the wheel and took the keys he held out to her. "Family tradition," she said, and closed the door. When she pulled away, the ranger still stood there in the rain, staring after her.

She didn't get far before the nausea hit her. Pulling into a dilapidated convenience store's parking lot, she managed to make it to a rest room before she lost control. But her heaving stomach couldn't produce anything anyway. She hadn't eaten since she'd had the call from the Texas Rangers, asking her if she had a sister, describing her, telling her to come down and identify the body.

She collapsed on the dirty tiled floor, her guts tied up in knots. If she could break down in rivers of tears, it might take the edge off. But she couldn't. She couldn't cry. Sometimes she thought she and Michele had used up all their tears that night when their father had finally hit their mother one too many times.

Years of abuse. Years of the two of them watching it, too young and afraid to do anything to stop it. Though Chelsea had wished a million times she had done something. She wished she'd murdered that bastard in his sleep. She wished she hadn't always cried when her father hit her because maybe then her mother wouldn't have always stepped in. Always deflected the bastard's anger—away from her daughters and onto herself. Chelsea should have killed him. Maybe Mom would still be alive. Maybe Michele wouldn't have grown up to repeat the same damned cycle.

To Chelsea, it seemed as if the men of this world had it in for the Brennan women. Which was why she'd long ago decided never to have anything to do with any of them. She'd die a virgin and of old age, not at an angry man's hand. And never again, no matter what else she might face, would she let another person take her place in battle. Any battle.

Like the battle she was facing right now.

Stiffening her resolve, Chelsea gripped the stall door and pulled herself to her feet. Her throat burned, and she reached into her coat pocket for a cough drop, only to encounter the plastic bag that was all she had left of her sister. Grating her teeth, she pulled it out, opened it and emptied its meager contents into her palm. There was her sister's high school ring. A pair of cheap metal earrings with gold-colored paint. And a locket on a thin silver chain.

Chelsea dropped the other items back into her pocket, letting the bag fall to the floor. She held the locket in trembling hands. It had belonged to her grandmother, Alice. Mamma had given it to Michele after one of their father's violent episodes. She'd given the matching earrings to Chelsea. She'd done that a lot. Given them gifts. As if she could ease their pain with baubles.

Chelsea opened the locket.

A red newborn face was framed inside the silver heart. Dark hair sticking up in odd angles, tiny hands clenched into fists, eyes squinting tightly.

"Ethan," she whispered, and she ran the pad of her thumb over that innocent face. "I'll find you, baby. I promise. I'll find you."

And then she turned the locket over. There was a tiny compartment in the back. You'd never know it was there unless someone showed it to you, the way their mother had shown it to Michele and Chelsea. And as she pried at it, Chelsea wondered if maybe she'd find a photo of the man who'd murdered her sister and taken her nephew. Maybe she'd have something to go on, some jumping-off point in her search for her sister's child.

Blinking rapidly, Chelsea succeeded in opening the tiny compartment, then gasped as a small, folded slip of paper fell to the floor. She dropped to her knees to retrieve it.

Her hands shook so badly she could barely unfold the thing without tearing it, but when she did, she almost sagged in relief at what she saw there. A name, and an address.

There was no doubt in Chelsea's mind that it was the name of the bastard who was responsible for her sister's death. And no doubt that when she found the scum, she'd find her nephew, as well.

Men had all but wiped out the Brennan women. First Mom, and then Michele. Chelsea stood straighter and lifted her chin. Well, it was high time one of the Brennan women fought back. And she was the only one left to do it. She'd taken all she could take. All those years of impotence against her father...well, it was over. She wasn't a helpless little girl anymore, and the rage she'd stored up back then would be all she'd need to keep her going now. Just long enough to unleash it on a worthless, abusive pig.

When she got through with the man whose name Michele had written here, he was going to wish he'd never been born. And if she had any doubts that this man had fathered her sister's child, they were erased as she reread the name.

Garrett *Ethan* Brand.

Someone tapped on the rest room door. "You all right in there, ma'am?"

"Fine. Just a minute." Chelsea took a moment to snap the locket closed again, then fastened the chain around her own neck. She dropped the note into her pocket and turned to open the door.

The young woman who'd pointed the rest room out to her lingered outside.

"Sorry I took so long," Chelsea said, stepping out of the rest room into the main part of the little store again.

The clerk looked worried as she surveyed Chelsea. Only then did Chelsea wonder about her appearance. Glancing down at herself, she saw the dirt smudged on her skirt and the runs in her nylons. No doubt her hair was wild, too, with the humidity and the rain.

"I was just gettin' worried, is all," the woman said. "Is everything all right?"

"Yes. Fine. Listen, do you have road maps in here?"

"Sure," the clerk said, looking relieved, maybe because the need for a map indicated the wild-looking woman in her store was headed out of town. "Where you going?" As she asked, she went to the counter to thumb through a rack of road maps, her back to Chelsea.

"To a ranch called the Texas Brand in the town of Quinn," Chelsea replied. Silently, she added, *to make one Garrett Ethan Brand sorry he ever heard the name Brennan.*

Chapter 3

Insistent wails broke through the satin bonds of sleep like a randy bull crashing through a fence to get to an in-season heifer.

Garrett pulled his pillow over his head and groaned. It was only Ethan's second night in the house, and Garrett's second without more than ten straight minutes of shut-eye. But it seemed as if it had been a year.

The crying didn't stop. Ah, hell, no wonder. Poor kid was among strangers, in an unfamiliar place. Was probably missing his mamma. Garrett dragged himself out of bed and slogged into the hallway. He wore shorts and a T-shirt, having learned last night that getting undressed with Ethan only a beller away was as useless as teats on a bore-hog. His bare feet scuffed the braided runner as he headed to the bedroom across from his. Aside from Adam's and Ben's, this was the only empty bedroom in the house. It had been his parents' room. Now it was reserved strictly for guests. Garrett had never had the heart to use his absent brothers' bedrooms for visitors because he was always half-hoping they'd just show up, home to stay, one of these days.

Garrett crossed the hall, opened the door and scuffed inside. Ethan stopped crying the second Garrett leaned over the cradle. Not a single tear dampened the little demon's cheeks. Not one. All noise and no substance, his crying. His eyes were far from red and swollen. No, they were bright blue, sparkling and wide.

They focused on Garrett's face and fairly twinkled at him. His little arms flailed as if he were trying to fly, and he flashed Garrett a dimply grin. Anyone would think the kid was glad to see him.

Garrett's impatience melted like butter in a hot skillet as he bent to scoop the baby up, and was rewarded by an actual, audible laugh. "Just lonely, aren't you, Bubba? Yeah, well, I know all about that." He carried the baby out into the hall and down the stairs, hoping his siblings would appreciate the trouble he was taking to let them sleep in peace. The rocker seemed to be the key. Little Ethan hadn't conceded to sleep last night until Garrett had rocked him.

Hmm, looked like ol' Blue was one step ahead. The hound stood in front of the rocking chair, head cocked to one side, tail upright, as if awaiting their arrival. Garrett eased himself down, and Blue laid on his feet with a contented sigh. Damn dog seemed to think a baby was exactly what had been lacking in this house.

Garrett moved to shift Ethan onto his lap, but the baby's face nuzzled into the crook between Garrett's neck and shoulder, the little body cozying closer to his chest. Some very odd, kind of warm, fuzzy sensation washed over him at the feel of that tiny, clingy body, so relaxed and trusting in his big arms. He pulled the blanket up over

Ethan's shoulders and patted the little back slowly and rhythmically with a hand that spanned its width. He pushed the rocker into motion with his feet.

If someone had told Garrett a week ago that he'd be sitting here cuddling a little baby in the middle of the night—and *enjoying it*—he'd have had them tested for drugs or alcohol. So small. He'd never held on to anything so small and fragile before. He'd been awfully uncomfortable at first. Garrett was a big man, and people tended to take one look at him and just assume he was rough and dangerous. He went to extremes to be gentle, moving slowly and speaking softly to counteract the impressions made by his size. But he still felt big and clumsy around tiny, fragile things. He ran one hand over Ethan's downy hair, as dark as Wes's.

That woman who'd left this bundle on the front porch...what had she been thinking? Did she have any idea what she was giving up? At that moment, as that little child clung to him, Garrett knew there wasn't a more precious treasure in the whole world than the one in his arms right now. And more love had never come in a smaller package. 'Cause somewhere between yesterday and the moment Garrett had leaned over that crib tonight, this baby seemed to have decided to love *him*. He practically bubbled over every time Garrett went anywhere near him.

"Dabababa," Ethan sang, his voice soft and sleepy as he cuddled closer.

Garrett rubbed circles on Ethan's back and inhaled the sweet baby smells as he rocked. "You're just a little bird, aren't you, Bubba? All the time singing."

Ethan made a motor noise with his lips that resulted in Garrett's T-shirt getting wet.

"Yeah," Garrett said softly, rocking and patting in time. "Your mamma must have known what she was doing, huh? I got a feeling she wouldn't have left you without some pretty big reasons."

Ethan wiggled himself into a more comfortable position, snuggling close again as one tiny hand gripped a fold of Garrett's T-shirt.

"She's a smart lady, your mamma," Garrett went on, his voice just a little above a whisper. "She had to know I'd realize you weren't my flesh and blood. But she also must've known how it would look to the kids if I turned you away. What a bad example it would've set."

Garrett didn't know who the woman might be. He knew beyond a doubt *he* hadn't fathered the child. Though knowing it wasn't as pleasant a feeling as it ought to be. Hell, being a daddy to something this cuddly wouldn't be much of a chore. Garrett wished to God he knew who the mother was, why she'd brought Ethan here. Only one thing was obvious. Whoever she was, she hadn't left the child at just any old ranch house. She hadn't chosen at random. Her note called Garrett by name. Hell, it went so far as to claim the child was named for him. So this action she'd taken had to have been well thought out, planned. She'd deliberately left her child in Garrett's care.

He was having serious second thoughts about turning Ethan over to Social Services come Tuesday morning. After all, he was the town sheriff. There was no reason he couldn't make a few inquiries on his own, try to find the woman himself. If she'd wanted Ethan in the system, she'd have taken him there, wouldn't she? And suppose she came back for her baby in a week, or a month? Lord knows, once kids go into foster care, it's sheer hell for a parent to get them back. All that red tape could be avoided if Garrett could just keep little Ethan here with him. Just for a short while. Just to give the woman a chance.

A little palm patted Garrett's face.

Oh, yeah, he was changing his mind, all right. Hell, he was smitten by the little mite already, and he'd only had him a couple of days. What must it have done to Ethan's mamma to leave him alone on that porch? Torn her insides out, Garrett figured. But she'd done it, and in doing so, she'd put her trust in *him*. No way was Garrett going to let her down.

He lowered his head to the side, so his cheek brushed Ethan's silky hair. "Don't you worry, little Bubba. I'm gonna make things right for you." Ethan heaved a deep sigh, and Garrett closed his eyes.

It was still dark outside when he heard a vehicle and felt the touch of headlights on his eyelids. He'd fallen asleep! Sitting right here in the rocker, holding that baby! Of all the idiotic things to do. What if he'd dropped Ethan on his head?

But his arms were still firmly anchored around that little body, as if they'd been on guard duty even as he'd slept. He squinted at the antique pendulum clock that sat on the mantel. Three a.m. He'd been asleep almost three hours!

And who the hell was pulling into the driveway at this time of night? Could be an emergency in town, maybe. He *was* the sheriff. But wouldn't someone have called instead of driving clear out here?

Garrett got up real slow, and turned to lay Ethan on the couch. Then he pulled the nearest armchair up beside it, back first, so there was no way the baby could roll onto the floor. He was just tucking the blanket over that sleeping angel when he heard the pounding on the front door. Not knocking. *Pounding.*

His stomach twisted a little as he thought about his gun, clear out of reach upstairs, and he tried to recall if he'd arrested any particularly ornery characters lately. But hell, aside from the occasional drunk and disorderly boys over at La Cucaracha, he rarely arrested *anyone*. Quinn was a quiet little town. Not much happened there.

Garrett hustled through the dining room, casting one last glance over his shoulder at Ethan as he went. Still asleep despite the racket at the door. Good. He paused in the kitchen only long enough to flick on the outdoor light so he could get a look at the rude S.O.B. who was trying to knock the door off its hinges. He parted the curtain and peered out.

Hostile eyes peered back at him. Hostile... and then some. The creature that stared back at him seemed, in that first instant, to be nothing *but* eyes. Huge, round, and wild. The impact when those eyes met his sent him two full steps backward before he'd even been aware of moving. Like he'd been kicked hard in the chest. Those eyes... they were hurting. Hurting like he'd never seen anyone hurt before, and it looked to him as if they intended to hurt back.

Garrett blinked and gave his head a shake. Hell, he'd best get a grip and look again. There had been more there than a pair of stricken eyes.

He leaned forward again, this time flicking the lock and twisting the knob. No use with the locks. It was a woman, even if she was all eyes. And he could handle a woman, no matter how crazed.

The door opened.

She shouldered inside before he stepped out of the way, then stood toe-to-toe with him. "Are you Garrett Ethan Brand?"

Her voice was like cherry-tree bark—stringy and coarse.

She had burnished bronze hair that seemed as riled up as she was. Her clothes were dirty and her stockings full of runs. Mud clung to her high-heeled shoes. She was a mess. He figured she must have had an accident or something. But unless she'd lost a limb—which she obviously hadn't—he couldn't see any explanation for the pain and rage in her eyes.

"Yeah, I'm Garrett," he told her. "Why don't you sit down and I'll—"

He reeled backward at the impact of her fist—not her hand, *her fist*—connecting with his left cheekbone and snapping his head sideways so hard and fast he thought he'd probably need a neck brace.

"Damn, woman! What the hell was that—hold on a minute!" He caught her fist in his hands before she could land another blow. So she kicked him in the shins with those muddy, pointy-toed shoes of hers. He yelped in agony. Damned if he wanted to hurt any woman, but this one was pushing even *his* legendary patience. He dropped her hands just long enough to wrap his arms tight around her middle, pinning *her* arms to her sides. At the same instant, he pressed her up against the door and pushed his body tight to her considerably smaller one. So tight she couldn't swing those deadly feet again. But even as he did it, he took great pains not to hurt her. She was so small he got the feeling she'd break easily.

And then he just stood there, his body plastered to hers, panting from the struggle and the surprise and, mostly to be honest, the pain. And he wondered what the hell to do next. Lord, her heart hammered like a scared jackrabbit's hind feet. Her lungs moved in and out too rapidly. She had cheeks as pink as a tea rose and eyes that damn near put him on his knees just with the force of the emotions he saw roiling in them as he stared down at her from a distance of well over a foot.

He caught his breath in short order, though she still breathed as if she'd just run a mile uphill. "You want to tell me why you're trying to cripple me now, ma'am, or on the way to jail?"

Her eyes narrowed and...they were green. Deep, forest green. Like pine needles in the sunlight. He'd never seen eyes like those.

"Where is he?"

Garrett blinked twice. "Where is who?"

"You know damn well who. Where is he?"

A bitter dread settled in the pit of his stomach. God wouldn't be so cruel, would he? This crazy woman couldn't possibly be little Ethan's mamma...*could she?*

He cleared his throat, trying to figure out a decent reason to lie to her, when Ethan made up his own mind. He let out a yelp. And an outright miracle happened. That wildcat in Garrett's arms went limp as a noodle. The fury left her eyes, and instead they softened, melted. A look of utter longing and bittersweet relief took over, and the tension left her so fast it felt as if her bones had turned to water. He wasn't sure she'd still be standing on her feet if he wasn't holding her.

"Ethan?" she whispered.

"Yes, ma'am, that's Ethan. But I'll tell you, I'm not inclined to let anyone as violent as you within a hundred miles of him."

Her eyes flashed up at him, anger flickering to life once more. Tempered now, though.

"Are, uh, are you his mamma?"

Soft auburn brows drew together. "You know perfectly well where his mother is, mister."

"No, ma'am, I surely don't."

"Yes, *cowboy*," she said, mocking his drawl and saying "cowboy" as if it were a cuss word. "You surely *do*." Her voice lowered until it became little more than a harsh, tortured whisper. "She's lying in a morgue in El Paso. And you put her there, you bastard."

She was shaking—*shaking*—like a road sign in a killing wind. Vibrating with the force of whatever emotions roiled inside her right now.

The kitchen light flashed on, and Wes appeared at Garrett's side. His open hand might look harmless to a stranger, but Garrett saw the way his fingers twitched just a little. He'd snatch that bowie from his boot at the drop of a hat.

"What's going on, Garrett?"

He didn't answer. His gaze remained fixed on the wild-eyed creature whose soul was crying, even if her eyes were not. "Ethan's mamma is dead?"

She didn't reply, only glared at him. He heard Jessi's soft gasp behind him and realized she'd come into the kitchen, too. And probably Elliot, as well. The scent of baby powder told him one of them was carrying Ethan. That and the way the woman trapped between his chest and the door suddenly stared at a point beyond him.

"Answer me. Is she dead?"

A single nod.

"Are you sure?"

Her eyes finally came back to his. "I just came from identifying my sister's body, you murdering slug. You're damned right I'm sure."

Wes stiffened, closed his eyes, shook his head. Elliot snorted, coming forward to stand at Garrett's other side. "Lady, you don't know my brother at all if you think he could hurt a woman."

His words had no impact on her. She merely lifted her chin and continued staring at Garrett. "I came for my nephew. Give him to me and I'll leave."

"Well, now, I'm real sorry, ma'am, but I can't do that."

"I'll kill you myself before I'll let you keep him." And Garrett believed she meant every word of it.

"You'll have to go through me," Wes told her, his eyes going cold. Wes's eyes, when they went cold like that, could make a rattler tremble. Two black marbles without a hint of feeling. "And going through me won't be an easy job, lady."

"Damn straight it won't," Elliot agreed. "And when you finish with Wes, you'll have to get by me."

"And then me," Jessi said.

Nothing fazed the woman. She didn't even blink. "If that's the way you want it." She faced Garrett again. "Let go of me, Brand. I'll leave, but when I come back it will be with the law."

"No need to leave for that, ma'am. I happen to *be* the law. 'Round here leastwise."

For the first time, he saw fear tinge her eyes. She glanced down at his arms, imprisoning her, and it seemed to Garrett she was suddenly afraid of him. He eased his hold on her that very second. Let her go completely, and even stepped back away from her. It stunned him, that fear. Made him feel kind of queasy. He didn't like scaring people. Especially women or kids. Though he usually tried to be less intimidating because of his size, he knew only too well it wasn't always enough. Hell, nothing made Garrett more miserable than people's being afraid of him.

Especially her.

She was very small, he realized. Smaller than Jessi, even. She'd been through some kind of hell tonight. And he figured she was probably telling the truth about having just identified her sister's body in El Paso. She certainly *looked* like someone who'd just lost a sister. And if she truly thought him responsible . . . well, hell, he'd have been just as angry in her shoes.

She didn't lash out at him again. Only stood there, looking like she'd fall down in a few more minutes. Looking like the stress was tearing her nerves right to shreds.

Garrett turned around and took little Ethan from Jessi's arms, though she protested. Ethan chirped and grinned and blew spit bubbles. He latched onto one of Garrett's fingers and held tight. Garrett turned back to the woman, who stood near the front door. "Come on into the parlor," he said to her, and he tried harder than he ever had to make his deep voice sound soft and gentle. "Sit down and hold your nephew for a while. We'll talk this out."

She blinked, licked her lips. "I just want to take him and go."

"I understand that. But you have to understand my position here. I'm a sheriff, ma'am. A woman left her child in my care. I can't just hand him over to the first stranger who comes along and claims him, now can I?"

She eyed him so skeptically he squirmed inside.

"I'll check out your story," he went on. It was more than her smallness that made her seem as fragile as bone china right now. And he felt big and awkward beside her. "If you are who you say you are, and Ethan really is your nephew, I'll let you take him. But, ma'am, even if I were sure right this minute, I wouldn't let you out of here now. You're in no shape to be driving tonight. Especially not with a baby in the car."

He had her there. She knew it. He saw the concession in her eyes. "I'm not leaving here without him."

"Then you're gonna have to stay a spell."

She looked at the baby he held and she put her arms out. Little Ethan looked back at her and smiled. Her white hands trembled as she took a step forward. Then she dropped like a sack of potatoes right at Garrett's feet. Garrett pushed little Ethan into the nearest set of arms, which turned out to be Wes's, and bent down to scoop the woman up off the floor. As he turned to carry her through the house and upstairs, he noticed that she smelled like violets.

Chapter 4

Chelsea awoke to hot sunlight burning over her eyelids and face, cool, crisp sheets against her skin, and the smell of coffee. Good, strong coffee.

The smell, she discovered after blinking the sleep haze from her eyes, originated from the carafe that sat on the round table beside the bed. A pink cloth with lacy white edging covered the table and draped halfway to the floor, leaving only the bottom portion of the broad, carved, totem pole-like pedestal visible. Chelsea wanted to reach for that coffee. And for the plate of the steaming, fragrant, omelet-type concoction beside it. But she couldn't summon the energy to move.

"Well, the beast lives," a feminine voice announced.

Chelsea jerked her gaze to where the young woman she remembered from last night stood near the window. The curtains were as pink as the tablecloth. In fact, so were the sheets. Pale pink fabric with lilac blossoms lined the two overstuffed chairs in the room, and the wallpaper matched. It was very loud, very flowery and *very* pink. A white vanity with more filigree trim than substance stood in one corner. It was laden with pretty bottles and jars of every size, shape and color.

"Looks like the inside of Jeannie's bottle, doesn't it?" The woman let the curtains fall closed. "My brothers think all the frilly stuff makes up for being the only female in a houseful of men. I let them indulge me."

She was young. Early twenties, Chelsea guessed. Her pixie-short hair gleamed a reddish brown like the coat of a deer. And those huge brown eyes of hers reinforced the image of a doe. She was taller than Chelsea, curvier, too.

"So, do I pass inspection, Your Majesty?"

Chelsea cleared her throat, trying to work up enough energy to put the spoiled brat in her place. All she managed was, "What do you want?"

"I don't *want* anything, least of all to wait on some lunatic in my own house. I wouldn't be in here at all if Garrett hadn't insisted I stay with you until you came around. He said he was afraid you'd be *scared waking up in a strange place.*" She said the last bit in a whiny, mocking tone, and Chelsea wished she could slap her. "So I suggested my room. At least here I can keep an eye on you."

"I wouldn't be here if I had a choice about it."

"You wouldn't be here if *I* had a choice about it, either, lady."

Chelsea closed her eyes at the look of hostility in the pretty face.

"You might as well eat." The girl pushed herself away from the wall she'd been leaning on and came to the bed to hand the tray of food to Chelsea.

"Thanks," Chelsea said.

"Don't thank me. I wouldn't cook for you if you were starving. Garrett brought this up."

Chelsea looked up from the plate of food on her lap to the glittering brown eyes. "Look, I don't have a problem with you. It's your brother—"

"You have a problem with one Brand, lady, you have a problem with all of them."

"He might have killed my sister." And why the hell was she suddenly qualifying her accusations with a "might have." Last night, she'd been so sure. Chelsea sat up straighter, suddenly losing interest in the food. "You can't expect me to just—"

"He didn't even *know* your sister! And *you* don't know Garrett. Of all my brothers, he's the most gentle, the sweetest, the kindest, the—"

She broke off, turning away fast and blinking tears from her eyes. As if she didn't want Chelsea to see her crying.

"Garrett wouldn't hurt a fly. You can ask anyone who knows him. The boys in town, they have a joke. They call him the gentle giant." She turned again, with one angry swipe at her eyes. "But *I'm* not gentle. And neither is Wes. And I'll tell you right now, we're not gonna stand by and let you hurt Garrett this way. You can't go around accusing him of murder. You do and I'll—"

"That's enough, Jessi."

The command was spoken softly, but in a voice so big it didn't seem likely anyone would disobey. The man Chelsea had believed to be a cold-blooded killer stood in the doorway, looking at his little sister with a frown, but adoringly all the same.

"But, Garrett—"

"No buts. Go on, now. Wes needs your help in the barn. That new calf got himself tangled in some wire and cut his hind leg up. He needs tending."

"Wes can handle a cut calf."

"Wes isn't the Brand one semester away from a degree in veterinary medicine, Jes. You are. Now get out there and see to the calf before he gets infected or something."

The girl—Jessi—blinked twice, and seemed to forget all about Chelsea. With budding concern in her eyes, she yanked open a closet door and snatched out a brown leather satchel. Then she headed out of the room, and Chelsea heard her feet taking the stairs at a trot a second later.

Garrett Brand came farther into the room, but he left the door open. He really *was* big. Not just tall, but as broad shouldered as a lumberjack. He had bodybuilder arms that bore the coppery kiss of the sun beneath a fine mist of dark hair. His eyes were as deeply brown as his sister's. Soft eyes, bottomless and kind.

Deceptively so.

"We ought to talk," he said in that slow, easy way of his. He moved slowly, too, as if giving her time to object with every step he took. When she didn't, he eased his big frame into one of Jessi's pink-and-lilac chairs, and Chelsea wondered if she were about to witness a scene from *Goldilocks and the Three Bears*. Nope, the fragile-looking chair legs held.

It was only when those deep brown eyes moved slowly down her sheet-draped body and then darkened that Chelsea became suddenly, acutely interested in what the hell she was wearing. She lifted the sheet, peeked down and gasped.

"I'm naked under here," she blurted, mainly because she was so surprised.

Garrett shifted in the chair, his face reddening all the way to his ears. "Well, I asked Jessi to get you out of your clothes last night. I mean . . . you were pretty well soaked from the rain and all, and . . ."

She scowled at him when he ran out of words.

"You want me to leave so you can get dressed?"

"In what? I don't see any of my things in here."

"Well, you must have luggage in your car, right? I can have Elliot go out and—"

"Just say what you have to say and get it over with, will you?"

He nodded fast, keeping his eyes carefully lowered, though whenever they did come up, they focused on certain strategic bits of the sheet and she wondered how much he could see through it.

"All right," he said. "For starters, ma'am, I'm not sure what—" he frowned, meeting her eyes "—what's your name?"

"My name?"

"I can't talk to you without even knowing your name. It feels too odd."

She closed her eyes, sighed. "Chelsea Brennan."

His lips curled upward just slightly at the corners. "I like it."

"I'm so glad it meets with your approval," she snapped, then saw a wounded look come and go in his eyes and almost regretted her words.

"I didn't hurt your sister, Chelsea Brennan," he said, and there was so much sincerity in his deep, steady voice that it made her wonder. "But I'd like to help you find out who did...if you'll let me."

Nothing he could have said would have shocked her more. Denials, she expected. Threats, even. But an offer of help? What was this? A trick?

"Why would you want to help me? You don't even know me."

"That's true, I don't. But I know Ethan." He licked his lips as if he were nervous or something, dipped his head.

"It might sound foolish to you, Chelsea, but I made that little fella a promise. I told him I'd make things right for him again, and that's what I intend to do."

She studied him, scanning the little worry lines—or were they laugh lines?—at the corners of his brown eyes. Telling herself that just because his appearance and demeanor were so damned gentle and approachable didn't mean that's the way he truly was. Inside. Where it counted.

Hell, her father hadn't looked like the monster he was, either.

"Why should I believe you? How do I know this isn't just an act? That you aren't just lying to throw me off track?"

"Why *shouldn't* you believe me?"

"You want me to list the reasons?"

He nodded, watching her with those soft eyes of his.

"Fine. I will, then. A year ago, my sister, Michele, got herself pregnant by the lowlife she'd been dating. She didn't tell me his name, but I saw him once from a distance. He was big...like you. And he wore a hat—" she pointed at the black hat he'd perched on the arm of the chair "—like that."

He glanced down at his hat with a frown, then picked it up. His lips pursed in thought as he turned the brim slowly in his big hands and ran his fingers around the edge and then through the dip in the hat's center in what seemed uncomfortably like a caress. "Most of the men in Texas wear hats like this one," he replied, calm and quiet. "And I imagine a lot of them are big."

He stroked the black felt over and over. Chelsea's stomach tightened and twisted, and she jerked her gaze away from those slow-moving hands.

"A week ago, Michele called me. She told me she had a son, Ethan, and she asked me to come down here right away to see him." Chelsea clenched her jaw, closing her eyes before rushing on. "If only I had, she might still be alive. But I knew I couldn't get time off work on such short notice. I promised to fly down in a couple of weeks, but..."

"There was no way you could have known," he said.

But she should have known. There'd been something in Michele's voice, something she should have picked up on. But she hadn't. Not until it had been too late. She'd live with that for the rest of her life.

"Then, yesterday, I got a call from the Texas Rangers, telling me they had a body they wanted me to look at."

"And it was her," Garrett finished softly.

Chelsea nodded. "Someone left her for dead, only she wasn't quite. But she didn't live long enough to make it to the hospital."

It surprised her when a warm hand slid over her cold one on the bed. And she stared at it for a long moment. A big, powerful hand, only it wasn't hurting. It wasn't controlling or cruel. She pushed her brows together at the unexpectedness of that. And then the hand moved away, and Garrett cleared his throat.

"They gave me her things," Chelsea went on. "There was a locket with Ethan's picture. Your name and address were in a compartment in the back."

"So you assumed I was the killer. And Ethan's daddy." Garrett shook his head.

"She named him after you."

"And I still haven't figured out why, or how she even knew me, or who she even was." He shook his head slowly, such sincere regret in his eyes that he had her almost believing him.

Chelsea sat up, clutching the pink sheet to her chest. She pointed at the floor, where someone had slung her mud-spattered purse. "Hand me my bag, would you?"

Garrett nodded and retrieved the bag for her, returning to his seat with those slow, careful movements of his.

Chelsea dug out her billfold and opened it to the photo of her sister. She handed the picture to the big man at the bedside. "This is Michele, Ethan's mother."

Garrett narrowed his eyes as he studied the snapshot. Then they widened in recognition, and Chelsea knew, whether he'd admit it or not, that he'd known Michele.

"I remember her," he said slowly.

"You do?" She hadn't expected him to admit it.

He nodded. "It was last summer. I saw her out on the River Road, middle of nowhere, alone, with a flat tire on her beat-up old car."

"And?"

"Well, I stopped and changed it for her, of course." He looked at her as if she should have known that much. "She seemed jittery, as I recall. Had a scared-rabbit look to her that worried me. I invited her back here for supper that night, and she came. Adam and Ben were here then, too, so it was a houseful." He shook his head, then his brows drew together again.

"Did she spend the night with you?" Chelsea knew her meaning was clear in her tone.

His head came up and he gave her a sharp look. "We invited her to stay over in the guest room. She refused. Said she had to be on her way. All told, she didn't spend more than two or three hours under this roof."

"It only takes a few minutes to get a woman pregnant," Chelsea said.

Garrett sighed hard. "She was already pregnant. Ma'am, do you think your sister was stupid?"

She blinked and sat up in the bed, holding the sheet to her chest. "No. Michele was irresponsible and flighty and drawn to bad men, but she wasn't stupid."

He nodded, handing the photo back to Chelsea. "You said you heard from her for the first time in over a year, just before she was killed. Now, why do you think she called you then, after all that time? Hmm?"

Chelsea drew a breath, braced her shoulders, taking full blame, which she deserved. "She knew...I think she was reaching out to me because she needed help."

"You think she knew this S.O.B. was after her."

Closing her eyes tight, Chelsea nodded.

"If it were you," Garrett said, his voice deep and smooth, "and you had your own little baby boy in your arms and a man trying to kill you and no one to turn to, what would you do, Chelsea?"

Facing him without flinching, she said, "I'd cut the bastard's heart out before he could do it to me."

Garrett blinked, maybe in surprise. It had to be surprise in his eyes the way he stared at her for a full minute before he finally nodded and spoke again. "I do believe you would," he said slowly, his gaze brushing her face from forehead to chin before focusing on her eyes again. "Fair enough, then. But what about Michele? Is that what she would have done?"

Chelsea's lips trembled as she imagined Michele's fear and desperation. She stared down at her sister's image, then closed her eyes. "She never fought back, never in her life. When things got tough for Michele, she'd run. She'd run right back home to me, and I'd take her in, find her a job, bail her out, whatever she needed. Until the next slug came along with a mouthful of promises. Then she'd take off again."

"So you think if she were scared this time, if she knew someone were trying to kill her, she would've run?"

Chelsea nodded.

"And what about the baby, Chelsea? It's hard to run for your life with a baby."

"She'd never have taken Ethan with her if she'd known she was in danger," Chelsea said quickly. "She'd never risk him that way. I know my sister. She'd have found a safe place to hide him and then she'd have run as far and as fast as she could."

She heard his sigh, his *relieved* sigh, and opened her eyes again to see him nodding in understanding. He held her gaze.

"Don't you see it, Chelsea? That's exactly what she did. We found little Ethan on our front porch day before yesterday. She left him here so he'd be safe." He must have seen the doubt in her eyes, because he went on. "I live right here on the Texas Brand. Have all my life," he said. "I run the ranch and I show up in a little bitty office in town every weekday with a star pinned to my shirt. Everybody in Quinn knows just about every move I make. I promise, I haven't had time to be terrorizing any woman. I haven't been to New York in years, either, and I can probably prove that if you'll just tell me the date this boyfriend of your sister's was there."

He meant it. She could tell he meant it, and her doubts about his guilt were stronger than ever.

"My sister ran away with that cowboy last year on April first," she said. "Bitter irony, isn't it?"

"April Fools' Day," Garrett observed. "Okay. I'll see if I can find some proof of my whereabouts that day for you."

She studied him, wondering why, if he really was innocent, he wasn't throwing her out on her backside. She'd stormed into his house in the middle of the night, accused him of murder and physically attacked him. He, in turn, had cooked her breakfast.

She looked down again at the omelet.

"It's getting cold," he told her.

"Doesn't matter. I'm not hungry anyway."

"When's the last time you had a meal, Chelsea Brennan?"

Every time she heard her name spoken in those slow, drawling tones, she felt a chill run up her spine. She tried to remember when her last meal had been, found she couldn't, then shrugged.

"You'll be skin and bone if you don't eat soon."

His words made her remember the way Michele had looked in the morgue, and she felt cold inside.

"Just a little," he urged. "I didn't put too much spice in 'em. If you want, though, I can run downstairs for the jalapeño sauce."

She almost smiled. Hot sauce on eggs? She forced herself to take a bite of the omelet, which melted on her tongue like butter. Garrett got up and poured coffee from the carafe, filling a fat clay mug with the steaming brew. He leaned close to hand it to her, and she caught his scent. It made her want to sniff more of it.

It scared her.

"I want my clothes," she said, feeling uneasy and suddenly wishing this man were far away from her. "I want to take Ethan and go back to New York this morning."

Garrett lowered his head. He looked truly sorry. "No. Not yet."

"What do you mean, not yet?"

"I'm sorry. No, listen, I mean it. I am sorry. But I can't just let you take off with Bubba until I know—"

"*Bubba?*"

"Er, Ethan. Look, you're stuck here for today. There's no two ways about that, so you may as well get used to the idea."

Her fork dropped onto the plate and she glared at him. "You *can't* keep me here against my will!"

"Sure I can. I'm the sheriff. And last night, you assaulted me. I can toss you in jail and I will, Chelsea Brennan, if you try to take Bu—Ethan out of this house today."

"You son of a—"

"You insult my mamma, Chelsea, and you're gonna regret it."

She blinked and defiantly stuck out her chin. "What are you going to do, *Sheriff* Brand? You going to kill me the way you did my sister?"

He closed his eyes, shook his head slowly from side to side. "Damn. I give up." He turned and left the room, closing the door behind him.

She knew it had been a cheap shot. Because she really didn't have a reason in the world to suspect that big man of murder.

Garrett stood in the hallway outside Jessi's room and took a long, deep breath. It had been a long time since anyone had tested his temper as sorely as that hellcat, Chelsea Brennan, was doing.

Worse than that, she was beautiful. All of her. And there hadn't been much hidden with nothing over her but that thin pink sheet of Jessi's. It had clung to her. There'd been a little indentation over her belly button, and her breasts might as well have been exposed.

They were small and firm and . . .

He clamped his jaw against the tide of reaction that tried, once again, to sweep him away. Tried not to think about the soft, pale color of her skin, or the satin texture of her neck and shoulders, or those pine-tree green eyes. Tried not to feel that small, china-doll hand, cool and trembling underneath his big callused one.

He couldn't afford to have tender feelings for her. Hell, she'd come here to take little Bubba away to Lord only knows what kind of life! She was accusing Garrett of murder, to boot!

Easy enough to solve the latter problem. The former one bothered him, though. If she turned out to be Ethan's aunt after all, then he'd have no right to keep that boy here.

Garrett sneaked into the guest bedroom where Ethan's cradle was, and saw the little pudge had decided to wake up at last. He was playing with his toes and drooling. A crooked smile tugged at Garrett's mouth, and he went to the cradle. "Morning, Bubba."

"Ga!"

He bent to pick up the baby, then thought better of it and removed the diaper first. Then the little T-shirt. He laid a fresh diaper under Ethan, but didn't tape it up. "You lie there and kick for a minute while I run a baby-size bath for you." Ethan's huge smile and gurgles of joy followed Garrett into the bathroom. "Never did know a fella who enjoyed being buck naked the way you do, Bubba."

He turned on the water.

Chelsea heard splashing. And the enthusiastic coos and chirps that went with it. Ethan! God, she'd come so far, waited so long to finally see him. That big lug of a sheriff might be able to keep her from taking him home, for the moment at least, but he couldn't keep her from seeing him.

She got out of the pink bed, holding the sheet around her in case anyone barged in, and went to the closet. She found a satin robe. Pink, of course, and a bit too long for her, but she belted it around her waist anyway, tying the sash nice and tight. Then she left the bedroom, barefoot, and followed the sounds into the big bedroom down the hall. A cradle stood empty beside a made-up bed with a wagon-wheel headboard. And farther inside, another door stood open.

Chelsea moved toward it, then stood stock-still just beyond the doorway, staring in utter shock at what she saw. The fat, laughing baby slapping his hands against the water in the tub so that sprays of droplets exploded all over the place. And the big man kneeling on the floor beside the tub, one hand firmly around the baby for support, while the other ran a washcloth over a round little belly.

Garrett had stripped off his T-shirt. Not in time, by the looks of it. It lay on the floor in a wet ball. Water dripped from that brick-wall chest and from those bodybuilder arms. And from his hair. Its thick, dark waves hung in straggles, some clinging to his face.

And he was laughing as much as the baby. A deep, rich sound that made her shiver.

Ethan. Her little Ethan. He was staring up at Garrett Brand with adoration oozing from his deep blue eyes.

Damned if the big cowboy wasn't looking back at the baby with something very similar shining from his brown ones.

Garrett turned, but never released his hold on Ethan. He'd tell her to get out, she guessed. He'd tell her to go back to the bedroom and stay there until further notice. He'd tell her—

"You mind handin' me that towel over there, Chelsea? I think I'm wetter than Bubba."

She blinked, gave her head a shake, then followed his gaze to the stack of towels on the washstand. She reached for one, handed it to him.

"Thanks." One-handed, he wiped his face and chest dry, then scooped the baby out of the tub and wrapped him up in another big, fluffy towel. The way he held Ethan, the way he cuddled him close... "Do me a favor and take it from here, Chelsea? I need some dry clothes, and then I ought to head out to check on that calf."

Her eyes burned and her throat closed too tightly for words to emerge as Garrett gently placed her sister's child into her arms.

"All his things are in that bag next to the cradle. You need anything, just step to the front door and holler."

She nodded, but mutely. She couldn't take her eyes from the baby. Garrett turned and walked away, leaving her alone with Ethan. She came as close to crying as she had since her mother died. No tears spilled over, but she felt them burning her eyes. Felt that choking sensation, the spasms in her chest.

"Ethan," she murmured, and she hugged him close. Felt his little fingers twisting and tugging at her hair. Smelled him. The little angel. The only family she had left. The best thing Michele had ever done in her short, misery-ridden life. God, how Michele must have loved this baby! "I'll take care of him," she whispered, praying somehow her sister could hear her and finally be at peace.

She carried the baby back into his room, walked to the wide, arching window and parted the curtains to stare out at the red-orange sky.

"It's all right now, Michele. I'll take care of him, I swear I will. I'll give him . . . I'll give him the things we didn't have."

Her voice trembled as she spoke, but she went on, feeling she needed to. She had to reassure her sister as well as herself. She had to speak the promise aloud to make it real, make it solid and attainable.

"He'll have a house, Michele. With a yard and room to grow. And . . . and he'll have a family. I'll love him so much . . . you'll see. And I'll never, ever hit him, Michele. No one will, I promise you that. He won't have to hide his bruises before he goes off to school, the way we did. I swear it. I'll protect him with my life. His grandfather will never even know he exists. And if his father tries to take him from me, Michele, I'll fight him to the death. I will. He's not going to grow up to be like them. He'll be . . . he'll be our son, Michele. Yours and mine. I'll tell him about you. I'll make sure he never forgets his mother."

Ethan's hand tugged at Chelsea's hair, and she smiled and hugged him again.

Jessi wiped the single tear from her cheek and tiptoed quietly back down the hall to her own room. Maybe . . . maybe she'd been a little hard on that strange city woman. She tried to imagine what her reaction would have been if their situations were reversed. If it had been one of her own precious brothers who'd been killed, and if she'd been convinced of who'd done it. Hell, she'd have been far rougher on the suspect than Chelsea Brennan had been on Garrett. She'd have probably shot first and asked questions later. And that would have been a crying shame, because Jessi never missed what she shot at.

Two things were for sure. Chelsea had loved her sister. And she loved little Ethan. And those were two things Jessi could fully understand.

That other stuff she'd overheard Chelsea talking about . . . about never hitting, and about hiding bruises . . . that stuff worried her. She decided to repeat the entire, one-sided conversation to Garrett just as soon as he came back inside.

Meanwhile, it was her turn to clean up the breakfast dishes.

Chapter 5

Garrett was more than a little put out to find that none of his normally well-mannered siblings had bothered to bring Chelsea Brennan's luggage in from her car. It was pushing nine a.m. by the time he'd finished tending the wounded calf, returned it to its mamma and ridden the fence lines, checking on the cattle as he did every morning and again every night. The two hours it took to cover the entire ranch did him as much good as it did the cattle, he thought. It relaxed him.

This morning, he'd only found one minor problem. Some brush had blown into the wire, shorting out the electric fence and leaving a portion vulnerable. Fortunately, the cows hadn't figured it out yet. Fat, happy Herefords stood around chewing grass and eyeing him while he cut the brush away and tested the fence.

When he and Duke galloped toward the barns again, Garrett saw Chelsea. She sat in the porch swing, Bubba in her arms. And she was still wearing Jessi's pink robe.

The picture she made there struck him hard for some reason, and he drew Duke to a stop and just sat there, not quite sure why or what to do next. Duke needed some oats and a good rubdown. But his unwilling houseguest was obviously being neglected.

Good manners prevailed, as they generally did with Garrett. He touched his heels to Duke's flanks and turned the horse toward the house. He stopped at the front porch and slid easily to the ground. He took a second to loop the reins around the hitching rail even though it was unnecessary. Duke wouldn't stray. In truth, he needed a minute to shake off the odd feeling the sight of her and Ethan sitting there in that porch swing—almost as if they were waiting for him—had caused in his gut. Like indigestion, only worse. He glanced around, looking everywhere but at her. Wes crouched near the gate to the horse pasture, tinkering with that loose hinge. Elliot held the thing in place for him as he worked. Both, though, were watching Garrett and Chelsea. Garrett saw the sneaky glances, the narrowed eyes.

His brothers didn't like Miss Chelsea Brennan very much, he deduced. And they trusted her even less.

"So, how's the calf?" she asked

Garrett brought his head around fast. Was that an attempt at civil conversation? Or was she just gearing up to make some nasty remark?

"Out in the pasture with his mamma. He'll be fine."

"Barbed wire is cruel," she observed, and though her voice was deep and soft, he heard the acid in her tone. "It ought to be illegal."

Garrett narrowed his eyes at her and tried not to notice the swell of her breasts peeking out at him from where the robe's neckline took a swan dive. "We've replaced it with smooth wire for that very reason. The piece that calf found was left over from days gone by. Grass had grown over it, so we must have missed it when we were clearing out the old fences.''

And just why the hell was he explaining himself to her?

"Electric shock therapy for cows," she decreed with all the pomposity of a haughty despot, "is just as bad."

"I have to disagree with you there, ma'am. The voltage is real low, and once they get bit on the nose, they tend to stay away from it."

She sniffed and looked away from him.

"It's better than letting them wander off and get lost," Garrett persisted. "Even a city girl ought to have sense enough to see that much."

She slanted him a glance that stung worse than any electric fence he'd ever accidentally grabbed hold of.

Garrett shifted his stance, regretting his hostile response. If he wanted to help Bubba, he couldn't go making this woman his enemy. He had to try to cozy up to her, keep her here until he figured out what to do. Okay, time to start over again. He cleared his throat. "I was thinking—"

"Did it hurt much?"

Garrett clenched his jaw. Cozying up to the hellcat wasn't going to be an easy task. "I was thinking," he began again, "you might want to drive into town with me."

"And why would I want to do that?"

"April first was a weekday. I ought to have something at the office to prove I wasn't in New York City."

"So make me a copy."

She was one ornery creature! "And have you accuse me of doctoring it up to cover my tracks?"

She met his eyes, and he felt heat. Only it wasn't from anger. And it had nothing to do with the sun already blazing down from the wide Texas sky. This heat was searing and electric. It sort of rushed up from his toes and made him a little bit dizzy. He had to look away first.

"What about Ethan?" she finally asked.

The screen door creaked, and Jessi stepped out onto the porch, wiping her hands on a checkered dish towel. "I'll take care of Ethan."

Garrett nodded, but Chelsea turned a wary gaze on his little sister.

"Don't do me any favors," Chelsea said.

Jessi had never had what Garrett would call tolerance. Her temper flared quicker than a sparkler on the Fourth of July. Hotter, too.

"Don't worry, I wasn't offering. I'll watch him for my brother. For you, I wouldn't cross the road, and if you think I—" Jessi stopped suddenly and bit her lower lip.

Garrett was perplexed. He'd never seen Jessi cut herself off in mid-tirade before.

Jessi shook her head, took a deep breath. "Sorry."

Sorry?

"Truth is, I just adore little Ethan. I'd love to take care of him this morning."

Garrett almost fell down in shock, and a quick glance at Chelsea's puckered brow told him she was as surprised as he.

Chelsea waited a moment and finally nodded. "All right, then. I'll need a few minutes."

Jessi came forward and took the baby from Chelsea's arms. She propped him on her slender hip. "You can use the shower in my room if you want."

Chelsea's eyes narrowed, but she nodded, got to her feet and walked into the house without another word.

Garrett tilted his head, fixing his baby sister with a questioning glance. "Why the change of heart, Jes?"

Jessi looked through the screen door into the house, and Garrett sensed she was waiting until Chelsea had moved out of earshot to answer him. When she finally turned back to him, she looked worried.

"Jes?"

She pressed her cheek to the baby's. "Garrett, I think somebody's hurt that woman. I think somebody's hurt her bad."

Garrett frowned. "Course she's hurt. She just lost her sister."

Jessi shook her head. "No, Garrett. I mean *really hurt* her. Physically."

Her meaning became clear, and Garrett felt a dark cloud settle right over his soul. A thundercloud. "Maybe you'd better tell me about it."

He kept looking at her. Not *just* looking, though. He kept searching her face as if trying to see something there, and it was making Chelsea damned uncomfortable.

She rode beside him in the oversize pickup truck, over dusty roads and finally paved ones, into the small town of Quinn. The truck was big. One of those kinds that needed two sets of wheels in the back just to push it along. Seemed everything about Garrett Brand was big. His home, his truck. Even his speckled horse had been huge. Then again, she supposed it would have to be to support a man of his size.

He pulled to a stop in front of an adobe-like structure with no curtains in the windows and a sign over the door that read Sheriff's Office.

"Here we are."

He got out and came around as if to open her door for her. She beat him to it. But then he took her arm to help her out, getting the best of her anyway.

Chelsea stepped out, stumbling a little because of her heels and the long reach to the ground. Garrett's big hands circled her waist surely and firmly, and he lifted her right up off her feet, setting her down again on the small stretch of sidewalk in front of the building.

But his hands remained for a second or two, even after her feet touched the ground. She felt every one of those fingers pressing into her flesh. The warmth of them seeped right through her silk suit.

His sigh made her look up to see him shaking his head slowly.

"What?"

His hands still hadn't moved away.

"I…" He looked down, took his hands away. "I'm just not used to handling tiny things," he said, and he looked embarrassed. "Like Ethan, and now you."

Her throat went dry. She didn't know how the hell to reply to a comment like that, so she said nothing. Garrett finally turned away and headed for the door. He used a set of keys she hadn't noticed to unlock it, then pushed it open and stood aside, waiting for her to go first.

The office consisted of only one sparsely furnished room, and two cells at the far back. That was it. She looked at him in surprise.

"Not much happens around here," he explained, reading her expression. He left the door wide open after coming in behind her.

"Obviously."

He shrugged and moved past her to the file cabinet, which wasn't even locked. After riffling through a drawer, he pulled out a folder, tossed it onto his desk and took a seat in the big hardwood chair behind it. As he began flipping pages, Chelsea felt restless. She prowled the office, examining some photos on the wall, and paused at one that had been taken right in front of the ranch house. A huge family. Five boys and a little baby girl. Two proud parents standing behind the group of smiling kids.

The oldest of the boys, she knew without a doubt, was Garrett. He stood taller than his father, with shoulders that seemed too big for his body. He'd been a gangly teen, she thought a little smugly. Long limbed and awkward.

Her gaze stole to him as he sat behind that desk, dwarfing the big antique. He certainly had grown into his body. His proportions were perfect now. He ought to be a centerfold.

She drew a little gasp at her uncharacteristic thought.

He looked up, caught her staring at him. He held her gaze with his for a long moment, and finally he smiled. His smile was a killer.

"That's a pretty suit, by the way."

Confusion made her blink. She glanced down at the forest green silk skirt and the sleeveless blouse that matched it. "It's too hot here for silk. I should have known better."

"It's the same color as your eyes."

Her head came up fast.

A deep red color crept up his neck into his face, and he looked for all the world as if his blurted compliment had been as surprising to him as it had been to her. "I mean . . . you know. Green and all." He quickly lowered his gaze to the papers in front of him again, shuffling madly.

"Yeah," she said in a voice just above a whisper. "Green and all."

"*Muchacho,* what *are* you doing here on a holiday?"

Chelsea turned, surprised by the frail, heavily accented voice coming through the open door.

"Hey, Marisella," Garrett said, and he rose, went to the door and took both of the deeply tanned, wrinkled hands in his. "How's my best girl?"

"Oh, now, Garrett…" The elderly woman—who wore jeans and a Travis Tritt T-shirt of all things—gazed up into the big man's eyes much like little Ethan had done earlier. Her black eyes beamed adoration.

"How's the arthritis, Marisella?" His tone was more serious now.

"No worse than usual."

"And ol' Pedro?"

She shook her head slowly, her dark eyes going sad. "He doesn't eat, Garrett. Pedro, he is turning his nose up at everything I offer. Doc Ramone is away at that veterinary convention, and I am sick with worry." Marisella glanced over Garrett's shoulder at Chelsea, then smiled. "And who is the *chica?*"

Garrett turned to her. "Marisella, I'd like you to meet Chelsea Brennan. She's staying out at the ranch with us for a few days."

A few days?

"Chelsea, Marisella del Carmen Jalisco. Prettiest widow lady either side of the Rio Grande."

Marisella's sun-bronzed face crinkled when she smiled, and she waved a dismissive hand at Garrett's compliments, nodding to Chelsea. "Good to meet you, Señorita Brennan. You are from the east, yes?"

"New York."

Silvery brows went up. "And which of the Brands is it you've come to…see?"

Chelsea frowned. "I'm not sure what—"

"None of them, Marisella," Garrett interrupted. "She's a friend. That's all. Now listen, I'll come by this evening to have a look at that worthless ol' cat of yours, all right? Maybe Jessi and I can doctor him up for you."

"It will be a relief to me if you do! When Pedro is not well, I feel as bad as he does."

"We'll be there."

She reached up to pat Garrett's cheek. "You do your papa proud, *hombre.* Never a time anyone in Quinn has trouble, but that you offer a hand. I do believe the woman who captures your heart will have her hands on a diamond." After the last pointed statement, she aimed a wink in Chelsea's direction, then turned to go.

Garrett hurried to grip her elbow and ease her down the steps, his hands touching her as if she might break.

He really did *seem* gentle.

As he stepped outside with Marisella, a breeze wafted in through the door, lifting the papers from the desk and scattering them. And then it died, leaving the air as still and muggy as before. Chelsea automatically went to pick the papers up, gathering them into a stack, one by one. But she paused with one sheet in hand because the date across the top caught her eye. April 1.

She froze, then hurriedly scanned the sheet, certain she was about to find a record of a return trip from N.Y. detailed there somewhere. But instead, she found the opposite.

Each sheet in the stack was a typewritten record of the day's events. Only they didn't read like dry, technical police reports. More like a journal or a diary. This particular page began with a single paragraph that took all the wind out of her sails.

Nine a.m.—Career Day at Quinn Elementary. Talked until 10:00 and answered questions till 10:40. Lord, but we have some characters in this town! Almost made me wish I had my own little brood at home.

Below that, marked with two stars, a postscript: "Note—check in on Brian Muldoon's mamma."

"Those are personal notes you're reading, Chelsea, not official records."

She looked up with a start to see Garrett lounging in the doorway, arms folded across his chest, looking at her. She swallowed hard, shook her head, added the sheet to the top of the stack and crossed the room to hand it to him.

He took the papers, glancing down at what she'd been reading, and nodded. "Career Day," he said. "How could I have forgotten that one?"

Chelsea tried to drag her gaze away from him, but couldn't. Had she been all wrong about him? She cleared her throat, searching for something to say, before latching onto the first thing that came to mind. "What was wrong with Brian Muldoon's mother?"

Garrett frowned down at the paper, then lifted his head and focused his big, soft brown eyes on her face. His voice more gentle than she'd heard up to now, he said, "Brian's daddy liked to hit her."

The pain sparked to life, though she slammed the door on her emotions before they could show. She fixed her face into an iron mask, refusing to flinch. "And what did you do about it?"

"Oh, the usual. We arrested him a couple of times, tried to talk her into pressing charges. She was too afraid of him to do it, though. And we couldn't blame her. We all knew he wouldn't serve enough time to do him any good."

"So he's still here in Quinn, beating the hell out of his wife?"

Garrett shook his head slowly. "We don't take to that kind of thing around here, Chelsea."

"Right. But your hands are tied, isn't that it?"

"Not by a long shot. I warned the worthless fool to stop...or else. He hurt her again. So my brothers and I went over there and...had a little talk with him."

Chelsea tilted her head, staring at him in disbelief.

"We made him see that the best thing for all concerned would be for him to get out of Quinn and never set foot here again."

"And he did? Just like that?"

"Well, we can be pretty convincing when we set our minds to it."

"You...you beat him up, didn't you?"

He drew a breath that lifted his shoulders and slowly let it all out again. Then he came forward and placed both his hands on her shoulders. She automatically shrugged away from his touch. She didn't like men putting their hands on her.

He frowned, but let his hands fall to his sides. "Chelsea Brennan, I'd rather be shot than lift a violent hand to anyone...or anything, for that matter."

"Oh?" He was too close to her. She could feel his warm breath on her lips. "Thing is, I'd have rather been drawn and quartered than to stand by and do nothing. So I told him to leave her alone in the only language he could understand. The way I see it, I didn't have much of a choice."

"And he never came back?"

"Nope. He never did."

"You violated his civil rights," she observed, but it was a weak argument. "You could lose your job and go to prison for that."

He nodded slowly. "No man has the right to lift a hand to a woman, Chelsea. Nor to a child. If you'd been in my shoes, would you have done anything different?"

She met his gaze head-on, and for just a moment the pain got the best of her. "If I'd been in your shoes," she said softly, "I'd have shot the bastard."

He narrowed his eyes as he studied her. "You're one angry woman, Chelsea Brennan."

She nodded. "You might want to take back your offer to help me find the man who murdered my sister, Garrett Brand. Because when I do, I'll probably kill him."

He smiled a little, and for a second she wondered why.

"I take that to mean you're finally convinced it wasn't me," he explained when she frowned at him.

She lowered her head, remembering her accusations, the way she'd hit him. If she'd been wrong... But it was pretty obvious she *had* been wrong, wasn't it?

"I probably owe you an apology."

"Probably."

He stood there, and his hands rose as if to touch her shoulders again. She stiffened, and he stopped himself, lowering them again with a thoughtful expression on his face. He was waiting.

"I apologize."

"I accept," he said with an abbreviated bow, really no more than a dip of his head and shoulders, but he never broke eye contact.

"Then you're more forgiving than I'd be." There was an invisible beam running between her eyes and his. Something that held her captive.

"Must be those green eyes of yours, making me feel generous." He moved a little closer.

Warmth curled in the pit of her stomach before she reminded herself he'd just given similarly effusive compliments to Marisella. "Then you won't object to my taking my nephew home anymore?"

Garrett stiffened and the smile left his face. "I'm afraid I have to."

Shock sent her backward. "Why?"

"I still have some unanswered questions, Chelsea."

"*Your* unanswered questions don't mean squat to me, Sheriff! We're talking about *my* nephew here. You can't keep him."

Garrett pushed a hand through his thick hair and turned to pace away from her. Then he came back again. "Will you just use your head for a minute, woman? Suppose you're right, and this no-account your sister was with *did* kill her. Don't you suppose he's looking for his son about now?"

"I'm sure of it, you big, dense *redneck!* That's why I want to get Ethan the hell out of here!"

"And you think this guy doesn't know about you? You think in a whole year with him your sister never once told him about you? Legally, he could still take his son from you, Chelsea. You wouldn't have a leg to stand on in court. Not unless you can prove your suspicions about him are true."

"He can't take Ethan from me if he can't find me," she argued, no longer sure why she was in such a hurry to get out of Texas and away from Garrett Brand. The man shook her in ways she'd never been shaken before.

"Hell, you said yourself you'd seen him from your apartment window. It kind of follows that he knows where you live!"

She opened her mouth, but lost the power of speech.

He knows where I live.

A gut-deep fear engulfed her—one she hadn't felt since she was a little girl lying in bed late at night, listening to

the thudding sounds of fists against flesh and the guttural groans of her mother. A man like that one knew
where she lived.

She'd sworn she'd never be afraid again. But she was
afraid now.

Two hesitant backward steps put her up against a wall.
One she needed, or she'd collapse. She was trembling.
God, she hated this kind of fear.

"Chelsea?"

He was there in front of her, looking worried and
scared.

"I'll kill him," she whispered, and for a second she
wasn't even sure if she was talking about her father or
Ethan's.

"Damn, your face is as white as a lily, woman." And a
moment later, he lifted his hands, hesitated and awkwardly gathered her close to him. He held her to his chest
and ran one hand up and down her back the way he might
do with the baby. Trying to comfort her. "I didn't say that
to scare you, Chelsea. I didn't mean to—"

"I'm not afraid of that bastard," she muttered.

"No. No, of course you're not. Hell, any woman who'd
march right up to a fella my size and deliver a right hook
isn't afraid of anything."

One of his hands ran over her hair, and she closed her
eyes. Then, realizing how very safe she felt in his arms, she
went stiff as a board. "I don't need any *man* to protect
me."

He stilled. Then slowly, his hands fell away and he
stepped back. "I didn't say you did. But let's just be
practical. If you go home to New York, he'll know where
to find you and Ethan. But right now, he has no idea
where you are."

"Assuming he's even looking for us. He might not care any more about his son than he did Michele."

"Maybe not. But why risk it?"

She searched his face as the answer was there.

"Just stay for a day or two, Chelsea. Long enough for me to try to find out who this man is and what he's capable of. Please. Do it for Ethan."

She lifted her chin a little. It galled her to admit Ethan was safer here with Garrett than he would be back in New York with her, but dammit, the man had a point. And she couldn't very well risk the baby for the sake of her pride.

"All right," she said at last. "All right, we'll stay. But only for a day or two."

Garrett smiled fully, and just for an instant, Chelsea forgot how to breathe. Now that she knew he hadn't killed her sister, she noticed that this man was attractive. Incredibly attractive. And that was something Chelsea had stopped noticing about *any* man a very long time ago. Maybe Garrett Brand wasn't physically dangerous to her after all. But she was only now beginning to realize how emotionally dangerous it might be to spend much time around him.

Because he couldn't possibly be as kind and gentle as he was pretending. No man could.

Chapter 6

Vincent de Lorean downed his third shot of tequila and lifted his gaze from the sparkling water in the terrazzo-tiled pool to scan the faces of the three men who stood in front of him. He didn't like the expressions they wore. He didn't expect to like the news they were about to deliver, either. Setting the cut-crystal glass down on the umbrella-shaded table beside him, he sent a pointed glance at Monique.

"Go inside."

She gave him a playful pout, but obeyed. She knew better than to question him. Smarter than the last pretty woman he'd brought here. Maybe she'd turn out better. Monique rose with the sensuality she knew he liked, lowering her long legs slowly, running one hand over plump breasts and then slowly over her belly before turning to click her heels across the concrete and wiggle her butt through the stucco villa's glass doors. The three men turned to watch her bikini-clad body as she moved away from them. They wanted her. Vincent knew it, and it pleased him. He liked other people to crave what was his.

As long as they didn't try to take it from him.

"Have you found my son?" he asked, and all three heads snapped around to face him again.

Jonas had been with him for ten years, and Vincent knew the fear in his eyes was real when he shook his head slowly from side to side. William, too, had the good sense to be afraid. But the third one, the new man...something was wrong there. Lash, he called himself, though Vincent was unsure whether it was a first name or last. He stood there, by all appearances, respectful. But there was no fear in his face nor in his blue eyes. In fact, Vincent smelled the smallest hint of defiance in the man.

He needed a lesson, this one. Vincent knew how to keep his men loyal. Fear. Once they knew he held their lives in his hands, they would never betray him. He sat quietly while Jonas spoke, assessing the best way to deliver the lesson.

"It's only a matter of time, boss. You know that we will—"

"The sister?" Vincent interrupted, having come to a decision on today's teaching methods. "What about the sister?"

"She was in El Paso," Jonas said. "She identified Michele's body, asked about Ethan, then left. She hasn't checked into any hotels in the area and she hasn't returned to New York."

"Then where the hell is she?"

Jonas closed his eyes, swallowed hard. "We have men watching her apartment, Vince. We'll find her. I swear it."

Vincent pursed his lips and shifted his gaze to Lash. "You. You were supposed to be staking out the medical examiner's office. You were told to follow this Chelsea Brennan when she left there. What happened?''

He didn't flinch or look away. He shrugged instead. ''I lost her. It was pouring rain and she was driving like a maniac.''

Vincent didn't like this man. He usually never hired men larger than himself or better-looking. He'd made an exception this time, because his oldest employee, Jonas, had told him what an asset this one would be. Furthermore, this Lash's voice held the slightest hesitation. The way a man spoke when he was lying...or when he was nervous. Vincent's ego preferred the latter theory to the former. Nervousness wasn't fear, but it was a start. The lesson he had in mind should solidify the man's loyalty.

Vincent drew a breath and released it slowly. As he did, he dropped his right hand to the folded towel beside his lounge chair. They couldn't see that hand. And they couldn't see the gun he pulled from beneath the towel, either. Not until he quickly leveled it on Jonas and pulled the trigger.

Jonas didn't have time to blink. His head snapped back. His knees buckled. He thudded to the concrete. William staggered a few steps backward before he started to cry and snivel, probably expecting to be next. The other one just stood there, staring right into Vincent's eyes, his own as cold as ice. Those eyes registered disgust and a little surprise. Still no fear.

''Jonas told me you'd be an asset,'' Vincent said softly, and he examined the silvery weapon in his hands. ''He was wrong. I don't tolerate mistakes in my employees. Do you understand that now?''

''Jonas was the smartest man you had working for you,'' Lash replied in a steady, controlled voice. ''He might have found your son for you. Now...who knows?''

Vincent stood up, walked closer to Lash. "*I* know. You will find him. And if you fail..." He said nothing more. Just sent a glance down at the body. "Now get him out of here. And find that woman. If she thinks she can keep my son from me, she's going to be very sorry. As sorry as her pathetic sister."

Garrett took his time. He drove Chelsea around Quinn, pointing out the shops he thought might interest her. Then he took her over the River Road to show her the Rio Grande. The idea was to calm her down a little bit. Because she'd been damned scared back there in his office. Hell, he'd never seen that kind of fear come over a person so suddenly or so completely as it had come over her when he'd pointed out that a killer knew where she lived.

She might talk a big game and she might be so filled with anger she was ready to take on the world. But deep inside, Chelsea Brennan was a frightened woman.

And she didn't like to be touched. He'd discerned that, as well. Whenever he'd had call to put his hands on her— which, as a matter of fact, he'd done more often than was probably necessary—she reacted like a skittish colt. Got all stiff and nervous and always ended the contact just as quickly as possible.

He was thinking that Jessi had been right about her suspicions. That maybe Chelsea had been hurt, physically hurt, by someone in her past.

He didn't like thinking that because it made him angry, and he hated being angry. He was too big to allow himself the luxury of a short temper. All his life he'd struggled to be calm and relaxed, no matter what. Hell, he hadn't even lost his temper when he'd put the fear of God into Brian Muldoon's heavy-fisted father. And the truth was, he'd taken his brothers along, not for support, but just to be sure he didn't actually *hurt* the man, much as the bastard deserved to be hurt.

He didn't like the feeling that came over him now, though, when he thought about someone lifting a violent hand to the woman beside him. Because it went beyond anger. It made him sick. He almost didn't *want* to know if it were true. He almost didn't want to know who had hurt her.

Almost.

She seemed a little calmer when they arrived back at the ranch that afternoon. Not much, but a little.

Ethan sat in a high chair in the kitchen, and Elliot was making motor noises and driving a spoonful of green goo into his mouth.

Garrett frowned. "Where'd that come from?"

"The baby food or the high chair?" Jessi asked after taking a bite of her fajita. Then she grinned. "Actually, it doesn't matter. Both of them were provided by our grouchy brother who claims to dislike babies."

"Wes?" Garrett shifted his gaze to Wes, who scowled back at him.

"Kid needed a place to sit, didn't he?"

Elliot grinned broadly at Wes's muttered reply. "Hell, I think Wes here would make a great little mother. Don't you, Jessi?"

"Of course he would. He ought to have a whole slew of babies crawling all over him, and maybe run a nursery school on the side."

"Old Mother Goose," Elliot sang, "when *he* wanted to wander, would fly through the air on a very fine, er, Paint. Gee, Wes, that doesn't fit. Any chance you can change Paint's name to Gander?"

Wes grimaced and attacked his fajita. Garrett just shook his head and went to the table. "Did you leave us any crumbs or anything?"

Elliot pointed to the heaping platter in the table's center. "I know it's not enough to fill *you* up, big brother, but it might make an appetizer."

"Come on, Chelsea," Jessi said. "There's plenty. Sit down and eat."

Garrett noticed Chelsea's surprised expression. She covered it fast and came forward anyway. Wes grabbed the platter and set it down in front of her, while Elliot popped a bite into the baby's mouth, then got up to go to the fridge. He poured a glass of milk and set it down in front of Chelsea. Without a word, he just set it down, then returned to his baby-feeding duties.

Chelsea looked disconcerted. "Th-thank you."

Wes cleared his throat. "We, uh, we were rough on you last night."

He turned those black eyes of his on her. Garrett saw it and half-expected her to melt into a puddle at his devilishly handsome, half-Comanche brother's feet the way most women did if he so much as glanced their way.

"I wasn't exactly polite," Chelsea replied, remaining solid.

Jessi passed the tossed salad. "We Brands are a tight bunch. We take care of our own. But we've been talking and . . . well, I guess you were just doing the same thing we'd have done in your shoes. So . . ."

"What my sister is trying to say, Chelsea," Elliot explained, "is that we're sorry about what happened to your sister, and we want to help you and little Ethan through this if we can."

Garrett felt his back straighten, and battled a smile. Maybe he'd taught them something after all. Chelsea sat at his right, and he thought he saw a lump come and go in her throat, but he wasn't sure. He thought he understood the change now. He was pretty certain Jessi had told the other two about what she'd heard and about her theory. He knew the thought of some bastard beating up on a little thing like Chelsea would turn their stomachs the same way it did his own.

"I, um . . ." Chelsea shook her head and pushed away from the table. "I have to go upstairs." She turned and quickly left.

"Garrett?" Jessi asked, staring after her.

"I don't know, Jes. Let's let her be for now. I'm going back to the office later to run a check on her and her sister, see what I can find out. Jes, I'll need you to come with me. Marisella's cat is off his feed again, and she's making herself sick worrying about him."

"Sure."

"Elliot and I can take care of things here tonight, Garrett. Leave whenever you need to."

Garrett nodded at Wes and, a few hours later, did just that.

But what he found out was not one bit pleasing to him, and it only made matters worse.

That evening, after he'd dropped Jessi at Marisella's, he'd spent a good hour sitting at his desk trying to get over the shock of it.

Chelsea Brennan's father, Calvin Brennan, had been arrested twenty-five times for spousal and/or child abuse. New York State Social Services had been called in when school officials reported the two girls often coming to school covered in bruises. But they hadn't taken action soon enough. Calvin was in Attica, serving the eighteenth year of a twenty-year sentence for beating his wife to death.

Garrett swore under his breath and thought again about the turmoil and the pain and the rage he saw every time he looked into Chelsea Brennan's eyes.

And he felt a burning moisture taking shape in his own.

Chelsea sat by the fireplace, imagining a cheerful fire burning in the grate. Anything cheerful would be a relief if it would dispel the grim mood that had settled over her.

Elliot and Wes bantered in the kitchen over whose turn it was to clean up the dinner dishes. From the wide window in the living room, Chelsea could see Jessi feeding carrots to a spotted horse. An ancient pickup truck with a driver Chelsea had recognized as Marisella del Carmen Whatever had dropped Jessi off twenty minutes ago, but Garrett still hadn't returned. She wondered what was keeping him in town. A woman, maybe? The idea gnawed at her a little more than it should have as she watched Jessi coax the beautiful animal closer and then stroke its muzzle as it snapped the carrots from her hands. Behind Jessi, the lush grass seemed to go on forever, a wide green blanket beneath a gigantic, sapphire sky as blue as little Ethan's eyes.

She remembered the photo she'd seen, the one of the Brand family taken years ago, and she thought this must have been a magical place for children. Room to run. Room to grow. This huge family surrounding them like a protective cocoon. A child would thrive here.

Ethan sat on the braided rug in the center of the polished hardwood floor, chewing on a worn-out old teddy bear's paw. Chelsea had no idea where the bear had come from. No doubt one of the Brands had dug it up from somewhere. They treated Ethan as if he were their own. Close beside Ethan—as always, she'd noticed—the big, gentle dog, eyes alert, watching the baby's every move and occasionally inching closer in hopes of a pat or a tug on the ear.

Chelsea battled the sense of unease that had settled on her like a shroud at the dinner table tonight. These people were good and kind. They had the type of happy, stable life she and her sister had always craved and dreamed about. And along comes Chelsea Brennan and her dead sister's baby, with maybe a killer on her trail. The thought that she might bring disaster raining down on this haven ate away at her. They wanted to help her but they'd only get hurt if they tried. The way her mother had. And she couldn't let that happen.

Yet, for the moment, Ethan was safer here than in any other place she could imagine. Chelsea was torn.

To battle her restlessness, she got up and headed into the kitchen, not the least bit worried about Ethan. She'd noticed the way the outlets in the living room had all been plugged and anything breakable had been moved out of Ethan's reach. Someone had placed an expandable gate across the bottom of the stairway. Ethan was safe here.

Safe.

She walked into the kitchen just in time to see Elliot snap Wes with the twisted end of a dish towel. Both laughed out loud, then stopped when they saw her standing in the doorway.

"Why not let me do the dishes this time?" she offered. "I know you have stuff to do outside."

"Hey, that's—"

"No way," Wes interrupted his brother. "You're a guest. Garrett would have our hides nailed to the barn wall."

"At least let me help. I need something to do, you know?"

Wes's dark eyes held hers for a moment. They were powerful, his black eyes. He was obviously part Native American, and Chelsea wondered why he seemed so different from the other Brands. He also had a way of looking at a person that was piercing and knowing. He nodded, snatched the dish towel from his brother and tossed it to her. "Okay. You can dry."

"Okay," she said, catching the towel and moving forward to the sink where Elliot had resumed washing dishes. Wes went back to clearing the table.

Chelsea could see these people had decided to make her welcome here. And though she was uncomfortable with them, she was grateful, too. If it hadn't been for this family, God only knows what might have happened to the baby.

"It's nice to see men doing housework and a woman outside with the horses," she said in an attempt at normal conversation. "Is it always like this?"

"We share the work around here," Elliot told her. "Garrett says he doesn't want Jess raised to think all she's good for is cooking and cleaning for a bunch of males. So we divide up the duties equally, inside and out."

She nodded. It was something she would have expected Garrett to think about. "I saw a photo in his office, of the whole family, I think, only you were all kids. You know the one I mean?"

Elliot suddenly stilled with a plate in his hand. Frowning, Chelsea turned to see Wes had paused in what he'd been doing, as well.

"I'm sorry. Did I say something wrong?"

"No," Wes told her. He gave his head a shake and gathered up a few more plates, turned and brought them to the sink. "We all have copies of that photo. It was the last one we had taken before Orrin and Maria were killed.''

She frowned. "Your parents?"

"Yeah," Elliot said softly. "Our parents."

"Orrin was my father, Maria my stepmother, but she treated me like her own son," Wes clarified.

"I'm so sorry. God, you were all so young. Jessi was just a baby in that photo. What did you do?"

"Garrett held things together." Elliot shook his head, plunging his hands back into the soapy water. "He'd only just finished high school when it happened and he'd already been accepted at Texas State, but he didn't go. He stayed home instead. Ran the ranch as well as any grown man could have done. And took care of this brood like a mother hen herding chicks."

"The state wanted to separate us," Wes said, picking up the story. "They wanted to send me to a family on the Comanche reservation, and the others into foster care elsewhere. If it hadn't been for Garrett, they would have."

"No wonder you all love him so much."

"We'd kill for him," Wes said, his voice low, his face expressionless, but Chelsea sensed the deep feeling underlying his words.

"We'd die for him," Elliot added with a firm nod and a slight crack in his voice.

It made her throat go tight to see such closeness in a family. It was the sort of thing she'd always fantasized about but had long since given up on finding for herself.

She dried the last cup and stacked it in the cupboard, swallowed hard and decided to change the subject. "There were six children in the photo."

"Yeah. Adam and Ben are the two you haven't met. Adam's in New York. Landed himself a job there last summer," Elliot explained.

"So far from home?" It seemed uncharacteristic in such a tight family.

"His fiancée dumped him for another man the day of their wedding," Elliot went on. "He couldn't stand being in the same town with her any—"

"Elliot."

Wes's voice held a warning. Family secrets, Chelsea supposed. And she wasn't family.

"I didn't mean to pry."

Elliot sent her a sheepish smile. Wes just sighed, shook his head and grabbed a sponge to begin wiping off the table.

"Hell, everyone in town knows about it anyway," Elliot added, unperturbed by his brother's censure. "And Ben, he's off in the mountains somewhere in Tennessee. Took off after his wife, Penny, died nearly a year ago, and we haven't heard a word from him since."

"Garrett has," Wes contradicted. "If he didn't know Ben was all right, he'd have hauled all of us over there to hunt him down."

"Yeah, but a postcard once a month telling us he's still breathing isn't what I call correspondence."

"He must be hurting," Chelsea said softly.

Elliot lowered his head in a sad, slow nod. "We Brand men haven't exactly been lucky in love."

"I just wish they'd both lick their wounds and get back here," Wes declared. "It's tough running a ranch shorthanded."

"What we need," Elliot remarked, pulling the plug and watching the water swirl down the drain, "is one good crisis. If they thought we were in trouble, they'd be here so fast—"

"Careful what you wish for, boy," Wes warned him. He gave the oval oak table one last swipe and tossed the sponge into the sink. Then he snatched his hat off the back of a chair and dropped it on his head. "Come on. We're burning daylight, and those two heifers are due to freshen any day now."

Elliot took the towel from Chelsea, wiped his hands and sent her a wink as he followed his brother outside.

Chelsea decided maybe Garrett had been right after all. It was safe here. In fact, while she hated to admit it after the way she'd initially treated all of them, she felt safer here than she'd ever felt in her entire life. Maybe it *would* be better to stay...just for a couple of days. Just to be sure her sister's killer wasn't a threat to her or to Ethan.

She picked up the phone. If she was staying, she'd need more funds, and she knew her last week's paycheck would be in her mail by now. She called her apartment manager, who was also a friend who lived down the hall from her, and felt lucky to catch the party animal at home.

"Mindy?"

"Chelsea? Is that you?"

"Yes. I'm—"

"Where *are* you? What's going on? Did you find Michele?"

That was Mindy. She talked a mile a minute and barely took time to breathe in between. "Michele..." Chelsea swallowed past the lump in her throat. "She's dead, Mindy."

"Oh, my God! What happened? Are you okay? Did you find the baby? Is he all right? What about—"

"He's all right. He's with me. We're both fine. But I'm going to be down here a while."

"You need anything, Chels? Anything I can do on this end, you know? Water your plants, send you something. 'Cause if I can do anything, I—"

"Yes. I do need you to do something."

"Anything. You name it and I'll do it. You poor kid, are you sure you're all right?"

"Fine. I need you to forward my mail for a few days, okay?"

"Sure. You got it. Let me grab a pen . . . Okay, here we go. Give me the address."

"I'm at the Texas Brand, Quinn, Texas."

"Sounds like a dude ranch."

"I don't know the zip."

"I'll get it from the post office, Chelsea. Don't worry, I'll send your stuff out tomorrow morning first thing, okay?"

"Thanks. I appreciate it."

"Chelsea?"

"Yes?"

"Michele's...funeral. You'll let me know, won't you?"

Chelsea closed her eyes as a deep shudder worked up from her feet all the way to her shoulders. She had to bury her sister. If this didn't kill her, she didn't think anything ever would.

"Yeah. I'll let you know."

"Thanks, Chels. You take care, okay?"

Chelsea didn't answer. She just replaced the receiver and turned her head to see sweet little Ethan on the floor. He'd fallen asleep there, and that old dog had curled up close beside him.

The creak of the screen door brought her gaze around, and it locked with Garrett's. His eyes—deep brown and soft as velvet—scanned her face, narrowed and probed. "Chelsea?"

She lowered her head. "I don't think I can do this."

He took a step toward her, then stopped, stood still. "Chelsea Brennan, I think you can do just about anything you set your mind to."

She shook her head.

He sighed deeply, his eyes roaming her face for a long moment. Then he came a little closer. "Did I ever tell you how much you remind me of my mamma?"

She looked up at him then, brows raised.

"She was the prettiest woman in the state of Texas. Her eyes were brown, not green, but they flashed with that same fire I see in yours sometimes. I never thought I'd know another woman with the kind of strength she had in her. But I was wrong about that."

"I'm not strong."

"To survive what you have, lady, you must have bones of solid granite."

Chelsea's eyes widened as she searched his face. And she saw the knowledge there, as plain as day. He didn't try to hide it. "You know, don't you?"

"About your father? Yeah, I know."

Chelsea closed her eyes, unable to look at him, knowing that her sordid past was an open book to him. She should have known that he'd find out. Her family history was largely a matter of public record after all, and he was a sheriff with access to all of it.

"I dream about him, you know," she whispered, not sure why her lips were moving, why she felt compelled to tell this man anything more horrible than he already knew. "I dream about the day he's released from prison. I'm there at the front gate, waiting for him. And as soon as he sees me, as soon as he looks straight into my eyes . . . I kill him." She looked at Garrett, half-expecting to see shock or disapproval in his eyes. But she only saw a reflection of her own pain. As if he felt it, too. "It scares me, Garrett. It scares the hell out of me because I think I could really do it."

"Then he'd win. Because you'd end up in prison, or dead, and every one of the Brennan women would be gone. And I think deep down, you know that, Chelsea. I think you're too smart to let him get the best of you that way. Even if you weren't, I don't think you'd kill him. Not when it came right down to it. Because deep down inside, you're not like him. Not at all."

"I wish I was as sure of that as you are," she whispered. "I hate him."

"I know." He took another step, this one bringing him close to her, but he didn't touch her. He just stood near enough so she could feel the heat from his body floating into hers. When she breathed, it was his scent and his breath she was inhaling. "I don't even know him, Chelsea, and I hate him, too."

"Why?" She looked up as she asked the question, saw him staring down at her.

"Because he hurt you."

"Why do you give a damn about that? You barely know me."

Garrett shrugged his big shoulders. "Damned if I know. Been asking myself the same thing all night. Doesn't matter, though, does it? Point is, I do give a damn. And right now, I'm fighting everything in me to keep from putting my arms around you, little Chelsea Brennan, and pulling you close to me and holding you until you stop shaking like a scared rabbit. Just the way I used to do with Jessi late at night when she'd had a bad dream. Or with Elliot when he'd wake up crying for Mamma. I'm fighting it because I know you don't like men putting their hands on you. And I can't say as I blame you for it."

He spoke slowly, his deep voice soft and steady and low. She realized he was trying to calm her, comfort her.

"M-maybe... it would be all right...."

He sighed, and his big hands slipped around her waist, their touch warm, but light as air. He didn't pull her to him. He just put his arms loosely around her and waited. Chelsea was the one who moved forward until her body was pressed to his. She turned her head to the side and rested it against his chest, right over the drumming of his heart. His arms tightened but only a little. One hand moved upward to stroke her hair slowly, soothingly, over and over.

"No one," she whispered, her words coming harder now, "has held me like this... since my mother..."

"It's okay," Garrett told her. "It's gonna be okay now, Chelsea."

"We heard him yelling at her. Heard the slaps. It was nothing we hadn't heard before. So many times before... She told us to stay in our room when he was like that, but I couldn't. It was different that time. There was something inside me, telling me... and I knew... I knew she was in trouble. I knew it when she stopped screaming. So I went... and she was just lying there... her face was so... it didn't even look like her."

His hand stilled in her hair, and she felt his muscles go taut. "And him?"

"Gone," she whispered. "Just gone. I bent over my mother. I touched her. I shook her. But she wouldn't wake up. She just wouldn't wake up."

His arms tightened around her convulsively. He held her hard now and rocked very gently from side to side. "Damn," he muttered.

"I was nine years old, Garrett. But it feels like yesterday."

He held her tighter.

"Mom," Chelsea cried softly, "Jesus, Mom, why?" Something warm trickled down her face, surprising her. Shocking her. Tears. She hadn't cried since that night. But she was crying now. And she couldn't seem to stop the tears. Garrett's shirt dampened with them, then became soaked with them, and still she cried. So many years' worth of teardrops and she wasn't sure she'd ever stop crying again.

Chapter 7

When she heard her brothers' booted feet coming up the steps, Jessi turned away from the screen door and put a finger to her lips.

Wes frowned at her. Elliot tilted his head.

She waved them closer, still shushing them, and when they were close enough, she pointed.

In the kitchen, Garrett held the mite of a woman in his great big arms. He held her very close and stroked her hair while she sobbed as if her heart were breaking into a million bits. And as they watched, Chelsea's hands rose slowly until they closed on Garrett's shoulders, and she clung to him as if she were holding on for dear life. The tears she shed were not pretty ones. She sobbed out loud with great heaving spasms that should have torn a woman her size right in half.

As tears brimmed in her own eyes, Jessi turned away and walked quietly off the big front porch. She didn't stop until she'd reached the gate to the east pasture, where horses grazed contentedly, and then she leaned against it, blinking her eyes dry.

She wasn't surprised when Wes's hand lowered to her shoulder. "What happened in there, Jessi?"

Jessi turned around and flung herself right into her brother's arms, and he hugged her tight. "Oh, Wes, it's more horrible than I thought! I know I shouldn't have been listening at the door, but I couldn't help myself when I heard what she was saying."

Wes eased her away from him and searched her face with those black eyes that seemed to see right inside a person.

Jessi wiped her eyes dry with the back of one hand, then shook her head. "We can't let her go back east. I'll tell you that much. That girl needs a family like nobody I've ever seen."

"She isn't a stray dog, Jessi," Wes said softly. "You can't just decide to keep her."

Jessi sniffed. "I've *already* decided. Now all I have to do is convince her she belongs here."

Elliot had joined them by this time and heard most of what they said. He stood very still, staring thoughtfully back toward the house.

Wes shook his head slowly. "We have enough trouble on our hands, Jessi. My gut tells me that this woman is only gonna bring more."

"I don't care," Jessi told him. "I want her to stay."

"Contrary to what you've been led to believe, little sister," Wes replied, "you can't have everything you want."

"Well, now, I wouldn't be too sure about *that*." Elliot looked at them briefly, then right back at the house again. "When's the last time *you* saw Garrett hugging on a female the way he was hugging on that one?"

"Don't be stupid, Elliot. Garrett's never given a damn about women."

"There's a first time for everything, Wes. And from what I saw in that kitchen, I'd say our big brother's perched himself right on the very brink of giving a damn."

"Yeah," Jessi said slowly, drawing out the word as the solution became clear in her mind. "All he needs is a little nudge."

"No way." Wes's narrow eyes went from Jessi to Elliot and back again. *"No.* You two stay the hell out of this. I mean it. We don't need any women cluttering things up around here, and...ah, hell, Jes, don't look like that. I didn't mean you. Just think about it for a minute. Look at Adam and Ben, both nursing broken hearts. You want to put Garrett through the same garbage?"

"Just because love didn't work out for Adam or Ben doesn't mean it won't for Garrett," Jessi argued. "Come on, Wes! Garrett is different."

"Chelsea Brennan is trouble."

"Maybe she is," Jessi went on with a little pout. "But she's *in* trouble, too. And since when has trouble been anything the Brands couldn't handle?"

Wes shook his head, turned on his heel and started to walk away.

"Wait, Wes." He stopped, but didn't turn to face her. "Just listen. Let me tell you what I overheard in that kitchen. *Then* decide whether you want to help her or not."

He turned slowly, grimacing. "I didn't say we shouldn't help her, kid, just that we shouldn't force-feed her to Garrett."

"Didn't see nobody forcing him just now," Elliot said, earning a scowl. He grinned at Wes and nodded to Jessi. "Go on, hon. Tell us what you know."

* * *

Garrett had never felt more big and awkward and clumsy than he had when he'd held Chelsea's small body in his arms. But he'd also never felt weaker. Made his knees turn to jelly to think about the hell she'd been through. And the thought that she'd actually talked to him about it, that she'd let him comfort her even a little bit, filled him to brimming with something else altogether, something he didn't even try to put a name to, because he knew he couldn't.

Chores were finished, dinner over. And, as was their habit of an evening, the Brands gathered in the huge living room to rehash the day. Elliot and Jessi sat close together on the sofa, exchanging glances now and then that told Garrett they were sharing a secret. Wes had the settee to himself and looked pensive. Garrett had opted for the big easy chair, and Chelsea sat in the rocker close beside it, while Ethan crawled around the floor in a diaper and T-shirt, rushing from one pair of legs to another with all the energy of a frisky colt.

This time, he headed for Wes's legs and turned himself around to plop down onto his backside, staring up at Wes expectantly. Wes didn't notice.

"Ga!" Ethan announced when Wes hadn't looked down at him quickly enough to suit him.

When Wes did look, Ethan put his hands up in the air. International baby code for "Hey, pick me up, you big dummy."

A panicked look came into Wes's eyes.

"Oh, go on, Wes. He won't bite you," Jessi teased.

When Wes still hesitated, Jessi jumped to her feet, scooped the baby up and deposited him gently on Wes's lap. Ethan grinned from ear to ear and reached up to grab Wes's slightly hawkish nose.

Elliot burst out laughing, and Wes scowled at him as he gently removed the baby's hand. Ethan snuggled into Wes's lap, resting, for the moment. Wes looked stunned.

"I still don't understand why his mamma left him here with us," Jessi mused, returning to the sofa. "And his name couldn't have been a coincidence. Garrett, are you sure you didn't—"

"Jessi, I've sworn on a stack of Bibles I didn't father this baby. You telling me you *still* don't believe me?" Being accused in front of Chelsea was somehow worse, though Garrett wasn't quite sure why.

"Of course I believe you! I was gonna say, are you sure you didn't meet Chelsea's sister somewhere, maybe a long time ago? I mean, she must have known you sometime."

Garrett looked at Chelsea, saw the silent question in her eyes. "No, I didn't tell them," he said. "Why don't you get that photo and show it to Jessi. See if she remembers." He hoped she would. Because he'd feel better if he were sure Chelsea believed what he'd told her, and having Jessi confirm his recollection would go a long ways toward convincing her.

"I don't know why I didn't show you all right at the beginning. Instead, I stormed in here like a..." She shook her head.

"Like a wet hen?" Jessi offered.

"No," Elliot said. "No, I'd say she was more like a wounded bear."

"She can't be a bear, Elliot. She's way too small," Wes countered. "She came in here like a Texas wildfire."

They were all grinning at Chelsea, treating her just the way they treated each other, and at first Garrett thought she'd be offended. But she shook her head again in self-deprecation and smiled back at them as she got up from the rocker.

She headed upstairs and Garrett watched her go, wondering how anything as delicate-looking as she was could have such a steel core. She came back seconds later and handed the photograph to Jessi, who waited at the bottom of the stairs.

Jessi studied it, tilting her head. "She looks familiar." Jessi passed the photo to Elliot, who passed it to Wes. "I know!" Jessi shouted, startling both Ethan and ol' Blue. "Remember, Garrett, it was about a year ago? That girl you found out on the River Road with the flat tire."

"That's right," Elliot said. "You changed her tire and then had her follow you back here and stay to dinner. I remember now! Hell, she was out to here!" He held his hands out in front of his belly in an exaggerated account of her size.

Wes shook his head. "She was *not* out to there, Elliot. She was only showing a little. But I do remember her. She seemed scared or something. Remember? We offered her a room for a night or two, but she was in a hurry to move on."

"Didn't she tell us her name was Ann or something? Ann Smith, wasn't it?" Jessi said softly as if thinking aloud. "Why would she have given us a false name?"

Chelsea came close to where Garrett sat, taking the photo from Wes as she passed, and stared down at it. "Maybe she was running from him even then. God, why didn't she just come back to me?"

"If she knew she was in trouble, Chelsea, she might not have wanted to get you involved. Or maybe...maybe she never got the chance to get that far," Garrett said gently.

Chelsea nodded.

"I still don't know why she'd name the baby after Garrett and then bring him back here," Jessi said.

"I do," Chelsea replied, her voice raw. She looked around the room at each of them. "Garrett told me about her visit here, and I've had some time to think about this. And I think I know exactly why she did what she did."

Garrett tilted his head, eager to hear Chelsea's theory.

"She was here even if it was just for a short time. And she knew . . . she saw what you have."

Garrett frowned, but Chelsea went on.

"When Michele and I were little, we used to pretend a lot. Our favorite make-believe game was the one where we had a big family. Lots of brothers and sisters. A nice big house, with a yard." She looked down at ol' Blue. He cocked his ears and whined, then hauled himself to his feet and came to her for a pat, which she gave. "Even a dog," she said, stroking his head and smiling. But it was a sad smile. "We'd get out all our dolls and stuffed animals and they'd all play a part in the fantasy." She drew a breath, swallowed hard. "When my sister walked through your front door, she must have seen our childhood make-believe world come true, in everything you have right here. And not just because of the big house, or the dog, or the number of people here. Because of the love that fills this old place. She must have thought this would be the happiest home in the world for a child. So later, when she had to find a safe place for her baby, she thought of this place."

"So, she brought little Ethan here and left him on our doorstep," Jessi said. "And it was probably the highest compliment anyone's ever paid us, Chelsea. Sometimes I forget how lucky I am to have these big lugs. Thanks for reminding me."

Elliot cleared his throat, averting his gaze momentarily. Wes just stared down at that baby in his lap as if he was seeing him for the first time.

"Chelsea, we haven't talked about this before," Garrett said as she took her seat in the rocker once more. "You don't have to now, if it's too much. But I checked with the Texas Rangers in El Paso earlier today. They said Michele died of a drug overdose and that they had no reason to suspect foul play."

Chelsea's eyes widened and she looked up at him fast. "You didn't tell them about Ethan—"

"No. Of course not. I don't want his father coming for him any more than you do. But that's going to have to be dealt with sooner or later. The man has a legal claim—"

Chelsea reached across the short distance between his chair and hers, clasping one of Garrett's hands with two of her own. "Garrett, no. You can't let him take Ethan. Not ever. He killed my sister. I know he did."

Her eyes were enough to send his heart slamming against his rib cage. But he was a sheriff after all. He needed facts. "Don't you think your...past experiences...might be clouding your judgment, though?"

She shook her head, squeezing his hand more tightly. "The heroin was injected. My sister never did drugs in her life. She was running scared and she left her baby. She wouldn't have done that just so she could go shoot herself up with drugs. She wouldn't have left Ethan unless she knew she was in danger. Those things alone would convince me, Garrett. But she also had a phobia about needles. She never would have injected anything into her own body. She'd have passed out at the sight of a hypodermic."

Garrett frowned. "Did you tell the Rangers that?"

"No. I wasn't even thinking clearly, and then I came here and..." She released his hand, closed her eyes. "I just left her there. I shouldn't have done that. I shouldn't have left my sister there alone."

"There's a family plot, Chelsea," Jessi said softly, and Garrett thought she sounded close to tears. "And, well, you and little Ethan, you're just like family now."

Chelsea opened her eyes with something like awe flooding their green depths. She stared at Jessi, then turned her gaze to each of the others in the room, one by one. And one by one, Elliot, Wes and finally Garrett nodded in agreement.

"You'd...you'd let me bring Michele here? Let me..."

"It's a beautiful plot," Jessi said.

"Mamma would approve," Elliot added. "She'd have said it was right."

Chelsea just shook her head, staring at them as if in disbelief.

"I'll take care of things," Garrett told her. "We'll do it quietly. No one besides us need know where Michele is laid to rest. For now, at least."

Chelsea's eyes grew moist as she scanned the faces in the room. "There is no way to tell you what this means to me...what it would have meant to my sister." Her gaze settled on Jessi. "Thank you, Jessi. I wish...I wish I could accept. But I can't."

Jessi frowned, tilting her head.

"Michele would want to be near our mother. I'm going to make arrangements to take her back home to New York." She lifted her gaze to Garrett's. "I'd like to do it soon. The idea of her spending even one more night in that horrible room..." Her eyes fell closed and she shook her head slowly.

Garrett bit his lip to keep his objections to himself. This was no time for Chelsea to be hightailing it back to New York. Deep in his gut, he had a feeling that told him not to let her go. Not now. Maybe not for quite a while.

"I think the littlest cowboy on the Texas Brand has fallen asleep," Wes observed, his voice a bit gruff. He rose awkwardly, moving slow so he wouldn't disturb the sleeping child in his arms.

Jessi rose. "I'll take him up."

"That's all right," Wes said. "I can handle it." He looked up from the baby, noticed the surprised gazes of his siblings and shrugged. "Passing him around would wake him up, is all."

Jessi and Elliot smirked, but Wes ignored them, tip-toeing up the stairs with the infant. Jessi turned to Elliot. "Guess I'll turn in, too. It's getting late."

"Late?" Elliot replied. "It's only—"

Jessi kicked his shin and scowled at him.

"Oh. Hey, it's later than I realized," he amended without a single glance at his watch. "Well, guess I'll hit the hay, as well. Good night, Chelsea. Garrett."

"Night," Chelsea replied.

Garrett only frowned. Those two rarely took to their beds before the late news, unless they were angry with him for something or other. Or up to no good. They hadn't been pouting, so he suspected the latter. The question was, what plot were those two villains hatching?

"I hope they understand," Chelsea said softly.

Garrett turned to her, stared into her forest green eyes and got lost for just a second. "Don't worry. They do."

"I should probably call that place tomorrow. Make arrangements to have Michele sent home."

"I could do that for you, if you—"

"No. No, Michele is my sister. The only family I have...had...except for Ethan. I'll take care of her."

He nodded, wishing this feeling of foreboding would leave the pit of his stomach. He really didn't have any legal grounds to keep Chelsea here. None at all. So he supposed he'd have to let her go.

The shrill of the telephone cut into his thoughts, and he got slowly to his feet to walk to the kitchen and pick it up. His greeting was cut off, as well, by a deep voice. A level voice. One he didn't recognize.

"The child's father is Vincent de Lorean. And he knows his son is with you."

"Who is this?" Garrett demanded, his grip tightening on the receiver.

"De Lorean wants Chelsea Brennan dead, Brand. She isn't safe. Not there and not in New York. She is the only person alive who could fight de Lorean for custody of that baby and stand a chance of winning. He wants to eliminate that possibility. He has men watching her apartment. They'll grab her the second she sets foot there. Do you understand?"

"How could he..."

"He's a powerful man, Brand. A dangerous man. Don't let the woman or the child out of your sight. Not for a second. If you do, he'll have them both."

"But—"

There was a click, then silence. Garrett jiggled the cutoff but to no avail. Finally, he hung up the phone, shaking his head, wondering what the hell he was supposed to do now.

"Garrett?"

Chelsea came to stand beside him, and she had to know damned well something was wrong. Garrett never had been any good at hiding his feelings.

"What is it?"

He shook his head. Not for all the world would he tell her anything that would put the ice-cold fear back into those pretty green eyes. He forced a smile. "Nothing, Chelsea. Nothing that can't wait until morning."

She relaxed a little. Still nervous. But calmer. It hit him that maybe she trusted him just a little bit. He vowed then and there he wouldn't let her down.

She yawned, and his smile became a genuine one. "You're sleepy. Go on up to bed, Chelsea. I'm gonna do the same myself soon as I lock up for the night."

She nodded, turned to go up the stairs, then stopped and faced him again. "You've been good to me and to Ethan," she said softly. "I owe you for that."

"You don't owe us a thing, Chelsea."

"I do. I'll repay you someday."

And she headed up the stairs without another word.

"Vincent de Lorean?" Wes shook his head, pacing the kitchen with a cup of coffee in his hand. The sun was barely peeking over the horizon, painting the ranch house's front windows a pale orange, like candle glow.

"None other. Biggest organized-crime figure in the state of Texas. Has ties to the Molinaire syndicate in New York."

"Well, hell, Garrett, we can't just let her go back there. She'd be walking right into their hands."

"Exactly. The question is, how do I convince her to stay?"

"You tell her the truth." Wes set his half-filled mug on the table and leaned over it, searching his brother's face.

"And see her go back to being terrified again?"

"What choice do you have? She's bound and determined to hop a jet for New York City at the first opportunity. Hell, Garrett, what else can you do?"

Garrett frowned. The same question had been nagging at him all night, and he thought he'd come up with some kind of solution. Not an easy one. But maybe the only one. "If I can do some digging, find evidence to tie de Lorean to Michele's murder, I can put him away, Wes."

"And since when are you some kind of supercop, big brother? You really think you can do what every cop in the state of Texas, not to mention the FBI, has been trying to do for five years or more? If it was that easy to get the dirt on de Lorean, he'd have been in prison years ago."

"So what would you suggest? Let her go to New York and read about her body being found the next day? Or maybe I tell her all this, and she takes off like a scared rabbit, goes into hiding somewhere with Ethan. How far did that kind of plan get her sister?"

Wes lowered his head and sighed. "Okay. Okay. When you're right, you're right. But while you dig up dirt on de Lorean, you have to find a way to keep Chelsea Brennan right here, where we can protect her from that bastard. What brilliant plan have you come up with to accomplish that?"

"Nothing." Garrett shook his head, feeling panic well up in his gut... again.

"It's simple." Jessi stepped in from the dining room, and Garrett started in surprise.

"Dammit, Jes, did you ever hear of a private conversation?"

"No such thing as privacy in this family." She walked to the coffeepot, took a mug from the tree and filled it.

When Elliot came in after her, Garrett stifled a groan. "Great. This is just great."

"You oughtta be glad we overheard you, brother," Elliot quipped, pulling out a chair and lowering his lanky body into it. "Sounded like you were fresh out of ideas."

"Oh, and I suppose you two have the perfect solution?"

"Sure we do." Jessi added sugar to her coffee and stirred slowly, her eyes twinkling. "If you want Chelsea to stay with us, Garrett, all you have to do is give her a reason."

Garrett rolled his eyes. "Now why didn't I think of that?"

"Don't be sarcastic," Jessi said. "Garrett, maybe you haven't noticed, but Chelsea Brennan... *likes* you."

"She likes all of us, Jes—"

"No. I mean... she *really likes* you."

Garrett went as still as stone as his little sister's meaning sank in. Then he battled an urge to strangle her. "Don't be stupid."

Jessi pouted. Elliot stretched his legs, leaned back in his chair and folded his hands behind his head. "Garrett Brand, you are one dense cowboy if you think Jessi's wrong about this. Hell, I didn't see Chelsea wrapped up in *Wes*'s arms last night. Nor mine, either, for that matter. It was you she was clinging to while she cried."

Garrett felt his jaw drop and his eyes widen. "You—"

"Now, Garrett, we weren't snooping. Just coming in from the barn, and there you were, big as life, hugging the stuffin' outta that little lady."

"You got it all wrong!" Garrett walked away from them, pushing his hands through his hair. "Dammit, she was upset, is all—"

"It was more than that, Garrett." Jessi came up behind him, put her hands on his shoulders. "Women know about these things. She's soft on you, I can tell."

"That's gotta be the most ridiculous... Why would she...? I don't..." He gave up trying to speak, because words just plain deserted him. Confusion took over instead, and he turned a questioning gaze on Wes.

Wes shrugged. "They have a point. Look, Garrett, nobody's saying you gotta go cow-eyed over the woman. But maybe if you just sweet-talked her a little—"

"I can't believe you guys!" Garrett spun around, ready to tell them all how ridiculous the very notion was—and saw Chelsea just coming into the kitchen. Her hair was all tousled and her big green eyes were sleepy. When she looked at him, she smiled softly, and Garrett's big heart flipped upside down and began to fill with a kind of panic he'd never felt in his whole damned life.

"Good morning," she said, her voice deep and rusty.

Garrett mouthed "mornin'" but no sound came out. He cleared his throat and tried again.

"You're just in time," Jessi said, grinning from ear to ear. "We were just saying how rude we've been. Why, we haven't even shown you around the ranch yet. And it's really something to see."

Chelsea's auburn brows rose.

"Do you ride?" Elliot asked her.

Garrett held his breath.

"No," she replied, and Garrett sighed in relief. "But I've always wanted to try."

His heart performed some more acrobatics he hadn't realized it was capable of.

"Good for you," Elliot all but shouted. "Garrett rides

the fence lines every morning to check things out. Perfect chance for you to try your seat. Isn't it, Garrett?''

"She can take Sugar. Oh, Chelsea, you'll love her. She's the most gentle mare on the place." Jessi's excitement was bubbling from her pores. "Wes, why don't you go saddle Sugar for Chelsea?"

Chelsea, too, seemed a bit caught up in their enthusiasm. But when she looked at Garrett, the smile left her face. "I really ought to stay here with Ethan," she said.

"Nah. Jessi can take charge of that little pistol for a while. I'll handle her chores for her," Elliot offered.

Garrett nearly choked. Elliot, offering to do extra chores?

Chelsea's eyes were still on him, and he squirmed. "It's okay. Really. I don't want to impose on your morning ride."

He lowered his head, feeling like a real snake. "No," he finally managed. "No, Chelsea, I'd really like you to come along."

"Really?"

When he looked into her eyes, he realized, a little slowly perhaps, that it was true. He would enjoy her company. "Yeah, really."

She smiled fully, almost blinding him.

"Come on upstairs, Chelsea," Jessi said, gripping Chelsea's arm and turning her around. "You need some jeans, and I have some that ought to fit you just fine. Might have to roll up the legs a little, but...oh, and some boots, too." Looking back over her shoulder, she sent Garrett a broad wink. "We'll be ready in ten minutes. Promise!"

When they disappeared up the stairs, Garrett pressed his fingertips to his forehead and groaned.

"Oh, come on, Garrett," Wes urged. "It isn't the end of the world."

"You can do this, big brother," Elliot added, a smug grin tugging at his lips, one he didn't try very hard to suppress. "And if you need any pointers on romancing a woman, you just come to me, okay?"

Garrett scowled at him, but Elliot and Wes just shared a laugh and headed out the door.

Chapter 8

The jeans were a bit long, but rolled up they were a fair fit. The boots were perfect. She and Jessi were both size seven, so their fit was comfy. Jessi had tossed in a rather tight-fitting tank top and a flannel shirt, insisting it would be hot by the time Chelsea returned, and she'd be glad to have the thin top underneath.

When Chelsea stepped out onto the front porch, two horses stood saddled and waiting. The gigantic dappled gray one she'd heard Garrett call Duke, and a smaller white mare with a handful of black spots on her rump, who had to be Sugar.

Garrett stood beside the horses, his big hand stroking Sugar's neck. He looked up at Chelsea, smiled a welcome, but she still had the niggling suspicion this little outing hadn't been his idea. And that he was less than happy about it.

She eyed the white horse, and her nerves jangled to life.

"Don't be scared, Chelsea. She's as gentle as a kitten. Come here." He held out a hand.

Chelsea went down the front steps and took it. When Garrett closed his fingers around her hand, he stilled for a second, staring down at their clasped hands as if in surprise. He drew her closer to the animal, laid her hand gently on the mare's neck, where his had been only seconds ago.

Chelsea stroked the animal's sleek neck and smiled. "She's beautiful."

"So are you."

She looked up quickly, only to see Garrett avert his face and pretend to tighten the girth straps.

"Now," he said, turning to face her again, "take hold of the pommel."

Licking her lips, she did.

"Put your foot in the stirrup."

She drew a breath and followed his instructions.

"Now swing your other leg over."

She nodded and pulled herself up. But the horse was tall, and she lost her momentum before she got her leg all the way over. Garrett's hands closed on her bottom, pushing her up, giving her enough of a lift to boost her into the saddle.

She felt her cheeks burn and couldn't look at him.

"Sorry," he muttered, handing her the reins. He walked around the mare, checking to be sure Chelsea had her foot firmly in the stirrup on the other side, then mounted his own horse in a move so smooth and effortless that watching him made her feel like a klutz. He held the reins loosely in one hand, and she imitated him. "Ready?"

She nodded once, then Garrett turned his horse and started across the lawn. Sugar didn't need Chelsea to tell her what to do. She turned, as well, and walked slow and easy beside Duke. They approached an open gate, and Wes, who was standing nearby, closed it behind them after they moved through.

"Squeeze your thighs around her, Chelsea," Garrett instructed, looking at her dangling legs.

She squeezed, and Sugar shot forward into a trot, causing Chelsea to bounce up and down until her teeth rattled. Garrett caught up to her within a few seconds, grabbed the reins and tugged gently. Sugar came to a halt.

"What did I do?" Chelsea asked, breathless.

"Dug your heels into her side. Just squeeze gently with your knees. You dig those heels in, she thinks you want to run."

Chelsea tried again, and this time the horse didn't take off. Garrett handed the reins back to her, his hand brushing hers as she took them. They started off again, side by side, and she knew he was going much more slowly than he probably would if he were alone. They rode into rolling green meadows, and soon she saw the curly coats of the white-faced Herefords dotting the grass in the distance. As they drew nearer, she saw calves running and jumping like children, and docile cows chewing lazily as if they hadn't a care in the world.

"They're something, aren't they?" Garrett remarked, drawing to a halt at a spot where they could look out over part of the herd.

Imitating Garrett again, Chelsea reined in her mount and followed his gaze. "I don't think I've ever seen anything that...peaceful."

It was true. Sitting here astride this gentle mare, beside this gentle man, with this gentle scene spread out before her, she felt that peace begin to fill her. This was a good place, this Texas Brand. A magical place. The vivid blue sky stretched wider than she'd ever seen it. And the sun beat down just as Jessi had predicted it would. Heat poured through her flannel shirt, and her skin dampened and prickled. Very carefully, she shrugged the shirt off one arm, but only got it partway down her shoulder before the horse danced a little, and she had to make a grab for the pommel.

"I...uh..." Garrett's horse sidled closer to hers. "I can get that." He reached out with one hand and pushed the shirt down her arm. She let go so he could tug it off, then held on with her other hand as Garrett's big, callused one pushed the shirt down from her opposite shoulder. His palm skimmed her arm all the way down, and she shivered. She closed her eyes without quite realizing she was doing so. She sensed him taking the shirt, and when she opened her eyes, she saw him staring at her. There was something in his gaze. Something new...and a little scary.

He blinked it away, tucking the shirt in front of him on the saddle, then nudged his horse into motion once more.

For an hour, they rode in silence, and Chelsea took in the beauty and tranquillity of the surroundings. The only sounds were the steady tromping of the horses' hooves, the creak of saddle leather, and once in a while, the gentle blowing sound made by the horses.

Garrett tugged Duke to a stop when they came to a small stream with a couple of trees on the far bank. He dismounted in one smooth motion and came to her side. "Better take a break," he said.

"Oh, but I'm fine."

He smiled, a big lopsided smile that made her stomach clench tight. "You think you're fine. But believe me, you're working muscles you didn't know you had. Come on, get down for a few minutes."

She nodded. "Okay, you're the expert." She braced one foot in the stirrup and tried to swing off the way he'd done. But Sugar sidestepped and she felt herself falling. Then two big hands curled around her waist from behind, lifting her gently, easily down. Her backside brushed over the front of him as he lowered her, and a shiver worked right up her spine. When her feet touched down, he didn't let go. Instead, his hands remained at her waist, holding her back against his body for a long moment.

"Damn," he whispered, and finally his hands fell away.

She turned around and stared up into his eyes. Dark brown, gentle eyes that held hers captive.

"Damn," he said again.

"Why do you keep saying that?"

He closed his eyes, breaking that tenuous hold, but only briefly. "Because I know you don't like being touched...and right now..." He shook his head in self-disgust. "I'm not good at this kind of thing, Chelsea. I don't know the kinds of pretty words that make women go soft inside. I'm a simple man, and I'm accustomed to just saying what's on my mind, straight out."

"So say it," she whispered, and her voice trembled, and fear danced in her veins. She felt more alive than she ever had.

"I want to kiss you."

She looked into his eyes, then at the expanse of green around them. They were alone here. But for some reason, she wasn't afraid. She'd never known a man as gentle as Garrett Brand. Not ever.

She tipped up her head and moved closer. "Then...go ahead and kiss me," she said, her words full of false bravado, but wavering all the same.

Garrett bent his head and touched his lips to hers. He didn't put his hands on her. He just kissed her slowly and gently, then lifted his head and searched her face.

"Again?" he murmured.

"Yes. Again."

This time his arms came up around her waist, his hands spanning the small of her back and easing her close to him. He kissed her again, nuzzling her lips until she parted them, then tracing their shape with his tongue.

Chelsea's pulse raced and nameless feelings swamped her mind. She put her hands on Garrett's broad shoulders and slipped them around him until her fingers tangled in his hair. She opened her mouth wider, ready now to experience more of this heady thing between them. Her heart pounded in her ears. Louder and louder, and when his tongue slowly slipped inside, it seemed the very ground under her feet trembled with—

He jerked away from her, eyes wide with alarm. And he swore.

"Garrett? Did I—"

"Stampede!"

His cry shocked her... then terrified her when its meaning became clear. She looked, and saw masses of frightened beasts churning the dust toward them. And even as Garrett reached for the horses, they bolted, wild-eyed, feet flying. Garrett's arm snagged her around the waist, propelling her forward. He shouted something at her, but the thundering hoofbeats of the cattle drowned out even his booming voice. As they splashed across the icy stream, she could smell the terrified cattle. Then her body was thrust against the trunk of a tree, and Garrett's ground tightly to her from behind, pinning her there. The animals were upon them, knocking into them on both sides, brushing, pushing. She felt Garrett's body being torn away from her and she turned to see, but couldn't.

Then she heard a shout and saw a horse at full gallop, pressing through the rampaging cows. A man she'd never seen before sat tall on a sable-colored, wide-eyed stallion. She watched as he bent low, reached down and pulled Garrett up. Garrett seemed to spring from the ground and onto the back of that horse. His gaze was glued to the tree as the cattle flew past, and Chelsea clung to it with all her might as their bodies jostled hers. But one hit her too hard, and her palms scraped painfully over the rough bark as she fought to hold on. Her back hit the ground hard, and she automatically curled into a ball, covering her face with her arms as her body was pummeled again and again. It felt as if several strong men were surrounding her, hitting her with hammers.

The blows stopped at last. Then the thunder slowly died away. And all that remained was the blackened earth and torn grass and the sound of her own heart beating more loudly than those hooves had done. She uncurled cautiously, every movement hurting.

The rider came forward. Garrett leaped from the horse and ran to her, dropping to his knees beside her. His hands gripped her shoulders, pulled her close to his big chest. She could feel the pounding of his heart there, hear the raspy rush of his quickened breaths.

"Chelsea, dammit, are you all right?" He held her so hard, so tight, she could barely breathe.

He eased back a little when she didn't answer. Brown eyes flooded with worry scanned her body. His shirt was torn, one arm dripping blood, and there was another ugly cut high on his cheekbone. She lifted a hand toward him. "You're hurt."

She heard galloping and jerked her head around, only to see Elliot and Wes approaching at top speed.

"The hell with me! What about you? Damn, Chelsea, when I saw you fall—"

"I'm all right." She put her hands on his shoulders and pushed herself to her feet. She hurt. She hurt everywhere, but she didn't think anything was broken. At least her arms and hands and legs and feet seemed to be in working order.

Elliot and Wes had jumped from their horses and were running toward them now. There was real fear in their eyes when they reached their brother.

"Garrett, are you okay?"

"What the hell happened?"

Garrett shook his head slowly, but his brown eyes narrowed dangerously as they found those of the stranger. "Something . . . or *someone* . . . spooked the cattle. Chelsea could have been killed."

The stranger said nothing. Just sat on that horse, holding Garrett's accusing stare. He was dark and whipcord lean, his face narrow and hard, with piercing pale blue eyes that even now seemed deathly calm. As Chelsea stared at him, something fluttered to the ground from his shirt pocket. A small slip of paper. She pointed at it and started to tell him, but Garrett's angry voice made her go utterly still.

"Who the hell are you, mister?"

"Name's Lash," he replied, his face every bit as grim as Garrett's.

"It wasn't him, Garrett," Elliot said quickly. "He was with us."

Garrett gave Elliot a brief glance, then turned a questioning one on Wes.

"Elliot's right. Lash drove in right after you two left. Said he was looking for work. Since we're shorthanded, I thought it wouldn't be a bad idea, and he was in a hurry to see you, so we saddled up and rode out here to run it by you."

"And it's a damned good thing we did, Garrett," Elliot added. "If Lash hadn't cut through that mess of frantic beefers to pull you up, you'd be hamburger."

"He saw you go down," Wes added. "We didn't."

Garrett heaved a thoughtful sigh, but his eyes remained wary. He walked over to the stranger, who'd dismounted by this time, and offered his hand. "Seems I'm indebted to you."

The man shook Garrett's hand. "You can repay me by hiring me on."

Garrett scowled. "Wish I could, friend, but this is a bad time—"

"Garrett, we could use the help."

Garrett turned to Elliot with a look that clearly told him to shut up. Elliot pursed his lips. "Hell, I'll go see if I can round up the horses." He headed for his own horse, jumped back into the saddle, wheeled around and rode off, leaving no one in any doubt as to his opinion of Garrett's decision.

Chelsea wondered why Garrett would be so distrustful of the man who'd probably saved his life. She knew Elliot was right. How many times had she heard them talking about how shorthanded they were right now?

"Like I said, it's a bad time," Garrett repeated, turning back to the stranger.

"I'm a good hand," Lash returned easily. "But if it's a bad time, it's a bad time." He shrugged as if he could care less. "You want some help herding those cattle back where they belong?"

"We can handle it."

"I got nowhere to go."

Garrett frowned. It wasn't like him to be rude, though Chelsea assumed that nearly being trampled to death would make even a saint grouchy.

"Fine. Ride along if you want." Elliot was riding toward them now, flanked by Duke and Sugar. Garrett returned to Chelsea and lifted a tender hand to push her hair away from her face. "You sure you're okay?"

"A few bruises, I think. Nothing serious."

"You up to the ride back to the house?"

She swallowed hard, but nodded. How else was she going to get back?

"The hell you are," he muttered.

Elliot jumped off his horse and led the other two mounts over to Garrett and Chelsea. "Garrett, why don't you take her back? The three of us can handle the cows. They've stopped running already. Tore through the north fence line, though. We'll drive 'em back in, repair the fence and meet you later at the house in time for lunch. All right?"

Garrett looked torn. For some reason, he didn't want to leave his brothers out here alone. Was he worried about the jumpy cows? From the wary look in his eyes, Chelsea thought his concern lay elsewhere. With the stranger. Why?

He glanced at Chelsea again.

"I can make it back on my own, Garrett. You don't have to—"

"No. Not alone." His forefinger lazily brushed her cheek, and she wondered if there was a bruise forming there already. It felt as if there was. "I'll take you back."

He went over to Wes, who stood a bit away from the rest of them, just watching them all with those sharp, probing black eyes of his. Wes inclined his head as Garrett spoke softly. Then nodded. Lash, meanwhile, had ridden over to Elliot and was conversing with him. The slip of paper blew closer to Chelsea's feet, and she bent to pick it up, turning toward the stranger.

But Garrett came back to her at that moment, and without warning, he put his arms around her and scooped her right off her feet. He settled her in Duke's saddle, then swung up behind her. One arm came snugly around her waist. He touched the stallion's sides, and the horse took off at a brisk walk, back the way they'd come. Chelsea sighed in resignation and glanced at the name and address on the scrap of paper before stuffing it into her jeans pocket and vowing to return it to its owner later on.

Cattle did not stand around chewing peacefully one minute, then stampede the next. Garrett knew that. He'd only witnessed one stampede in his life and he'd been in the ranching business forever. It was rare. It didn't just happen.

Something had spooked those cattle. And spooked them in the direction he and Chelsea had taken. Garrett couldn't convince himself it was a coincidence. Especially after that odd phone call last night. And that the appearance of this stranger—this *Lash*—could just be happenstance was a bit much to swallow.

Somebody wanted Chelsea Brennan dead. The voice on the phone had identified that somebody as Vincent de Lorean, a man as evil as Satan himself. And then she'd nearly been trampled to death. All within twenty-four hours.

No way could he have let her return to the house alone. And he couldn't trust her safety to his brothers. He had to see to it himself. Much as he disliked leaving Elliot and Wes out there with a stranger who might or might not be involved in all this, he'd had little choice. So he'd warned Wes about his suspicions. Wes could handle himself. Hell, Wes could handle himself and any six fighting men. He'd be all right.

Duke gave a little leap when he came out of the stream and started up the slight incline of the bank. Chelsea's bottom bounced down on the saddle, and she gave a little squeak of pain. Dammit, she was hurt, much as she might deny it.

"Don't sit so stiff," he instructed. "Just relax against me, and it won't hurt so much." He punctuated his advice by pulling her back closer to his chest. Her buttocks rocked between his legs, rubbing him in all the right places. Dammit, he should have left well enough alone.

No, he shouldn't. She leaned her head back against him. Oh, did he like that. He opened his palm on her flat belly. His hand itched to creep up higher. To cup her soft breasts, and squeeze them. His lips itched to kiss her. Her smooth-skinned neck was looking more tempting with every step Duke took.

"Why were you so suspicious of that man?" she asked softly.

Garrett clenched his jaw. He hadn't meant to be so obvious. The last thing he wanted was for her to think that the stampede had been an attempt on her life. He was afraid that knowledge would send her running scared. And if she ran, how the hell could he protect her?

"I don't like strangers nosing around," he tried.

"You took me in. Let me stay. *I'm* a stranger."

Garrett never had been any good at subterfuge. "You're a sight prettier than Lash is."

"Be honest with me, Garrett." As she said it, she turned her head so she could look up into his eyes. Her green ones searched and dug into his. Into his heart, too.

"I am being honest. You really *are* prettier."

She frowned at him.

"Okay," he said slowly, wondering how little he could get away with revealing. "We want it kept quiet that you're here, right? Why broadcast it to some drifter?"

She nodded, licked her lips. He ached to do the same. "So you really think Ethan's father will come after him if he finds out where we are?"

"He might. But—" Garrett cut himself off in midsentence as he was sharply, painfully reminded of Vincent de Lorean's other objective. His son. And Bubba was currently alone in the house with Jessi.

He tightened his grip on Chelsea. "Sorry about this, darlin'. Hold on." He kicked Duke's sides, and the horse obeyed instantly, beginning to gallop at a speed Garrett hoped wouldn't send more spasms of pain through Chelsea's slender, bruised body.

When he jumped off Duke's back and ran up the front steps, leaving Chelsea sitting alone on a horse the size of a small elephant, she mentally cussed him.

But he only made it as far as the screen door. One look inside and his frown lines eased into a smile. "Everything okay here, Jessi?"

"Sure. Fine. Why wouldn't it be?"

"No reason." Garrett turned around, smiling. But his smile died when he saw Chelsea glaring at him from the saddle. "Sorry," he muttered, and came back to her, put his hands on her waist and lifted her down.

She shook her head. "You're crazy, Garrett Brand. What were you trying to do, making that mastodon run with me on his back? Kill me?"

"Course not! Hey, I just got worried about Jess and Bubba, is all."

"His *name* is Ethan, you big lug."

He opened his mouth.

"And why would you suddenly get so worried that you had to race all the way back here and scramble my insides in the process?" She poked him with a forefinger. "You are keeping something from me. Something about that stampede, and that stranger, and—"

"Stampede?" The screen door squeaked and Jessi stepped outside, Ethan anchored on her hip. "What stampede?"

"The one that almost killed us," Chelsea replied, still glaring at Garrett.

"Now, it wasn't that bad. Don't look like that, Jessi. Everything's fine. No one was hurt."

Jessi's gaze dipped to Garrett's torn and bloodied shirtsleeve. "Liar. Look at you! And you, too, Chelsea! What in all hell happened out there?"

"Watch your mouth," Garrett told her.

"I will not watch my mouth." She pouted, then shook her head. "Ah, get in here, both of you, and let me have a look. And while I'm looking, Garrett Ethan Brand, you better tell me what this is all about!" She spun around and slammed back into the house.

Chelsea took the first step, but Garrett gripped her shoulder gently, stopping her. "Wait."

She sighed, but turned to face him.

"Before all that craziness out there, Chelsea . . . something was . . . happening . . . between you and me."

She lowered her head. Something *had* been happening. Something that had been dizzying and wonderful at the time. But in hindsight, it scared the hell out of her.

"It's just as well we were interrupted," she whispered, but the words were coming hard.

"I have to disagree with you there."

She forced her head up and tried to hold on to his gaze, but couldn't. She had to look away again. "I'm not ready for anything like this. I don't *want* anything like this."

"Like what? Hell, Chelsea, I'm still trying to figure out what *this* is."

"It doesn't matter. It shouldn't have happened, and it's over. Let's just forget about it."

"I'm not real sure I can do that. Forget it, I mean." He searched her face, trying to smile, but it was bitter, and she thought maybe she'd hurt this big, gentle man.

But she barely knew him, after all. His gentleness could fade as fast as the sun when a storm cloud rolls in. He could turn out to be as dangerous as her father had been. And she'd decided a long time ago that she would never trust any man long enough to find out. She would never fall in love. Besides, just because this man was physically attracted to her didn't mean he *felt* anything for her, so she was way ahead of herself anyway.

"It will be easier once Ethan and I are gone," she said.

His lips thinned. He seemed a little desperate and maybe at a loss for words. "I don't..."

"What?"

He lowered his head. "I don't want you to go, Chelsea."

She stared at him in surprise and more than a little confusion. What was he saying? He barely knew her, had only kissed her once, for God's sake. Well, okay, twice. How could he stand there and say—

"Will you two get in here already?" Jessi called.

"What do you mean, you don't want me to go? What do you want me to do, quit my job, give up my apartment and stay here? For a fling, Garrett? Well, I'm sorry to disappoint you. I don't do flings."

She turned away and marched up the steps and across the porch. But as she went, she heard his voice following her.

"Neither do I, Chelsea Brennan."

Chapter 9

Maybe one of those stupid cows had stomped on her head. That must be it. Maybe she had a concussion or brain damage or something. Or maybe Garrett did. Because she could have sworn the man she'd actually begun to see as some kind of big, honorable, gentle-as-a-teddy bear kind of guy had just propositioned her. Suggested she hang out at the ranch for a while, his meaning glimmering clearly in those formerly harmless brown eyes. He wanted her, the jerk. And he thought she was willing to put out. All on the basis of a couple of innocent kisses!

Man, his ego must be as big as he was!

She tried to hurry through the kitchen and dining room, straight on into the living room and up the stairway, but winced with every single step. It hurt, dammit. Him and his hormones! She should have known all along he only had one thing on his mind. Why hadn't she seen it coming? He'd probably only stopped the stupid horses so he could paw her, not so she could rest. And it was only just now occurring to her how utterly stupid she'd been to go along on that ride in the first place. Putting herself out of sight and shouting distance of anyone. Putting herself alone within reach of a man. Even this man. Because they were all the same underneath. Hadn't she learned anything?

A hot bath, she thought as she started up the stairs. It hurt to flex her thighs, and she grimaced. A long, hot bath. She tried envisioning it to get her up the next step. Her back screamed in protest. Steam, rolling off the water, she thought determinedly. Scented water. Hot, steamy, scented water and— She sucked air through her teeth at a new jab in her side. "Dammit!"

Big, strong arms swept under her, lifting her like a knight lifting a damsel in a fairy tale. Well, she was no damsel, and this horny lug was no knight. There were no such things as knights. Not even in Texas.

"Put me down."

"Not on your life, lady. Don't worry. I won't trouble you with my presence any longer than it takes to drop you on your bed."

"Drop me at my door, Hulk. I don't trust you anywhere near my bed."

Garrett took the stairs at a brisk pace. "I didn't say I wanted to sleep with you, woman."

"You want me to stay for what, then? My sparkling wit? My charm and sweetness?"

"What sweetness? You're as sour as a barrel of pickles." He set her on her feet, opened the bedroom door and waved a hand. "We'll talk about this later."

"I won't be here later."

"Fine."

"Fine." She slammed the door. Leaning shakily against it, she closed her eyes hard in an effort to fight the fragile whisper of doubt that flitted through her mind, trying to make her wonder if maybe she'd jumped to the wrong conclusions about Garrett. But, hell, he'd been so uncharacteristically sweet—for a male—to her ever since she'd arrived. And now that she thought she knew the reason—that he was hoping for some easy sex—it made perfect sense.

Didn't it?

She groaned softly and hoped to God she was right. If she wasn't, she'd just made a total fool out of herself. She walked into the little bathroom, depressed the plunger and turned on the hot water. They'd moved her into the guest room where the baby had taken up residence, apparently having decided she could be trusted around her own flesh and blood.

As the water flowed into the bath, Chelsea remembered the way Garrett had looked in here yesterday, shirtless, soaking wet and grinning like a fool as he bathed little Ethan. And she tried to think of why he'd been so nice to the baby. What could he be hoping to get out of him?

Nothing, of course. And it couldn't have been to impress Chelsea because he hadn't known she'd be watching. How could he have known?

God, could it be the man was just genuinely nice?

Nah.

Chelsea stripped off her clothes and sank into the bathtub, resting against the cool porcelain as the hot water slowly rose around her.

"Well, Jessi, so much for that stupid scheme you and Elliot came up with!"

Garrett slapped his dusty hat onto the back of a chair. His little sister set Bubba down and promptly knocked Garrett into the same chair.

"Sit still so I can look at this." She promptly tore his shirtsleeve off, grimacing. "This is nasty, Garrett."

"It's nasty all right. I told her I wanted her to stay. Now she thinks I'm some kind of sex maniac."

Jessi pressed her lips tight, but a gurgle of laughter managed to escape anyway. She turned quickly to the sink, taking a clean cloth from a nearby drawer and wetting it down.

"Oh, yeah, you think you're so smart."

"Well, jeez-louise, Garrett, you can't just blurt it out like that. You gotta build up to it. Give her some time."

"I don't have any damned time. She wants to leave today, for crying out loud!"

Jessi came over and pressed the damp cloth to the cut on his shoulder. "Sounds like that would really bother you."

"Only because it might get her killed."

Jessi's hands stilled on his shoulder. "Killed?"

"Vincent de Lorean would do anything to get his child back," he said grimly, "including murder."

Jessi's eyes opened wider. "God Almighty, Garrett, we can't let him!"

"No, we sure as hell can't. And we won't. We just have to convince Chelsea to stay put until I can figure out how."

"Guess you'll just have to sweep her off her feet."

He grunted. Then he stilled, searching her face. His little sister was dead serious here.

"Tell her she can't leave until tomorrow, Garrett. Make something up. Tell her the flights out today are all booked. Anything. Then, tonight—"

"Tonight she isn't speaking to me."

"Tonight you'll give her an evenin' she'll never forget."

Garrett shook his head. But his sister's eyes were sparkling, and he had a feeling he wasn't going to have much say in the matter.

"Now, about this stampede . . ." she began as if it were all settled. Sure. Just leave it to Jessi. She'd take care of everything. Oh, God help him now.

Dinner was a strained affair. Garrett was damned near squirming in his chair when he thought about what he had to do tonight. He wasn't eating with the others. Just sitting here for the company and the conversation, really. He'd eat later.

Jessi had worked it all out.

And there was this whole other matter to contend with. Lash. Elliot had been raving about how terrific the man had been with the spooked cattle. Even Wes had grudgingly admitted the guy knew his stuff. The damage to the fences had been worse than Elliot had realized, so the three had only come in briefly for a quick sandwich and then headed right out again. Elliot couldn't stop talking about Lash and his way with the cattle.

Even Jessi seemed impressed. She'd gone oddly quiet and suddenly learned some table manners. She was smiling more than usual, too.

Lash looked at her as if he were looking at a little kid, which was yet another mark in his favor.

Hell, Garrett would have hired the stranger in a minute under any other circumstances. But with the threat of danger hanging over all their heads, he didn't think he could afford to trust a stranger.

Even one who'd saved his life.

Maybe later, after all this was worked out and Chelsea was safe.

Chelsea.

She hadn't come down for dinner. She'd said she'd rather skip the meal and go to bed early. He hoped that was because she was mad at him and not that she actually wanted to go to bed early. Because that was certainly not what she was going to get.

Chelsea wore an oversize T-shirt she'd snatched from the clothesline out back in response to the sweltering heat outside. She'd have preferred to remain wet and wear nothing at all, but there were simply too many males in this house. So she closed the bedroom door firmly and lay in the bed in the T-shirt, with the window wide open. She tried to rest, but she couldn't get comfortable no matter which way she turned. Everything hurt. She couldn't relax, either, because she kept expecting someone to come through that door to put little Ethan to bed.

It was late before she heard the hum of vehicles rumbling away. A few minutes later came footfalls on the stairs, then the knob turned and the door opened.

Garrett Brand stood in the doorway with his hat in his hands. "You awake?"

"Yeah."

He came the rest of the way inside, flicking on the light as he did. "We need to talk."

"You think so?"

"Yup." He nodded to a chair near the dressing table. "Mind if I sit?"

"It's your house."

He pulled the chair close to the bedside, sat down slowly, then frowned, his gaze fixed on her bare thigh. She felt her blood rush a little more loudly in her ears. Then she followed his gaze and saw the vivid purple bruise and realized his look wasn't lecherous.

"I thought you said you didn't get hurt."

"It looks worse than it feels."

He got to his feet, headed out of the bedroom and returned within five seconds carrying a white plastic jar with a black lid. He didn't settle back in his chair again. Instead, he lowered his bulk to the edge of the bed, and Chelsea battled the urge to brace her feet against him and give a good shove.

He twisted the cap off the jar and scooped out a gob of ugly brown stuff with his fingers. She caught a whiff of it then and wrinkled her nose.

"What is that? It stinks."

"Liniment. Jessi made it up for the horses."

"The horses?"

"Yeah. They get stiff sometimes, go lame. It's good stuff. Trust me. Jessi's studying veterinary medicine, you know."

"I trust you about as far as I can throw you," she said.

And when he set the jar aside and moved his handful of goo toward her thigh, she pulled her leg away. "Wait a minute! You're not putting any horse liniment on me."

He met her eyes, and his held a definite twinkle. "Just lie still. It'll make you feel better."

She had a feeling this was a form of petty revenge for her determined low opinion of him. But she decided it might not be, and that maybe it was worth the risk. Anything was better than the way she ached right now.

He put his fingers on her thigh and gently rubbed some of the stuff onto the purple bruise. And though it should have hurt just to be touched there, it didn't. The ointment—or was it his fingers?—spread warmth over her flesh. Warmth that seemed to penetrate and slowly sink into her.

"Better already, isn't it?"

She released the breath she hadn't been aware she was holding and relaxed back on the pillows. "Yeah. It is."

"I told you." He scooped out more gunk and leaned over to her other leg, this time massaging the stuff onto the sore spot on her shin. Chelsea closed her eyes. Then his other hand slid behind her knee, lifting it until it bent upward. He started to rub some more of the liniment into the back of her calf, where some nasty cow had pinned it between a hard hoof and the ground.

An involuntary sigh escaped her. She bit her lip when she heard it, but it was too late.

"Where else?" he asked.

Her eyes flew open.

"Lift up the T-shirt, Chelsea."

"Not in your wildest dreams, cowboy."

His lips thinned. "You really think I'm gonna try something, don't you?"

She didn't answer, just looked into his eyes. But she saw nothing there to frighten her, or give her cause to mistrust him.

"I'm only trying to help you. You're hurting and I want to make it better." He shook his head, studying the brown gob on his fingertips. "Hell, maybe I am out of line. Taking care of people just…well, it's sort of ingrained in my bones, you know? Got so used to doin' it for the kids—"

"The kids?"

"Wes, Adam, Ben, Elliot…and Jessi. Especially Jessi."

She swallowed hard; he'd reminded her of who he was. The man who'd raised five children and kept a ranch going single-handedly after his parents had been killed. The man who treated a little old lady in town like the queen of Spain and even worried about her cat. The man who'd taken little Ethan in when it would have been just as easy to turn him over to the local social services. And who had sheltered her from the battering heads and hooves of a horde of crazed animals—sheltered her with his own body.

Did she *really* believe he was anything like her father?

"You were holding your back before. I just thought..." His words trailed into silence as Chelsea stared at him, probing his eyes for answers, finding only more questions. She chewed on her lower lip for a moment, then nodded once. She rolled onto her stomach and lifted the T-shirt above her waist.

"Damn, Chelsea, you look like you've been beat with a club."

"I feel like it, too."

His fingers touched her then. Warm. Soothing. He rubbed the stuff into her lower back, and it felt good. Maybe a little bit too good. When he stopped, she started to lower the shirt, but he covered her hand with his.

"Shhh. Just be still."

He began touching her once more, sliding one hand higher as he lifted her T-shirt with the other. He rubbed the ointment over both her shoulder blades and then the spot between them. She closed her eyes again, wondering if anything in her life had ever felt this soothing.

She'd never been touched this way before. She'd never expected a man's touch could be anything but hurtful and cruel. But Garrett's was gentle and healing and good.

He lowered the shirt down her back again. Chelsea rolled over, wincing as the gooey ointment stuck to the material.

"I'm ruining someone's T-shirt with this stuff," she said. She felt she had to say something, and that seemed like something safe.

"That's okay. I have others."

She blinked. "It's yours?"

His eyebrows rose. "Who else around here would need an extra-extra large?"

Her throat went dry. Why? What was so intimate about wearing Garrett's T-shirt? Why did she suddenly feel as if it were him wrapped around her, instead of just a piece of white cotton?

"What about your front?"

"I—"

But he was pushing the shirt up carefully and slowly. She didn't grab it and yank it back down. She waited, almost unable to breathe, telling herself this would be the proof she needed of what kind of man he truly was. When he yanked it up to her neck and tried to grope her breasts, she'd have no more room for doubt. And then . . .

He stopped, letting the shirt rest below her breasts. And though there was a definite yearning in his eyes as he gazed down at her bared waist, he didn't grope. He didn't make any lewd remarks. He didn't smirk.

"Your ribs are bruised to hell and gone. Damn, Chelsea, maybe we oughtta drive into El Paso and get you some X rays."

She shook her head. "Nothing's broken."

"You sure? Would you even know what a broken bone felt like? I mean, if you've never—"

"I've had plenty of broken bones, Garrett. I know what they feel like."

"You . . . ?" He stopped without finishing the question, but it was in his eyes as they met hers, searching.

"Yeah. A wrist once. A couple of ribs another time. And then there was the collarbone."

He swallowed so hard she saw the way his Adam's apple swelled and receded like a wave moving under his skin. "Your father?" The words were like a croak.

She only nodded.

Garrett closed his deep brown eyes very tight.

"It's okay," she said. "I survived it in one piece."

He opened his eyes, facing her, shaking his head. "But you didn't, Chelsea. You think every man who cares for you is gonna hurt you somehow, and that just isn't true."

"Isn't it? I don't know, Garrett. I think believing that is what got my sister killed."

He sighed long and deep, but said nothing more. Instead, he looked again at her exposed skin and resumed the process of smoothing ointment over her bruises. His fingers trembled a little. But he finished, wiped his fingers on a rag and recapped the jar.

"I have something that needs saying," he told her. "And I want you to listen and not think about your father or about your sister, if you can manage it. Just think about me and about you, okay?"

She nodded, but felt suspicion welling up in her heart.

Garrett cleared his throat. "When I said I wanted you to stay...it wasn't because I thought I could get you into bed. It was because...because I care about you. And I—"

"You can't care about me. You barely know me."

"Now I thought you were gonna let me finish."

She clamped her lips together, crossed her arms over her chest and waited.

"I don't know you very well, that's true enough. The point is, I *want* to know you. I like being with you, Chelsea. I like spending time with you and I like the way I feel when I'm near you."

She stared at him, sure there was a punch line coming. But there didn't seem to be one imminent. His eyes were intense and so damned sincere that he almost had her believing this bull.

"How...how do you feel when you're near me?" she asked, surprised to find her voice had gone whispery soft.

He shook his head, his gaze turning inward. "I don't know...like...like maybe I'm more than just a stand-in parent to the kids. Like maybe I'm more than just the guy everybody brings their troubles to. More than just a small-town sheriff. I feel...I feel like a man. A flesh-and-blood man. I feel...alive."

She drew a deep breath and told herself his sweet talk wasn't working on her. Then she denied that her stomach had gone queasy at his words, or that her pulse was pounding in her temples. And that little shiver up her spine had certainly never happened.

"That's lust," she told him. "That's all it is."

"I know lust, Chelsea Brennan. I haven't lived like a monk, you know." He let his gaze roam down her body, but quickly jerked it back up to her eyes. "All right. It's lust. I won't deny that I want you. But it's more than that, too. There's something happening here, and I want to find out what it is, because it's something I've never felt before."

She closed her eyes. "Look, I don't think I want to hear any more of this right now."

"Will you at least think about it?"

She nodded, because she knew there was nothing she could do to keep herself from thinking about it. Hadn't he told her he didn't know the kinds of pretty words that could make a woman go soft inside? Well, for someone who didn't know them, he was doing a pretty good job of reciting them all.

"Good. Now that that's settled, will you join me for dinner?"

Another surprise. The guy was full of them. "The ointment helped, Garrett, but I'm still too sore to go out."

"I know. That's why we're having dinner here."

"I thought everyone had already eaten." She scowled at him, growing suspicious all over again.

"They did. And now they're gone. There's a big she-bang in town tonight. Memorial Day lasts all week around here. Dancing and fireworks. Jessi took Ethan along."

Chelsea felt her eyes widen.

"Don't worry. She's telling people he's our cousin. So what do you say, Chelsea? I want to be with you tonight. Just the two of us."

Panic made her throat go dry.

"And just so you know, under no circumstances am I going to lay a hand on you tonight. I just want to spend some time. Get to know you. I promise, that's all."

She was alone in this house with him. She ought to be bounding out of this bed right now and running away from him. But she wasn't. Instead, she was lying here, thinking about how much she could enjoy an evening in his company.

She must be losing her mind.

"All right," she heard herself say. "B-but I still have to leave tomorrow."

"You can make that decision tomorrow," he told her. Then he rose slowly from the edge of the bed without touching her. "I'll leave you to get dressed. Just come downstairs whenever you're ready."

She nodded and watched him as he left the room, closing the door gently behind him.

Oh, God, this was not what she'd expected. Never in her life had she thought any man would care enough to try so hard to work his way past her defenses. She didn't know how to deal with this. She didn't *want* a man in her life. Not ever!

All right, so she'd just explain that to him. He could be Prince Charming, she'd tell him, but it still wouldn't matter. She'd made a decision never to fall in love with a man, and it was a decision she was going to stick to. And if it hurt Garrett's feelings, then that wasn't her fault. He'd get over it.

Garrett closed the bedroom door, leaned back against it and wiped the beads of sweat from his forehead. Dammit, but he'd never felt more like a schoolboy than he did right now. And the scariest part of the entire experiment was that it had worked! He pulled the index cards from his pocket, scanning the lines quickly to be sure he'd covered everything.

Never felt like this before…like the way I feel when I'm with you…more than just a small-town sheriff. Yup, he'd covered everything Jessi had written down. And tossed in some of his own lines to boot. He'd thought Jessi had gone plum out of her mind when she'd set him down to coach him on what to say. But maybe she knew a little something about what made women tick after all. Hell, she was one.

Imagine that. Little Jessi, a woman. All grown up. He'd never thought of her that way before. But she obviously understood this stuff. She'd told him these kinds of words from a man would make her melt inside, then assured him they'd work just as well on Chelsea. And by heaven, she'd been right.

Garrett flipped through the cards to the ones yet to come.

Let's see. Music. Candles. Wine. And the compliments. Dammit, if they weren't the most flowery things he'd ever heard, he didn't know what were. But the other stuff seemed to have been effective.

Besides, he'd taken his own precautions as backup. He'd reserved every single seat on the two flights to New York tomorrow. Just in case.

Chelsea came down the stairs, and Garrett turned when he heard her steps. He was ready to tell her she was "a vision too beautiful to be real." But when he saw her, he forgot his lines. Everything rushed right out of his head because the sight of her hit him right between the eyes.

She wore a silk sundress that was the same deep green as her eyes. Thin straps held it up, and it fell over her slender curves like a caress. Her vivid red hair was caught up in the back, leaving delicate curls springing free around her face. The high heels made her legs seem like weapons, deadly weapons that could bring even a man his size right to his knees. For just a second, he felt they were aimed at him.

"Damn, you look good." Garrett bit his lip after the words escaped and tried to recall his lines. "I mean—"

"Thank you." Her face flushed with pleasure, and she smiled. Well, hell, he hadn't blown it with that slipup after all. She reached the bottom of the steps and gazed past him. "This is nice. You did all this for me?"

He turned to survey the transformed living room. There was a small fire snapping in the grate and a little round table set up by the picture window. Two tall candles glimmered on the table, their light sparkling off the bottle of chilled wine and the dishes set there.

Garrett would have preferred a cold beer, but hell, if it kept the lady alive . . .

"The music is nice, too. Did you pick that out?"

He listened to the crooning of some fella named Bryan—with a *Y* of all things—Adams, and thought he'd greatly prefer Hank, Jr. "Yeah. You like it?"

She nodded, then came forward.

Garrett racked his brain to figure out what came next. The wine, that was it! Oh, wait, she was heading for the table. He hurried after her to pull out her chair. Then he got lost looking down the front of her dress because the gentle swell of her bosom had captured his eyes and wouldn't let go.

Damn.

He shook himself, dragged his gaze away and reached for the wine, filling her glass first.

"Thank you."

Thank God Jessi hadn't suggested he drink some from her shoe. The things had open toes anyway.

She sipped, licked her lips. Garrett's mouth went dry. He picked up his glass and drained it, then poured more and finally sat himself down. He didn't think he'd be able to sit still for very long, though. He was damned nervous.

"So," he said.

"So?"

"So tell me about yourself, Chelsea." He belatedly remembered his lines. "I want to know everything there is to know about you."

She ducked her head quickly. "You already know all my secrets."

"I don't even know what you do back in New York."

"Oh. No, I guess you don't, do you? I work for an ad agency."

"Doing what?" He tried to inject sincere interest into his tone, tried to maintain eye contact, which was, Jessi had insisted, vital.

"I do the artwork for print ads."

His brows rose in surprise. "You're an artist?"

"Some would call me one. Others might argue." She shrugged. "I love to paint, though. But it's best when I'm at home and I can paint what I want instead of what's been assigned to me. My apartment gets great morning light to work by."

"I wish I could see your paintings," he said, forgetting about the lines he'd rehearsed. "What are they like?"

"They're children mostly. I like painting children. Happy children. Loved children."

He swallowed hard. "Because you never were. Happy. Loved."

"Maybe." She averted her eyes. "You did a wonderful thing for your family, Garrett. I don't know if you realize just how much they needed you after your parents died."

"I needed them just as much," he said. Then he tilted his head. "What happened to you and Michele after your mamma went home?"

"Went home. That's a sweet way to put it, isn't it?"

He shrugged, unable to take his eyes off her. The candlelight made her green eyes shine, and he thought he might lose the entire thread of the conversation if he looked into them much longer.

"We went into the system. Foster care. Got shuffled around a lot until we were old enough to be on our own." She shook her head. "I wish we'd had a brother like you to watch out for us."

"I don't want to be your brother, Chelsea."

She bit her bottom lip, maybe a little frightened.

"But I'd like to watch out for you. You and Ethan. Even if you do go back to New York. You remember that, okay? If you ever need me, I'll be there in a heartbeat."

Her green eyes widened a little. Then she shook her head. "You really are something, Garrett Brand."

He wondered if she meant something good, or something bad. He was straying too far from Jessi's script here. Time to get back on track.

"Will you dance with me, Chelsea?"

She smiled a wavery little smile, took a sip of wine and slowly, gracefully, got to her feet.

Oh, God, that must mean yes. Garrett got up, too, and stepped close to her. He slipped his arms around her waist, but loosely, just anchoring his hands atop her hips. She clasped hers at the base of his neck, and he began to move with her in time to Bryan-with-a-*Y* Adams as he crooned a heart-wrenching love song. Didn't the guy know anything else?

Chelsea sighed, and her breath fanned his throat. His stomach clenched into a hard knot, and he told himself it was just because he hadn't eaten. It was hard to keep that in mind, though, what with Chelsea so close and Bryan-with-a-*Y* singing about how to *really* love a woman. Come to think of it, the song was downright erotic if you listened to the words. And Garrett was listening. Mental pictures were forming in his mind. Pictures that distracted him from the lines he'd rehearsed and his step-by-step plan of how this evening was supposed to go.

"I have to tell you something, Garrett," Chelsea said, and her voice was as soft as goose down.

"What's that?"

She drew a breath, sighed again. Those damned sighs of hers were tickling his skin, and he battled the urge to pull her closer. So he could really *feel* her, as the singer kept suggesting.

"I'm scared."

She said it in a sudden gust as if forcing the words out. Garrett's feet stopped moving, and he looked down into her face. Her beautiful face. He was beginning to feel like a real jerk for leading her on like this. If it wasn't for the fact that she'd end up dead if she ran off, he'd cut the act here and now. It wasn't exactly the most chivalrous thing he'd ever done.

"Of me?"

"No. I tried to be, but... you're just not a very scary kind of man."

He lifted his brows. "Is that a compliment or a slam, lady?"

"Compliment. I've never met a man I wasn't afraid of, deservedly or not. But you... you're different."

"Different how?"

She shrugged and moved closer, laying her head on his shoulder, nudging him into motion again. He tightened his arms around her waist and held her close, then began dancing again.

But now the singer was advising him to really taste her, and it was beginning to get on his nerves.

She'd probably taste just like sugar.

"I'm not sure," she said, and he had to think a minute to remember the question. "You're gentle, for one thing. Everything you do, you do... gently."

"And you like that?"

"Mmm."

"Glad to hear it. I'm doing one thing right, then."

"More than one thing," she said, and her voice was beginning to take on a lazy quality that made him nervous. "You're also honest. You don't play games, just say what you mean straight out. I like that, too."

Garrett closed his eyes as a shaft of guilt the size of a Mack truck drove right through him.

"So the least I can do is be honest with you in return."

Taken aback, he stopped dancing again. Hell, she had been. Hadn't she? "About what?" he asked. He looked into her eyes again, saw them staring up at him, trusting him. He was scum.

"About . . . us. This . . . thing between us."

Wait a minute. There was no *thing* between them. He'd made that up. No, Jessi had.

"I feel it, too," Chelsea went on.

"You do?"

She nodded. "I . . ." She licked her lips, lowered her head. "I want you just as much as you want me."

"You do?" It was all Garrett could do not to stagger backward.

She looked up again, smiled just a little. "Yeah, I do. So you have to believe me when I tell you that if I were going to get involved with any man, it would be you."

"It would?" Dammit, couldn't he do more than repeat her every word?

"But I'm not. I made that decision a long time ago, Garrett. There will never be a man in my life. And I will never, ever, fall in love."

He sighed in abject relief. Thank God. Thank God. At least this way, she wouldn't be hurt when she found out this had all been an act to get her to stay here.

"I just thought you should know that. So you won't be . . . you know . . . hurt. When I leave."

"Leave?"

Was there an echo in here?

"I'm glad you told me how you feel about me, Garrett. It's just one more reason for me to go. It will be easier on you when I'm back in New York."

"But Chelsea—"

"I can't stay, Garrett. Especially now." She lifted a hand to the side of his face. "You're a special man. You deserve so much more than I can ever give."

"I didn't ask you to give me anything," he said, which was, he figured, better than parroting her words and adding a question mark, but not by much.

"That's good, because I don't *have* anything."

He felt like swearing. Like stomping or hitting something. Jessi and her dumb ideas. All he'd done was give Chelsea another excuse to run off. Now what the hell was he supposed to do?

He gave himself a mental kick. "I moved in too fast, scared you, didn't I?" She shook her head in denial, but he caught her chin and stared down into her eyes. "Chelsea, I want you to stay. I want you to stay because I like you and because I'm nuts about Ethan. Because I'm scared to death of what will happen if you run off to New York alone. This maniac is still out there somewhere."

"I can take care of myself."

"I know you can. Hell, that's what you've been doing your whole life, isn't it? But this is different, Chelsea. You have to think about little Bubba now."

"I am thinking of him. And I owe it to him to see that his mother gets a proper burial—at home, where she belongs."

"Dammit, Chelsea, you can do it from right here. Ship the body. Make the arrangements over the phone."

"And miss my own sister's funeral?"

Garrett closed his eyes, trying hard to rein in his temper. She was frustrating!

"We can have a memorial service in Quinn. We can send a bushel of flowers. Hell, Chelsea, what do you think Michele would have wanted more? You and her son safe here with us, or standing beside a hole in the ground in New York waiting for that bastard to..." He bit his lip. Too late, though.

"What bastard?"

He shook his head.

"Garrett, you know something about Ethan's father, don't you? Something you're not telling me. What is it?"

The timer bell pinged from the kitchen.

"That's dinner." He said it with all the relief of a boxer teetering at the edge of consciousness and saved by the bell.

"I don't give a damn about dinner. What do you know?"

He sighed long and hard, seeing defeat in those sparking green eyes. "All right. I didn't want to tell you this because I knew it would scare you. But...I found out who Ethan's father is."

She stood away from him, braced and waiting.

He lifted his hands to her shoulders, but she pulled free. He cleared his throat. "Did you ever hear of Vincent de Lorean?"

"Maybe. The name is familiar, but... Should I?"

He drew another long breath. "He's one of the most wanted criminals in Texas, Chelsea."

She jerked back as the shock hit her. But she recovered fast, and he saw something else forming in her eyes. "Wanted...for what?"

"You name it. He's head of the biggest organized-crime syndicate in the state. A real mover and shaker in the drug trade. Suspected of tax evasion, conspiracy, fraud, extortion...and murder. But so far no one's ever been able to get enough evidence to put him away. He's a powerful man, with powerful connections.''

She closed her eyes slowly, backing up until her legs hit the rocking chair and then sinking into it.

"He has people watching your place in N.Y., waiting for you to show up there with Bubba."

She swore, using words he never would have imagined were in her vocabulary.

"You can't go back there, Chelsea. Don't you see that by now?''

She swallowed hard and nodded.

"You're scared. God, I knew this would shake you. That's why I . . .''

Her head came up slowly. "That's why you what?'' Then she swung her gaze around to the table, the candles, the wine. And he saw knowledge there he'd much rather not have seen. "That's what all this was about, then? You were trying to seduce me into staying here? You thought you could make me fall head over heels in love with you and never want to leave? Damn, Garrett, what the hell were you planning to do with me once the crisis was over?''

"Chelsea, it's not like that.''

"Don't make it worse by lying even more. You arrogant son of a . . . God, you must really be vain to think a little attention from you would be enough to. . .'' She shook her head hard, closed her eyes. "And I fell right into it, didn't I? Sinking into your arms and telling you. . .'' She got to her feet, but not too steadily. "You and your brothers will have one hell of a belly laugh when you tell them what a sap I was, won't you, Garrett?''

"No! Dammit, Chelsea, shut up and listen for a minute.''

"No, you listen. I'm leaving here. I'm taking Ethan and I'm leaving. But before I go, I need to know one thing."

He shook his head. She was not leaving. He wouldn't let her leave. Dammit, not when he knew she'd end up...

"Where does this bastard live?"

His thoughts came to a grinding halt at the pure venom he heard in Chelsea's voice.

"You can't—"

"I damn well can! And I damn well will, and if you won't tell me where to find this animal, I'll find someone else who can. I've waited almost twenty years to..." She stopped, breathing rapidly.

He shook his head and went to her, and he did touch her this time. He took her shoulders in his hands and stared hard at her. "Listen to yourself. Dammit, Chelsea, you're transferring all the rage you feel toward your father—rage you've been hanging on to way too long—onto a man you don't even know. What do you think you're gonna do? Hunt the man down and kill him?"

"Yes! Yes, dammit!"

"No. Chelsea, you gotta let go of this. It's eating you alive."

"I can't let go. They have to pay. Both of them. All of them. Every man who's ever lifted a hand to a woman...or to a child.... God, Garrett, when is it going to end? Somebody has to stop them. Somebody has to say it's enough. It's over. No more. No more!"

She was shaking all over and was as white as a sheet. He pulled her tight against him, stroked her hair. "Chelsea, you're right, so right. Somebody has to stop them. But you can't do it alone. I know you want to, but you can't. No one can. And you can't do it by hunting every one of them down like the vermin they are. You might take out a few, but then you'd end up in prison and all the passion you feel for ending this nightmare would be wasted.''

The first sob ripped through her, followed closely by another. It tore at his guts to feel the power of her pain wrenching through her small body. He ached, dammit. He bled inside.

"I...c-can get my father...and Vincent. And after th-th-that...it's all frosting...."

"No, baby, no. Not that way. Not that way."

"Then h-how?"

He hooked a finger under her chin, tipped her head up and saw the tears flooding her face. He meant to look into her eyes, try to see if he could make her see sense. But instead, he lowered his mouth to her trembling lips and kissed her. He tasted the salty tears. He tasted *her.* She shuddered with her inner anguish, but she held on to him. And she opened to him. He pushed his tongue between her moist lips and met hers. He licked the roof of her mouth and then drew her tongue into his, held it there, sucked at it. Wanted more.

Then she pushed him away, and he went. He released his grip on her at the first sign she'd had enough and stood there panting as she glared up at him.

"You don't have to pretend anymore, Garrett. It's not going to change my mind."

She turned and fled up the stairs.

Garrett sank into a chair, whispering the words that had leaped to his lips without rehearsal. Without one of Jessi's little cards. Without a well-laid plan.

"I wasn't pretending." He blinked, feeling as dazed as a shell-shocked warrior. "Hell and damnation, I wasn't pretending at all."

Chapter 10

Despite the liniment, Chelsea ached more in the morning than she had the night before. She rolled carefully out of bed, sending a jealous glance toward Ethan. He'd slept the night through in the hand-tooled hardwood cradle and still lay there, peaceful. Content. His legs drawn up underneath him made his little butt poke upward. Chelsea smiled, wondering how anyone could sleep in that position. He seemed comfortable, though.

She pulled on a bathrobe and slipped quietly out of the bedroom. Another steamy bath would have been nice, but the running water might disturb the baby. She'd just wait until later to soak her aching muscles again. Right now, she'd settle for a cup of coffee and the soothing feel of early morning.

The kitchen was deserted. Chelsea glanced at the little clock. Only 5:13. No wonder. The others wouldn't wake for a little while yet. She put on a fresh pot, located a cup and waited for the coffee to brew. When it was done, she took her steaming mug out onto the front porch. She sat down on the swing, leaned back and let the morning work its wonders on her. The new day crept in with its fresh, dewy air and its bird songs. The horizon glowed with brush strokes of fire and gold.

She sipped the coffee. It was beautiful here. Tranquil. But she couldn't stay. Not now.

Her serenity slipped a notch as she recalled what a fool she'd made of herself with Garrett last night. Telling him she wanted him. Confessing she had feelings for him. For God's sake, the man must be sadistic to let her go on like that when his side of the exchange had been no more than an act to keep her at the ranch. And that would have been reason enough to run. But what clinched it was the *reason* he wanted to keep her here. To protect her from an abuser and a killer. Just the way her mother used to step in and try to protect her.

And look where it had gotten Mom.

No, Chelsea didn't have it in her to watch anyone else, even someone as misguided as Garrett Brand, step in to take on a fight that belonged to her. She couldn't see another person hurt in her stead. And she most certainly couldn't stay here now.

Problem was, she couldn't go home, either.

She stared out at the horizon. There must be somewhere in the world that would be safe for her and Ethan. Somewhere, there must be a haven.

Then again, Michele had thought the same thing. She'd been running, searching for a safe haven, too. But this Vincent what's-his-name had found her anyway. And killed her.

A nicker came from the stable, just beyond the bigger barn. Then another.

Chelsea looked in that direction, frowning. A whinny followed, and she found herself getting to her feet, tilting her head, squinting. She knew next to nothing about horses. But what she'd heard struck her as odd. Not the normal, soft sounds animals made, but more a cry of alarm. Or something.

She took another sip from the mug and lowered it to the railing. Then she started down the front steps, pausing before she stepped into the still-moist grass to remove her slippers. No sense soaking them. She tossed them behind her onto the porch and hurried barefoot across the front lawn. The dew chilled her feet and sent a little shiver dancing up her spine. It felt good.

She reached the big front doors and lifted the crosspiece that held them closed, as she'd seen Garrett do. She tugged one of the huge doors open and stepped inside.

Dimmer in here. Cooler. The sweet smell of what must be grain, but smelled faintly of molasses, and the sharp odor of the animals themselves filled the place. Chelsea walked down the center between the stalls that lined either side of the stable. Huge brown eyes followed her progress as she moved slowly along. She spotted Sugar when she was almost all the way to the other end of the long, narrow building. She went over to her, stroked her white muzzle. But the horse seemed nervous and jumpy for some reason, dancing away, eyes too round.

Chelsea wrinkled her nose as she caught a faint whiff of something else. Something that shouldn't be here. But her attention was distracted from the task of putting a name to the scent when she heard a gentle creaking. She turned to see the big door she'd left open slowly swinging shut.

She blinked and her throat went dry.

"The wind," she whispered, sending the mare a nervous smile. "Just the wind." Wind or not, she'd had enough of this place. There was a door at the far end, exactly like the one she'd come through. It was closer than the other, so she headed toward it. Now that she'd checked and seen that the horses were fine, she could leave with a clear conscience.

The spotless concrete floor was cold on her damp feet anyway. She should have worn shoes. She walked quickly to the door, but it took only a single try to tell her that it was not going to budge. Probably a crosspiece, same as on the front door, holding it closed from the outside. Chelsea licked her lips. There was a smaller door on her left. Not an exit by the looks of it. Probably a tack room or something. Though...oddly, she didn't smell leather. More like...

She opened the door. Saw nothing out of the ordinary. But that smell. And...hey, that window was broken. What the...? She was only vaguely aware of a sudden movement outside the broken window. A pinprick of light, flicking from the window to the floor. Lightning bug. Only when the match landed in the puddle at her feet did she realize...

The gasoline on the floor made a *woof* sound and sent her sailing backward. She landed on the concrete floor, hitting it so hard she lost her breath. The fire followed her.

The baby was crying. And strangely enough, Chelsea hadn't done anything to stop him. Garrett grumbled under his breath, but dragged himself out of bed anyway. Even if Chelsea were mad enough to shoot him, she shouldn't take it out on little Bubba.

Nah. She *wouldn't* take it out on little Bubba. So what was up?

He pulled on his jeans. Ethan kept on yelling. He tugged on socks and stomped into his boots, waiting.

Chelsea still hadn't picked the kid up. He gave her every opportunity, even shrugging on a shirt to put off the moment when he'd have to go into that bedroom and maybe see her lying there all sleepy and sexy. He didn't want to see her. Not after what she'd confessed last night.

That she wanted him.

Damn, but the look in her eyes when she'd said it had kept him awake all night. Haunting him like a ghost. Didn't matter if his eyes were opened or closed, he could still see her there.

And he'd blown it. Sure as all hell, he'd blown it. He supposed he was a little bit slow. He must be, not to have realized sooner that his part in this little play was more than just an act. The little hellcat meant something to him. Though he doubted he'd ever be able to convince her of it now.

Ethan howled, and Garrett sighed in defeat and stepped into the hall. Tapping once for politeness, he opened the guest-room door. Ethan sat up in the bed, playing with his toes and hollering largely for the pleasure of hearing his own voice, Garrett thought. He looked up when Garrett stepped inside and grinned his fool head off.

Garrett gathered him up and scanned the room, the unmade bed, the empty bathroom. Chelsea wasn't here. Frowning, Garrett looked around for the diaper bag.

"I'll get that, big brother." He spun to see Jessi, sleepy-eyed and ruffly-haired, smiling at him from the doorway. "Here, hand over the little pudge. I'll give him his morning bath. Meanwhile, you can tell me how last night went. You were already in bed by the time we came home."

Garrett frowned as a high-pitched whinny, which sounded an awful lot like Duke, drifted from the stable through the open bedroom window. "Later, Jes."

He handed her the baby on the way past, took the stairs at a trot and headed into the kitchen. Fresh coffee. Sugar out on the counter. A spoon.

"Chelsea?"

No answer. He frowned, studying the room, the beginnings of worry gnawing at his stomach. She shouldn't be out alone. Not with Vincent de Lorean after her. But as he glanced at the front door, he saw that it was unlocked. Somebody had gone out this morning. He crossed the kitchen quickly, opened the door and looked over at the porch swing, half-expecting to see her scowling at him.

She wasn't there. But a half-filled coffee mug sat on the railing. And her slippers lay on the steps.

Duke squealed again, drawing Garrett's gaze toward the stable. That's when he saw the smoke.

He turned just long enough to bellow, thankful for once for his booming voice. "Fire in the stable!" And then he was racing across the lawn, his heart in his throat. He told himself there was no reason in the world to think Chelsea was in that stable. But he believed it anyway. His heart damn near pounded a hole through his chest.

No. She couldn't be inside. The crosspiece still held the front doors closed. Garrett lifted it, tugged the doors open. Flames roared in front of him, a solid wall of fire blocking the entrance. Garrett turned away and raced around the side of the building, up the ladder to the second story where the grain was stored, and climbed inside. The place was sweltering and beginning to fill with smoke. But no flames licked at the granary. He got down on all fours, felt the searing heat scalding his palms as he searched for the trapdoor. He coughed, swiped sweat from his brow, found it and jerked it open.

Light, heat and smoke poured through. No flames, though. He couldn't see any directly below, so he swung his legs down through, and let himself drop.

The floor met him halfway, it seemed. Knocked the wind out of him. Damn. He coughed, wheezed, knuckled his stinging eyes and tried to see. He shouted Chelsea's name, but it was useless. The horses had taken to shrieking in terror. Walls of fire rose at both ends of the stable, blocking the exits, and the flames had spread, licking at the rafters and the stalls at either end.

Sugar reared and kicked the wall behind her again and again. Her stall was on fire, and she was crazed. Garrett staggered to his feet and started toward the frightened animal. Only then did he stumble on Chelsea. She lay on the floor, barely visible in the smoke haze that filled the place. If he hadn't tripped over her, he might never have found her.

Garrett bent down and scooped her up. She hung limply in his arms, head hanging backward. Her robe was smoldering, he realized with a start, and he quickly stripped it off her. Then he moved back to the trapdoor. He slung Chelsea over his shoulder, gripped the ladder and started up. Flames roaring in his ears now. Searing his flesh. Smoke choking him. He was weakening, dammit. Wheezing, gasping like an old man.

He emerged into the loft, but it was no longer any better here. Worse, if anything. Hotter. Smokier. Flames were now licking up through the floorboards here and there, and the roar was deafening. Horses screamed in an agony of panic.

He took a step toward the opening he'd come through. Then another. And then the floor beneath him just dissolved, and he and Chelsea crashed down into the hubs of hell.

* * *

"Garrett!" Jessi screamed. "Garrett!"

She stood as close as she could to the blazing stables, which wasn't close enough. But she had little Ethan on her hip and didn't dare go any closer. The place looked like a giant torch, and her beloved brother was inside. It was a nightmare. Elliot manned a hose, trying to soak down the blaze in the doorway enough to get inside. Wes had raced back to the house for a chain saw and now he was revving it and running, which was none too smart, but he did it anyway.

He headed around the side of the stable, and Jessi raced after him. Wes lifted the saw and sank its ripping teeth into the side of the building. The machine whined and growled. The horses shrieked and the fire roared. Ethan took to crying, too, and soon the noises all blended together.

Jessi dropped to her knees right there in the dirt, hugging the sobbing infant to her breast and praying out loud for the volunteer firemen to show up fast. She watched as her brother wielded the saw, and as soon as a jagged, gaping hole was made, Wes tossed the chain saw to the ground, lifted his arms over his face and charged right on inside.

"Wes, no!" Jessi shouted, but she knew it was useless before the words were out. Then Elliot came charging around the side of the burning building, as well, and dived inside after Wes. Blue stood beside Jessi, all four legs braced as he leaned forward, barking at the fire, the hair on his haunches bristling. The dog ran a few steps forward, then backed away, whimpering over and over again, torn between the age-old instinct of self-preservation and the love of his masters.

The fourth time he lunged forward, ol' Blue didn't come back. He leaped through the opening and vanished into the billowing gray smoke.

"Oh, Lord," Jessi cried, kneeling and rocking as unchecked tears flowed down her face. "Lord, don't take my brothers. Don't do that to me...please...."

She heard sirens. Time ticked by. Endless moments passed like hours, though it could only have been seconds between the time she heard the sirens and the time the trucks came barreling into the drive, bounding over the grass. Then men were running this way and that, voices yelling orders.

"Jessica?"

A warm, big hand closed on her shoulder, and she dragged her gaze from the fiery maw that had swallowed almost all of her family except for Ben and Adam. She saw the worried face of the stranger who'd come to dinner last night.

"Lash...God, Lash, my brothers..."

His dark brows rose over those pale blue eyes. "In there?"

She nodded, returning her gaze to the hole, praying, hoping.

"There are people inside!" Lash yelled at the men who were even now manning fire hoses. He touched Jessi again. Both hands this time. "Come on. Get away from here before you and the baby end up hurt." He pulled her to her feet. But she tugged her arm free as soon as she was upright. "Jessi, there's nothing you can do here. Come on."

Fresh tears spilled over as he guided her away from the building at a run. He pointed her toward the house, then left her, heading back to join the fire fighters. Jessi didn't go far, only halfway, and she never took her eyes off the inferno. The roof was ablaze now, as well. But the flames in the doorway had subsided. She caught her breath when she saw Lash don one of the heavy yellow coats and a helmet, then head inside with the others.

Only seconds later, big old Duke was led through that doorway with a neckerchief over his eyes. Behind him were Sugar, whose rump bore charred spots, and Paint, dancing and kicking wildly. The man who led them out was Jason Pratt, a local merchant she'd known since kindergarten. He ran across the lawn, releasing the animals into the corral and closing the gate before hurrying back to the blazing stable.

Marisella's battered pickup bounced into the driveway, and the elderly woman jumped out with the agility of a sixteen-year-old. She ran up to Jessi. "Give the child to me before you drop him, *chica*. Here." She pried Ethan from Jessi's arms, and the baby stopped crying.

Then Lash came through the front door, half-dragging Elliot. Elliot's arm was wrapped around Lash's broad shoulders. They ran several yards from the stable, then Lash eased Elliot to the ground, whirled and raced back inside. One of the volunteers who hadn't gone in rushed over to Elliot with an oxygen tank and a mask. Jessi took a step forward, but Marisella's firm hand on her arm kept her from running to him, as well.

Two more men came out, Wes suspended between them, his face blackened with soot. He was coughing uncontrollably, and it looked as if he were fighting his rescuers. They dumped him on the ground and one of them stayed with him, trying to hold him there by all appearances, while the other rushed back inside. On his way in, this fire fighter passed another, coming out carrying Chelsea in his arms. He laid her beside Wes and Elliot.

Jessi did rush forward now, ignoring Marisella's warnings. She fell on the ground beside her brothers, not caring that she was in the way of the paramedics who tried to tend them.

"Elliot! Wes! God, I thought... Are you all right?"

Wes coughed some more, but tore the oxygen mask away from his face and struggled to his feet. Elliot lay on his back, blinking slowly and breathing deeply from the mask over his face.

"Garrett's still in there," Wes growled at the fire fighter holding his shoulders. "And you damned well can't stop me from going in after my brother."

Elliot muttered something that sounded like "Garrett" from beneath the mask. Jessi smoothed his sooty hair away from his black-streaked face. But her eyes were on the door. More horses emerged, then more. She counted them and knew they were all safe. But no sign of Garrett. She glanced Chelsea's way, but so many people were bending over her it was impossible to see. Fear gripped Jessi's heart.

Part of the roof fell in with a deafening roar and an explosion of sparks and cinders. The flames shot skyward, and Jessi screamed Garrett's name. Wes shoved the fire fighter so hard the man went flying and hit the ground, then Wes surged forward, running flat out toward the stable.

But he stopped short at the doorway. Garrett and Lash came stumbling out, and it was unclear who was helping whom. Blue lumbered along beside them. They staggered forward, and Jessi ran to meet them. Wes already had his arms around Garrett, so Jessi took hold of Lash and helped him back toward the others.

The remaining part of the roof and one whole side of the stable fell inward with a thunderous crash. But Jessi was too busy thanking God to notice it much.

"Chelsea . . ." Garrett coughed and pushed the oxygen mask away from his face. He glanced once toward the burning building. Not much was left but a blazing framework. And then that even collapsed in on itself, leaving only charred ruins.

Jessi knelt beside him, crying, holding his hands. "They got her, Garrett." She nodded to his left, and Garrett saw Chelsea lying there, surrounded by men who worked on her. But her eyes were closed and his heart turned over.

He drew a raspy breath, swallowed, but his throat felt raw. "Wes and Elliot?"

"They're okay, Garrett." This from his left, and he turned to see Lash sitting upright, back bowed forward slightly, holding a mask to his face, breathing several times before moving it aside to speak again. "They took in some smoke, but they're okay. We got all the horses out, too, I think."

Garrett took only a second to look for his brothers. Elliot seemed shaken, dazed, but all right. Wes had wandered over to the corral and was trying to soothe the horses there. Garrett brought his gaze back to Lash and narrowed his stinging eyes. "What the hell are you doing here?"

"Garrett, he saved your life. Elliot's, too," Jessi said. "Thank God he was here."

Lash held Garrett's gaze. "I saw the fire trucks heading this way, and I followed."

"Why?"

Lash shrugged. "Thought I might be able to help. I used to do this crap for a living."

Garrett frowned. "You're a fire fighter?"

"Used to be. In Chicago."

Garrett nodded, digesting the information and still wondering what this stranger was really doing here. Why did he leave Chicago and show up in a speck on the map like Quinn? Why did he just happen to be around every time disaster struck?

Chelsea groaned, a hoarse, guttural sound, and putting his questions aside, he got to his feet and went to her. He knelt beside her, brushing her hair away from her face.

"She took in quite a bit of smoke, Garrett. Has a few burns, but nothing life threatening. We need to get her to the hospital."

He nodded to the anonymous voice of a paramedic, not bothering to link a name to it or to check the face of what was, in all likelihood, one of his neighbors.

"You could use some treatment yourself," the voice said.

"I'm fine. See to Chelsea." The man didn't argue. Garrett watched helplessly as Chelsea was bundled onto a gurney and rolled to a waiting ambulance. He turned once, found Wes and Jessi standing nearby. "You all right, Wes?"

Wes nodded, grim-faced. "Some of the horses have burns. They'll need tending."

"Can you and Jessi handle it?"

"Sure," Jessi said quickly. "I'll ask Marisella to stay and take care of Ethan for us."

"I want Elliot at the hospital. He doesn't look good."

"Neither do you," Wes replied. "I'll see he gets there."

"Send him along by ambulance. I want you to stay here, Wes. I'm thinking this fire was no accident."

Wes's black eyes narrowed, again reminding Garrett how appropriately his Comanche mother had named him. Raven Eyes. "Vincent de Lorean?"

"Probably."

"You think he'll try again?"

"He might."

"I'll watch things. He tries anything today, he's gonna be one hurting son of a—"

"You watch things. Don't let little Bubba out of your sight. Not for a second. I'm going with Chelsea."

Wes nodded, for once not making smart remarks about his love life. Garrett climbed into the back of the ambulance and found a seat. He clutched Chelsea's dirty hands in his and closed his eyes as the doors slammed shut. Then the vehicle bounded away, its siren wailing.

She stirred awake. Pain seared her right arm and both feet. Her lungs burned. Her eyes stung, and it hurt to breathe. But all of that faded when she brought her vision into focus and saw Garrett sitting in a hard little chair beside her bed, staring down at her. Black soot coated his face and neck and arms. His dark hair curled unnaturally at the ends, singed, and she realized what had happened. She'd been trapped in the burning stable, and he had come in after her.

His brown eyes widened when they met hers. "Thank God Almighty, Chelsea. I was beginnin' to think you'd never come around."

She opened her mouth to speak, but only a hoarse croak emerged. She glanced down at herself. She lay in a white bed, wearing a pale blue hospital gown, and her right arm was bandaged and both her feet were wrapped in gauze. No soot coated her skin, and she realized someone had cleaned her up. No one had tended to Garrett, though.

She cleared her throat. It hurt. "You're a mess," she whispered.

"You should have seen yourself."

She mustered a smile.

"Are you hurting, Chelsea?"

"A little." She closed her eyes, licked her parched lips. "A lot."

"I'll call a nurse, make them give you something for—"

"In a minute." She covered his hand as he reached for the call button clipped to the edge of her pillow. "Garrett, there was someone outside the barn."

"You saw someone?"

"I saw...a shape. Movement. I smelled gasoline, and..." She closed her eyes, shivering at the memory of the instant when she'd realized what was happening.

He left the chair, bending over the bed and enfolding her in his arms before the chill even left her spine. His big, solid chest was under her hands, and his strong arms held her gently. She thought she felt him tremble. And when he spoke, his voice was rough from more than just the smoke he'd inhaled. "Dammit, Chelsea, you could have been killed. I could've...*we*...could've lost you."

She didn't fight her instinctive response to him. She let her arms slide around his waist and hugged him back, resting her head on his shoulder. He smelled smoky. But even that didn't make his embrace less soothing.

"I was scared, Garrett. I haven't been that scared since those nights when I'd sit in my bedroom and listen to my father's slaps and my mother's tears."

His sigh warmed her neck. Then he loosened his grip and moved back a little. He looked down at her and smiled softly. "I smudged your face." He took a tissue from the box on the bedside stand and wiped at a spot on her cheek.

She drew a calming breath, wishing she could steady her pattering heart, but finding it difficult.

Garrett dropped the tissue into the wastebasket and sat in his chair again. "So what were you doing in the stable, Chelsea?"

She shrugged. "The horses sounded jumpy. I thought I'd check on them." She studied his face as he listened carefully to her answer. "How did you know I was out there?"

"Saw the coffee on the porch, your slippers. Then the smoke." He shook his head and swore. "You'll never know how I felt when I yanked those doors open and saw that wall of fire."

"But you came inside anyway."

He held her gaze a long moment, his brown one darkening. "Because I had this gut-deep feeling you were in there."

"You could have gotten yourself killed trying to get me out."

"What was the alternative, Chelsea? Just leave you there to burn to death?"

She shrugged. "I'm beginning to think my nephew would fare just as well being raised by you as by me. Maybe better."

"And you think your nephew is the only reason I risked my neck to get to you?"

She lifted her chin. "What else would I think?"

He hooked a finger beneath her chin to raise it, then settled his mouth over hers. His kiss was gentle. Healing, almost. Warmth and life seemed to flow through him into her. He lifted his head.

"Think that," he said softly.

She blinked up at him, confusion swirling like a tempest in her mind. "I don't..."

"Doesn't matter, Chelsea. We have time. Right now, all that matters is that you're okay and you're coming home with me."

She drew a slow breath as Garrett settled back in the chair. "I'm not sure that's such a great idea."

He frowned, didn't speak, just frowned and nodded at her to continue.

"Garrett, if that fire was deliberately set, then this Vincent character knows where I'm staying. He knows where Ethan is. And he'll keep trying until he gets to us."

"He can keep trying until hell freezes over, Chelsea. It won't do him any good. He's got a truckload of Brands to go through before he can get to you or Bubba, and he's gonna find that isn't exactly easy."

Chelsea closed her eyes. "That's exactly what I'm afraid of."

Garrett shook his head slowly, a puzzled look creasing his brow.

"You could have been killed in that fire, Garrett. Elliot or Wes—God, even Jessi—might have died today. I don't *want* all of you standing between this gangster and me. I don't want anyone else suffering because I showed up in your lives."

"No one's going to suffer—"

"No? Tell my mother that, Garrett. She died because she tried to protect my sister and me. I can't live with that happening to anyone else."

He stared down at her in silence as if he didn't know what to say. Finally, he just sighed hard. "We'll take precautions. I'll contact Ben and Adam, get them back here to help out. Everything will be just—"

"No."

He frowned at her, seeming unable to understand what she was getting at.

"He murdered my sister, Garrett. Not yours. This is between Vincent de Lorean and me, and nobody else."

"And Ethan," Garrett whispered. "Don't you forget about Ethan."

Licking her lips, swallowing hard on a decision that went down like a brick, she nodded. "I'm not forgetting him."

"Chelsea…" He shook his head, leaned over and took her hand in his. "All that crap before, the wine and the music, that wasn't me. It was bull. But I realized that night that—"

"I don't want to hear this. Not now, Garrett. Please."

He stared down at her, and she knew she'd hurt him. God, could the big lug actually have developed a soft spot for her after all?

"You aren't alone anymore, Chelsea. Dammit straight to hell, I know you've had to be your whole life. I know every battle you fought, you fought by yourself. But you don't have to do that this time. Damn, woman, why won't you let me help you?"

Because I love you.

The words whispered through her mind like a sudden breeze, startling her enough to make her eyes widen. She loved him. The way she'd loved her mother and her sister. She loved him in spite of the fact that he was a man and that she'd vowed never to love one of that gender. And she trusted him. There wasn't a single doubt in Chelsea's mind that he'd never harm a hair on her head. No doubt in her mind that he'd do everything in his power to protect her.

Her mother had tried to protect her, too. From a man a lot like Vincent. Her own father. Oh, Chelsea and Michele had taken beatings. Lots of them. But whenever she could, Mom had stepped in, diverted the bastard's rage away from her daughters, deliberately directing it at herself instead. And she'd died because of it.

And Michele. Michele had found a safe haven for her baby son and then run off in another direction. She'd become a moving target for Vincent's rage in order to save her son from the monster. And *she'd* died because of it.

Chelsea couldn't let someone—especially Garrett—try to take her place as the target of Vincent's vengeance. And she wouldn't run. Running didn't do any good. No place was safe as long as that man remained on this planet.

"Come home with me, Chelsea. The doc said you could leave whenever you felt up to it."

She nodded slowly. "Okay. I'll come." But she knew in her heart she was lying.

Chapter 11

Something was on her mind. Garrett knew it as well as he knew his own name, but she wouldn't open up. Wouldn't tell him about it. Wouldn't let him in.

And he wanted to get in more than a hairless pup in a blizzard. The more she withdrew, the more edgy he became. Until it seemed to Garrett that nothing in his life had ever been as important to him as his new mission. Getting to Chelsea Brennan. Making her let him help her. Let him see what she was thinking, what she was feeling. Let him . . .

Ah, hell, he didn't know what.

The stable was nothing more than soaking wet ashes and a few chunks of charred beams here and there. The horses were stuck in the corral for the night. Elliot was still complaining about his lungs hurting. Wes, Garrett suspected, was hurting a lot more than Elliot, but typically, he hadn't said a damned word to indicate it. Jessi was still shaky, jumping at shadows. He'd heard from Elliot that she'd been target shooting while he and Chelsea had been at the hospital. Target shooting, when they all knew damned well and good that Jessi could outshoot any of them. She didn't need to practice. He hated to see his tomboy sister all nerved up.

He'd been nerved up, too. So much so that he had a call in to the Texas Rangers asking for background information, an address and anything else they had on Vincent de Lorean. They hadn't got back to him yet, but Garrett thought it wouldn't be much longer. The second he knew where he could find the bastard, he planned to pay him a visit. And not a pleasant one.

Only Ethan seemed unaffected by it all. He played with the new set of soft-sided, brightly colored building blocks Wes had brought home from one of his trips into town. Kid loved the things. Especially seemed to like bopping ol' Blue on the head with them, not that Blue minded any. In fact, the old mutt actually batted one across the floor a second ago the way a playful puppy might do.

Little Bubba had a way of making everyone feel younger, Garrett supposed. He glanced into the kitchen at Chelsea and swallowed hard. Yup. He knew he for one felt like an awkward twelve-year-old eyeing potential dance partners at his first boy-girl party.

He girded his loins and stomped into the kitchen. He'd taken a lot of pains today while Chelsea had been lying upstairs in bed recuperating. Now, dammit, he was going to give this thing one last, all-out shot.

"Chelsea?"

She turned toward him with a head of lettuce in her hand, auburn brows lifted. She'd trimmed off the edges of her hair where it had burned a bit, so now it framed her face in a way it hadn't before. He liked it. She seemed softer, and maybe a little more approachable. Her eyes were not hostile when they met his, and he thought they might've come to some kind of a truce back there at the hospital.

God, when he'd realized she might be trapped in that fire...when he'd seen her lying so still on the ground while those men worked on her...

His world had tilted. Looking into those deep green eyes, he felt that way again right now. Like looking way down into a pine-bordered lake. He could see himself in their reflection. He could see...

Good grief. He guessed he'd better get her alone before he made a damn fool of himself in front of everyone. They'd never let him hear the end of that. He took the lettuce from Chelsea and set it aside. Then he reached for her good hand, closed his around it and gave a gentle tug as he turned toward the door. "Come on. You and I are going out for dinner."

"We are?"

"Yup." He pulled her a few steps closer to the door.

"Don't you think you might have asked me first?"

"Nope."

"Shouldn't I at least change my clothes?"

He glanced down at the snug jeans and T-shirt she wore, smiled, then checked it so she wouldn't see what was in his eyes. Truth to tell, she looked a little bit too damned good. The jeans hugged and the T-shirt revealed and he wanted to touch her all over. But not if she was going to be cringing and getting all skittish with him. He wanted her to want his touch. He wanted her to...

He closed his eyes, drew a breath. "You're perfect, Chelsea. We're not going anywhere fancy."

She shrugged. "If I said no?"

"I'd stand outside your window and do my lonesome coyote impression until dawn."

Her lips curved into the delicate smile he'd been getting all too used to seeing. And even though he was getting used to it, that slow, slight curve of her lips made his stomach turn cartwheels and his heart break into a gallop.

"Then I guess we're going out," she said softly. "Though I might want to hear that lonesome coyote impression some other time."

He grinned at her and pulled her to the door. Duke and Paint stood saddled and waiting.

Chelsea frowned. "Where's Sugar?"

"Burned her rump a little bit this morning. Nothing too serious. Jessi tended her and she'll be fine. But a saddle would chafe."

Chelsea stroked Paint's neck and moved around to the left side. Garrett helped her into the saddle.

"Isn't this Wes's horse?"

"Yup."

"Won't he mind?"

"He insisted. Said Paint was the most well-trained, intelligent animal on the place, and if you were riding at all, you ought to be riding him."

"He said that?"

Garrett nodded. "My brother pretends to be made of stone, Chelsea, but he isn't really. It's just tough to crack through that granite shell sometimes."

"Wasn't very tough for Ethan, though."

"No, Ethan got to him right off. We could all see it." Garrett checked the bulging saddlebags and then swung into the saddle.

"What makes him like that? So... hot tempered and hard?"

Garrett glanced sideways at her as the horses turned side by side and started across the lawn, not toward what used to be the stable this time, but around the house, behind it and across the back lawn, as well, toward the sparse clusters of little trees scattered here and there.

"My brother spent two years in prison, Chelsea. That's enough to harden a man."

She opened her mouth, closed it again and stared at him. "Wes?"

"Yup. Some guys he was hanging with robbed a bar. Beat the hell out of the owner. Wes had left them before it happened, but he got blamed all the same."

"You mean he was innocent?"

"I'd stake my life on it."

"But..."

"I wasn't a sheriff then. The circumstantial evidence was stacked against him so high, I'm not sure I could've done anything even if I had been. Bought him the best lawyer in the state, for what it was worth. But he ended up being sentenced to five years hard time. We got him paroled after two, though. I'm not sure that would have happened, either, except one of the men on the parole board was a friend of my daddy's a hundred years ago."

"That's awful." She turned in the saddle, looking back toward the house and shaking her head. There was real regret in her eyes. "Two years for nothing."

"After Wes went up, I ran for sheriff. Figured if I couldn't beat the damn system, I might as well join it and try to change things from the inside. My brother... well, it's taken him a while to understand that. He was none too happy to come home and see me wearing a badge."

"I can imagine. He must have thought you'd joined the enemy."

Garrett nodded, studying her face. "You have a way of nailing things right down, Chelsea. That's exactly how he felt."

She stared into his eyes, and he could see her feeling for him, as well as for his brother. She had a heart as big as all outdoors. Though she didn't even realize that. Odd the way she could feel for the pain of others, but couldn't let anyone else—couldn't let *him*—feel for her. Share her hurts.

She did once, though. She did when she told him about the night her mamma died.

"What about now?" she asked. "Does he understand now?"

Garrett had to blink and focus hard before he came back to the subject at hand. "I think so. There's something...something lacking in Wes's soul." Garrett walked Duke up to a little tree and drew him to a halt. "I've raised him just like the others, but it wasn't enough somehow."

He slid from the saddle, pulled off the bridle and didn't bother picketing Duke. He wouldn't wander far. He removed the saddlebags and slung them over his shoulder.

"But, Garrett, Wes isn't just like the others."

"No?"

She shook her head. "Elliot told me he's half-Comanche."

Garrett nodded, not minding at all that Elliot had told Chelsea about it. "My father left us for a time. It was before Elliot and Jessi were born, and I was just a kid. Never did know the whole story until a good deal later."

He slipped his free arm around Chelsea's shoulders, moving a little bit away from the horses and into a shady spot as he spoke. Compelled for some reason to tell her everything about himself, about his family.

"What was the whole story?" she asked in that deep, soft voice that sent chills up his nape.

Garrett cleared his throat. "Her name was Stands Alone," he said, "and I wish to God I'd known her. She was one hell of a woman, Wes's mother."

She frowned at him. "I'm surprised you'd feel that way about the woman your father had an affair with."

Garrett shrugged. "She was orphaned as a child, married young and widowed a short time later. Hence the name. But she never knew my father was married. They had a brief affair, and she fell deeply in love with him. But she was a wise woman and she knew, somehow, that his heart belonged to someone else. When she called him on it, he told her the truth. Then she sat that man down and gave him hell. Told him she wanted nothing to do with a man who would betray a good woman who bore him sons. Lectured him on the value of a good man. On how honor and trust and fidelity were more precious than riches, and how a man's children should mean more to him than his own life. She made him feel about two inches tall and sent him home to us, telling him not to ever try to see her again. What she didn't tell him was that she was pregnant with his son."

He looked into Chelsea's eyes, saw them wide and interested.

"How did your father ever find out about Wes?"

"He didn't," Garrett told her. "My mother did. Stands Alone changed my father. When he came back to us, he was the most devoted husband and father anyone could ask for. He felt bad for hurting our mother and did his damnedest to make up for it. Some years later, my mother heard talk of a young Comanche woman who'd died and left her son, Raven Eyes, alone."

"Raven Eyes?" Chelsea said it softly, then nodded. "That fits him."

"Mamma claimed she had a feeling, and to her dying day she swore that feeling was the spirit of Stands Alone, whispering to her. Whatever it was, she went to the Comanche village and asked around. Before long, she learned the truth—that Raven Eyes was my father's illegitimate son. She brought him home and treated him like one of her own, right from day one."

"How old was he then?" Chelsea asked.

"Seven."

She nodded.

"He seemed happy enough. But there's always been that shadow in his eyes. I just wish I knew what it was." He looked down at her, saw her gnawing her lower lip. "What? You're thinking something. I can see it. Go ahead. Tell me."

Chelsea nodded. "He spent the first seven years of his life in an entirely different culture. Then, just like that, he's removed from it. If it were me, I'd feel as if I were missing half my identity. He doesn't even seem to acknowledge the Native American blood running in his veins, but he must know it's there. He must remember his life before, but he acts as if it never happened."

Garrett moved closer to her, taking her waist in his hands, so she faced him. "You think that's what it is?"

"A tree can't grow without roots, Garrett. Your brother only has half of them and a whole pile of anger to boot. I'd say that's it. He probably doesn't even know that's what's bothering him, but I'll bet if he were to spend some time getting in touch with his heritage, he'd realize what he's been lacking in a heartbeat."

Garrett nodded, studying her pretty face and wise eyes. Pained still, but wise. "How can anyone be so smart about other people's demons, Chelsea, and so blind to their own?"

Her smile died slowly, and she averted her face. "I'm not blind to them. I just..." She shook her head.

"Just don't like looking at them."

She nodded.

"I want to make this better for you, Chelsea. I want to make it all go away so you can heal."

"Why?"

He lowered his forehead until it rested lightly against hers. "A broken heart can't be filled. It just keeps leaking. I want those cracks all patched up, Chelsea."

She looked down. But he kissed her anyway. He nudged her lips into parting, he tasted her mouth, he slipped his arms around her and held her tight. The way he'd wanted to all day.

"I think I might be—"

"Don't." She pulled free of him and turned back to her patient mount, pulling the bridle off the way Garrett had done with Duke. "Not yet, Garrett. I'm not ready."

"Okay."

She faced him, bridle dangling from one hand. "Okay? That's it?"

"Yup."

Her eyes were wary, then relaxed and maybe even just a little bit grateful.

He slung an arm around her shoulders and walked her along a trail, leaving the horses to graze. "Come here. I want to show you something."

Chelsea walked along beside him, and he thought she seemed a little better since coming out here. Maybe this would help. "What are you going to show me?"

"This." He led her around the last tree and waved an arm toward the huge pond that filled what was once just a small valley before Garrett and his brothers had diverted a tiny stream to fill it. The shore was grassy and level, and she took a deep breath, eyes glittering, lips curving.

"It's beautiful."

"Yeah, I thought so, too. Until I saw you."

She blushed a pretty shade of pink, and Garrett felt his chest swell a little. Maybe he didn't need Jessi and her silly cards after all.

"You know the other night, all that candlelight and wine and crystal and china?"

She lifted her brows, nodded.

Garrett cleared his throat. "Well, uh, none of that was me. I mean, it wasn't . . . genuine. You know?"

"I think so."

He nodded toward the pond again. "This is me."

Her eyes narrowed a little, but she nodded.

Garrett let the saddlebags slide from his shoulder to the ground. He hunkered down, unfastened the straps and opened them up. Then he pulled out a folded gray-and-white checkered tablecloth, took it by the edges and gave it a shake.

Smiling, Chelsea grabbed the opposite edges and helped him settle the cloth smoothly over the grass. Then she sat on it, curling her legs underneath her.

Garrett allowed himself the pleasure of watching her sit, then dived back into the bags for the paper plates and plastic utensils. Then a big Tupperware bowl full of cold fried chicken and another one with leftover chili. And one with fresh tossed salad. And a pitcher of iced tea that was all dewy on the outside. And two plastic tumblers. Some pita bread. Some cheese. And a saltshaker.

By the time he finished, Chelsea was laughing very softly, and he slanted her a sideways glance. "What?"

She shook her head. "Just wondered if you left anything at all in the fridge for the others."

He grinned at her. "I only took as much as I could carry." He continued arranging the food on the blanket. Then sat back, surveyed it and nodded once. "See this spread?" he asked.

"Yeah."

"*This* is me. I'd a hundred times rather have a picnic under the sky than a fancy-schmancy candlelight dinner indoors."

"Oh."

Holding his plastic cup in one hand, he poured it full of iced tea with the other. Then he held the cup up. "See this?"

She nodded. "Is that you, too?"

"Uh-huh. Nothing comes close when the sun's been beating down for days on end. I don't even like wine. I wouldn't know a blush from a rosé, nor would I care to. Don't know which kind you'd have with chicken. Don't rightly give a damn, either. Give me a tall glass of good, sweet water, or some iced tea, or an ice-cold beer on occasion, and I'm a happy man."

"I see."

Garrett handed her the glass of tea and filled another for himself. He swallowed it in one gulp. Then he reached into one of the bags and pulled out a little portable radio. He flicked it on. Mellow country music came from the tiny speaker. Whining steel guitar, then some fiddle, and a plaintive voice that could break a heart.

"Hear that?"

She smiled. "Not really a Bryan Adams fan, are you?"

Shaking his head, he frowned and said, "Well, actually, that song we were dancing to the other night began to grow on me. But this is what I'd have picked." He reached down and snapped the radio off. "Or maybe not.

'Cause this is the real music.'' She frowned. He held up a hand. "Shhh. Just listen."

He knew she was doing what he told her. And he was glad. He watched her pick out the sounds one by one. The gentle grinding sound the horses made as they chewed grass. The lapping of the pond when the breeze pushed at it. The occasional banjo strum of a bullfrog. The birds. The rustling leaves. The horses, moving their hoofs against the grass. The whirring wings of a dragonfly. All of it.

"You're right," she whispered. "This is the real music."

He sat there, stared at her and was plunged into a depth of longing he'd never experienced in his life. Her eyes closed. Her head tilted as she listened, and the slight breeze wafted through her hair, like invisible fingers threading through it to feel its silkiness.

It occurred to Garrett that she belonged here. Right here, right in this very spot. It was as if it had been created just for her. And she belonged in this family. She was good for them. She saw things he couldn't see, hadn't seen. And something else occurred to him, too. Something that made him feel like he was coming down with a bad stomach virus.

Chelsea opened her eyes only to see Garrett looking a bit sickly. His face had gone unusually pale, and his eyes looked unfocused and distant, maybe a little shell-shocked.

"Anything wrong?"

"What? Uh, no, nothing's...I'm fine. Here, have some chicken before it gets cold." He pushed the bowl toward her.

Chelsea grinned. "Garrett, it already *is* cold."

"Oh. Yeah, right." He yanked out a drumstick, looked at it and grimaced.

"Are you sick or something?" She felt a new worry creeping up on her. He really didn't look well, and she thought of all the smoke he'd inhaled and wondered if he might be having some delayed reaction to it.

"Probably just a stomach bug," he said, and set the chicken down on his plate. He refilled his glass and took another swig of iced tea. "You go ahead. Don't want all this food to go to waste."

Chelsea frowned at him, but helped herself to a bit of everything and ate. Garrett mostly shoved food around on his paper plate and watched her. He took a bite or two, but looked as if he were eating cardboard sandwiches filled with sand. Chelsea had witnessed this man's appetite firsthand. He did not pick at food. He inhaled it.

She finished eating and started cleaning up. Garrett's hand covered hers, stopping her. "Let me get that."

"No, it's okay. I don't mind." She went on with what she'd been doing. Garrett finally shrugged and joined in. When everything was packed away, she stood and stretched, gazing out at the pond again. She'd like to take a closer look, but if Garrett didn't feel well . . .

"Pull off your shoes, Chelsea. Put your feet in."

"But you're sick."

He waved a dismissive hand. "Go on. Coming out here and being with you is the best medicine for what ails me."

She met his eyes, but he blinked and looked away. Chelsea shrugged and sat down, pulled off her shoes and socks and rolled up the legs of her jeans. Then she walked slowly toward the water's edge.

She stuck one foot—the one that was no longer bandaged and sore—in the cool water, down onto the smooth pebbles at the bottom. Something slippery brushed her ankle and she jumped backward with a gasp.

Garrett's booming laugh reached her just before he did. "Just a little fish, Chelsea. Don't tell me you're scared of a little fish. Didn't you ever swim in a pond before?"

She slanted him a narrow-eyed glare. "No. Only pools where you can see all the way to the bottom." She glanced warily at the water again. "What else is in here?"

He shrugged. "A few frogs. Maybe a mud turtle or two."

"Turtles?" She took another step backward.

"Nothing that will hurt you, Chelsea."

She turned slowly, tilting her head. "You sure?"

"Nothing's ever gonna hurt you. Not when you're with me."

Only, she wasn't going to be with him much longer, was she? She bit her lower lip, let her chin drop down. He came closer, caught it and lifted it again. His brown eyes scanned her face. Chelsea stared up into them. Then at his lips. She wanted to kiss him more than she'd ever wanted anything. The knowledge surprised her. He'd kissed her, yes. He'd even asked permission to kiss her, and she'd given it. But for her to want to touch his mouth with hers badly enough to take the initiative was something entirely foreign to her. Hadn't she decided the touch of a man was something she could live without? Something she didn't need? She needed it now.

And he knew. She could tell he knew. Because his eyes darkened as they plumbed the depths of hers. But he didn't move. Just stood there, waiting, the picture of patience and kindness and understanding. But with his eyes, he spoke to her, encouraged, invited, even dared. And without a word, he drew her closer. A force beyond understanding pulled at her, until she stood on tiptoe and lifted her face to his, then fitted her mouth to his and tasted his lips.

They trembled so slightly she barely felt it. A faint ripple seemed to emanate from somewhere deep inside his big body and from his lips to hers, and then it echoed right to her soul. Her hands slid up his chest to curl around his neck, and Garrett bowed over her, gathered her close and moaned deeply and softly as he kissed her. She parted her lips to him, and he touched her with his tongue, tentatively at first, then boldly, probing her mouth in tender strokes that sent fire searing down into her spine and weakened her knees.

His lips slid over her mouth, skimming her cheek and jawline, then the hollows underneath. She shivered, letting her head fall backward to ease the way for his explorations. He kissed a path down the column of her throat, nuzzled the collar of her blouse out of the way, then tasted the skin over her collarbone and along the top of her shoulder. His hands pressed flat to her back, and he kissed the uppermost curve of her breasts and the spot in between them. Then he trailed hot, wet kisses back up the front of her, not missing an inch of skin on the trip to her mouth. His hands slid upward, tangling in her hair. Chelsea ached with a burning need she'd never felt for any man. A need she'd vowed she never would feel.

She kissed him back, not wanting this forbidden feeling to end. Not ever. When his mouth left hers again, she moved over his throat the way he had moved over hers. She felt every corded muscle under her lips. She tasted the salt of his skin. His pulse thudded wildly against her mouth, filling her and melding with her own rapid heartbeat until she couldn't distinguish one from the other. And she wasn't sure she wanted to.

His hands rose to cup her head, and gently he pulled her away. He was breathing rapidly now, and all of his color had come back and then some.

"Chelsea, if we don't stop—"

"I don't want to stop," she blurted, surprised she'd said it so fast. But it was like that with Garrett. She could say anything to him and know he wouldn't laugh at her or use the knowledge against her. He wasn't that kind of man.

"What *do* you want?"

Her answer was to crush herself against his chest and lift her head in search of his lips once more. He didn't hesitate to answer her quest. As he kissed her, he slipped his arms underneath her and lifted her up. Still kissing her, holding her, cradling her in his strength, he took long strides, bending once to snatch up the checkered tablecloth, then continuing along the shore. When she felt the sun's absence from her heated flesh, she opened her eyes to see a small cluster of scraggly trees surrounding a blanket of grass. He let the tablecloth fall and lowered her on top of it. He knelt beside her, bent over her and kissed her mouth some more. As if feeding on it, he drew on her tongue and lips as if they tasted sweeter than honey. A sweetness he craved. Hurriedly, he smoothed out the cloth before he lay down beside her, wrapped her in his arms and gently eased her off the hard ground until she lay only on his body.

The sensation was intense. The rugged length of him beneath her. Her breasts crushed to his chest. His hands slipped up underneath her shirt, roughened palms sliding over the skin of her back, up to her shoulders to pull her closer. Hold her tighter. Lick more deeply into her mouth. Let her more deeply into his. Still, it wasn't enough. She wanted to feel his flesh. She wanted to be naked with him. She wanted him inside her.

She braced herself up with one hand, tugged at the buttons of his shirt with the other. Her hurried movements made her clumsy. His big hand covered hers.

"Easy. It's all right, beautiful Chelsea. We have all night."

She met his blazing hot gaze, nodded once and tried again to free a button. His hand remained on top of hers, eyes locked with hers, as she released it and moved lower to the next and then the next. When the last button was freed, she pushed his shirt open, ran her hand over his muscled chest and felt the fine hairs there tickling her palm. She ran her fingertips over his nipple, and he clenched his jaw, grating his teeth. A rush of desire surged through her at the way his face changed just by her touch. She wanted more of that, so she scratched gently at his nipple with her nails, and he closed his eyes, drew three quick, openmouthed breaths.

It was good to do this to him. To make him gasp with pleasure. It was something she'd never dreamed of doing to a man. The thrill of it coursed through her like a drug, adding to her own arousal until she felt herself quivering like the reed of an instrument when its player's lips are over it. She moved her hand aside, lowered her head and kissed his chest. She flicked her tongue over his hard little nipple and scraped her teeth over it, too, while she used her hand to torture its mate.

His chin pointed skyward, and he panted, his chest rising and falling under her. His arms stretched out to either side, and she knew he was letting her lead the way in this. Letting her do what she wanted. Letting her call the shots. Because he didn't want to push her or scare her or...

"Chelsea...*dammit,* Chelsea, you're killing me...."
But his words were only hoarse whispers.

She sat up, staring down at him, feeling a power filling her. Feeling more alive, more utterly female than she ever had.

He lifted his hands to her blouse, took hold of the top button, searched her eyes. "Can I?"

Nodding, she sat still as he released every button. He put his hands on her shoulders and pushed the blouse open then down her arms. Lowering his eyes to look at her, he stared at her unbound breasts with something like reverence in his eyes. His hands slid very slowly down the front of her. She didn't tell him to stop. The heels of his hands and then his palms slipped downward over her breasts, and her nipples stiffened and pressed against his hands. She understood then the cause of his rapid breathing because she could barely control her own. Closing her eyes, she fought to regain it. Warmth and a tingling sensation rose up from the core of her and seemed to pool where he touched her. He drew his fingers downward, closed them on her nipples, the slight pressure and movement causing her to gasp.

He slid his hands around to her back and pulled her gently lower, and lower still, so that she was over him where he lay on the ground. She didn't resist. She could do this. She could let him guide her, let him have some of her, because she trusted him as she'd never trusted another man.

When she'd bent so low his warm breath caressed her breasts, he lifted his head to kiss the very tips. One and then the other. The contact too brief and too light. But his head remained there, close to her, and he parted his lips and ran his tongue over one yearning nipple, pushing it this way and that for a moment, only to leave it wet and aching for more as he moved to the other. Only when she felt ready to cry in sweet anguish, did he finally capture one of those throbbing nubs in his mouth. He suckled her, very gently at first. Then with more pressure and still more. It felt good. It felt so, so good. Her hands caught his head to hold him there, and she fed him her breasts for a long time. When he lay back, they were wet from his mouth, and the soft breeze wafted over their sensitized peaks and he watched them lengthen as if reaching for him.

Her mind began spinning because the longing wasn't just where he'd fed on her. It was everywhere. It was all through her body. And the epicenter was between her legs, where she felt hot and wet and empty. Straddling his body, she rubbed herself against him and felt his answering hardness bulging and pushing at her there.

She slid down a little to look at him, swelling behind the jeans he wore. With hands that trembled and a heart that did likewise, she touched the shape of him. As he'd done before, he lay still, arms returning to that nonthreatening position, stretched out at his sides. He let her touch him. Let her run her fingers along the swollen length of him and finally stop at the button of his jeans. Licking her lips, Chelsea freed it. And carefully she lowered the zipper. Parted the fly. Saw his shape and size and hardness even more clearly, outlined in white briefs.

She took hold of the jeans at the waist and pushed downward. Garrett obligingly lifted his hips, but when he arched up that way she almost forgot what she'd been doing. She pushed the jeans down to his knees, then pulled away the white fabric and pushed that down, as well. She sat there, astride his magnificent thighs and looked at him. Smooth and dark and so aroused. She moved her fingers closer, touched, traced his length right to the tip, then over it and down the other side. He groaned, and she looked up at his face to see undisguised agony twisting his features. She used her nails, very lightly, on the tip of him, and he lifted his hips off the ground in supplication. She bent her head and kissed him there. That skin tasted different somehow. Musky and male. Erotic. She followed the path her fingers had taken, with her tongue this time, and he moved and twisted and clenched his hands into trembling fists at his sides. If it killed him, she knew he'd let her explore him and learn him until she was ready to take the next step. Whatever she asked of him, he'd do. Whatever she needed, he'd give to her. It was just the way he was.

She cupped him underneath, massaging gently as she closed her lips around him in the most intimate kiss imaginable. And only then did he pull away from her lips, shaking his head when she looked up in question.

"Give...me...a minute," he gasped. She nodded, amazed she could reduce this giant of a man to this. She sat still, waiting for him to compose himself. He opened his eyes, met hers, smiled at her. "Okay. All right. Is it my turn now?"

A tiny ripple of nerves danced along her spine, but she nodded. She could give as well as take.

He caught her waist in his hands and lifted her up onto her knees. Then he undid her jeans and pushed them down. Chelsea twisted her body to the side and took the jeans off for him. He kicked his off, too, his eyes never leaving hers. When she began to move toward him once more, he whispered, "Wait. The panties, too. I want to see you, Chelsea."

Her throat had gone as dry as sandpaper. Not from fear—from sheer, gut-wrenching desire. She stood while he lay there watching, and she pushed her panties down and stepped out of them. Garrett blinked as if a sudden bright light had flashed in his eyes as he took in all of her from head to toe, utterly naked.

"You're...you're...you're perfect, Chelsea."

"I'm not—"

"Shh. Don't argue, baby. I know perfect when I see it and you're it."

She sat down, feeling too exposed standing while he burned her with his gaze.

"Lie down on your back for me, Chelsea. Will you do that for me? The way I did for you?"

She faced him, eyes widening.

"Do you trust me, Chelsea?"

She nodded. Slowly, she lay back on the ground with her thighs pressed tightly together.

Garrett rose up on his knees, near her feet. "Let me look at you. Let me kiss you, Chelsea. I want you to feel the way I was feeling a second ago. Let me give you that." His hands touched her inner thighs. "Open for me, sweet Chelsea."

Shivering with passion and nerves and who knew what else, she spread her legs for him. Garrett's eyes focused on the center of her. Then he lowered his head and kissed her there. His hands moved to open her wide, making her feel utterly vulnerable. Part of her wanted to push him away and cover herself as he looked at her. But he'd remained still for her and she would do the same for him. She kept her hands to the ground on either side of her. And he kissed her again, this time touching places that made her shake and burn and cry. Again and again he pressed his mouth to her. Then his tongue stroked over her in a hot path of fire. He drank from the very depths of her like a man possessed. Craving more. Until she cried out for him to stop because she felt herself losing all control.

So he stopped and he lifted his head. Her body ached for something she couldn't understand. It yearned and pleaded for fulfillment.

He met her eyes. "I want to be inside you, Chelsea. I want it now. But only if you—"

"Yes!"

She reached for him, and he lowered himself onto her, nudging the tip of his arousal into her wet opening. She planted her feet and arched to receive him further. Garrett slid his hands under her buttocks, held her tight and tipped her up. Smoothly, gently, he sheathed himself completely inside her.

She felt a momentary flare of pain. But Garrett moved slowly, pulling back until she quivered with need, only to plunge himself to the very hilt again. And then again. She found herself moving with him, arching to meet his every thrust, her hands clawing at his backside, clenching and kneading. He claimed her mouth. Took it, this time. She knew now he was beyond thinking about asking permission. His tongue filled her mouth as he drove her to some point beyond rational thought, her insides twisting tightly as he moved with her. And then she exploded around him, crying his name aloud without a thought to whoever might hear. He drove into her again and again until he went stiff all over, shuddering violently.

Then his muscles uncoiled, and he lowered himself down, not on top of her, but beside her. He pulled her head down to his chest, and whispered something she didn't want to hear. So she pretended she'd imagined it, then climbed on top of him and started kissing him again.

Chapter 12

Mercy.

Chelsea curled in the crook of his arm, naked as the day she was born except for his denim work shirt, which he'd used to cover her a short while ago. Her head rested on his chest, and her fiery hair tickled his skin. Her breaths were slow and rhythmic. Waves of air rushing into her, rolling down to the furthest reaches of her lungs, pausing, and then slowly receding back out to sea as she exhaled.

He hadn't seen her this relaxed since he'd met her. Which hadn't been all that long ago. A fact that made him wince. This kind of thing wasn't like him. Outside, in front of God and everybody, and he'd done things with her he'd never done with any woman.

Outside, for heaven's sake! And though she was covered—from her shoulders to her thighs at least—*he* was still lying under the stars fully exposed.

He reached for his Stetson and settled it over his most

vulnerable area before laying his head back down on the ground.

She sure had been something.

One of his hands came up to stroke that reddish gold hair of hers, and Garrett closed his eyes, sighing inwardly. Hell, he hadn't thought it would ever happen. Not to him. Not like this.

She stirred in his arms, and he could tell by the change in her breathing that she was awake. He kept stroking, liking the feel of the silky strands under his palm. And he rather thought she was liking it, too.

"What time is it?" she asked, her voice husky.

Garrett peered up at the stars for a second. "Almost midnight."

She sat up, his big shirt slid down her back to the ground. Her breasts moved freely and he found himself wanting her again.

Again?

Yup.

"Garrett, what are the others going to think?"

He smiled at her. "They'll probably think exactly...this."

She groaned and pulled the shirt over her again. "We'd better get back."

He frowned as she got to her feet and started pawing the ground in search of her clothes. "I kind of thought we ought to...maybe...talk first."

She located her blouse, and it seemed to him that she was real careful to keep her face averted. "About what, Garrett?"

"Well...about this. About...you know...*this.*"

She found her jeans next and stepped into them. "This? You mean the sex?"

The way she said the word made it sound like something simple. Like eating or breathing or something. It wasn't, though. Hell, Garrett's entire world had been altered here tonight. "Yeah," he said. "About the sex."

She pulled on her blouse and tossed his shirt to him. "There's nothing to talk about," she told him. "It was just sex. Gee, Garrett, you didn't think it was anything more than that, did you? I mean, I already explained it to you. I'm not going to get involved with a man. Not any man. Not ever. And just because we had a little fun tonight doesn't mean I've changed my mind about that."

He took the blow admirably, he thought. Felt an awful lot like it had landed hard, right in the solar plexus, and he did lose his breath and feel like throwing up. But he managed not to double over or gasp aloud like a fish out of water. He figured those were major coups by themselves. This was all wrong. He knew it was all wrong on the practical plane of his mind, but the problem was, on the emotional plane of his heart, he was too busy bleeding to notice what the practical side was saying.

She'd hurt him. Taken a blade and driven it in right to the hilt, then given a little twist for good measure. She gathered up the tablecloth they'd been lying on, wadded it into a little ball and carried it back to the spot where they'd had their picnic a lifetime ago. She stuffed it into his saddlebag without pause. Garrett would have folded it with exquisite care, stroking the fabric where her body had touched it. Wondering if the material could retain some of the magic that had happened between them tonight.

But it was pretty obvious the magic was all in his head. She thought they'd had a little fun. Nothing more. And damned if he hadn't thought she was anything *but* that kind of woman. He'd believed her to be a lady. A wounded, frightened innocent. An injured doe he could nurture and care for and maybe, if he were lucky, make his own.

Well, he'd been a fool, then, hadn't he?

He dressed quickly, yanking his clothes on, taking his anger out on them. Then he went for the horses. They'd wandered off, but not too far. Hell, in the heights of ecstasy, he'd forgotten all about them. He doubted Chelsea had been anywhere near as moved.

He walked the horses back to the pond, saddled Paint up for Chelsea and quickly did the same with Duke. When he went to help her climb on, it was to see her swing herself into that saddle all on her own. Quick learner, he thought. Damn her. She hadn't learned half-enough. Garrett swung onto his own horse and dug his heels in. It was only as Duke leaped into a gallop that Garrett caught hold of his temper and throttled it until it cooled. He couldn't run ahead and leave Chelsea to play catch-up. Cold as she might be, Vincent de Lorean was still after her. He reined Duke to a halt and waited. When Chelsea rode up beside him, he started off again, at a walk this time.

But nothing could make him look at her. Or talk to her. Not now. If he so much as opened his mouth, he was going to make a blubbering fool out of himself by telling her what had happened to him tonight. And she'd probably laugh at him. Hell, the way she acted, it was easy to imagine she'd had plenty of sex, with plenty of men. Men she hadn't cared for any more than she cared for Garrett. She probably thought he was just a big, dumb cowboy. *He* probably thought she was right. He *must* be pretty dumb to let himself fall so hard.

* * *

If Garrett so much as looked at her, she'd lose it. She knew she would. If he said a word, those gut-wrenching sobs she was battling would break loose and tear her apart.

She'd never dreamed she could trust any man enough to do...what they'd done. She'd never believed herself capable of letting herself be utterly free and unreserved in a man's arms. But she had been just that with Garrett. And it was only possible because of his exquisite tenderness, the caring in his eyes when he looked at her, the gentleness of his every touch.

There would never be another man like him.

She hoped to God little Ethan would try to emulate the big, gentle man who was going to raise him. It was the right decision. It was what Michele had wanted, what she'd known all along. Her sister must have sensed how perfect Garrett would be for Ethan. Somehow, she'd known.

Chelsea was no good for him, because she was too filled with anger. Only the anger had changed now. It had eased and softened. It was no longer the futile raging of an abused child against an omnipotent parent.

This was different. Not wild and undirected anymore. She knew Vincent de Lorean had murdered her sister. But that wasn't why she had to kill him. The need for revenge had somehow lost its force. Or maybe she'd just lost her taste for it.

No. Her reasons now were utterly different. Ethan. Little Ethan would never be safe until Vincent de Lorean was out of the picture. Utterly eliminated from the baby's life. It had to happen. If it didn't, Ethan might grow up the way Michele and Chelsea had. Oh, not the poverty. De Lorean was a wealthy man, Chelsea knew that.

But the abuse. The lack of love. The broken heart. She couldn't let that happen.

And as long as de Lorean lived, no one who cared for Ethan would be safe from his wrath. Not Chelsea, even if she took the baby and ran away and hid. Not Garrett. Not any of the Brands. De Lorean would extract his own kind of vengeance on every one of them. And that would destroy them. All of them.

It was up to Chelsea. This was her ball game, and she was calling the shots. By herself. Just the way it had always been.

The horses stopped in front of the house, and she slipped down. Garrett took the reins from her without a single word and headed out toward the pasture where the other horses grazed. Chelsea watched him go, blinking back tears. Then she went inside and directly up to Garrett's room.

The house had a still, eerie feeling that told her everyone inside was asleep. Garrett would be a while coming back inside. He'd rub those horses down and hang the saddles and bridles along the split-rail fence, where the few others that had survived the fire were already hanging. He'd go out to that big barrel Wes had filled with grain from the feed store, and he'd scoop some out and feed the horses. Then he'd check their watering trough to be sure it was filled.

He'd take care of everything, Garrett would. He'd take care of her, too, if she'd let him. Just the way Mom always had. And he'd probably get himself killed the way she had, too.

Chelsea opened Garrett's nightstand drawer and took out his revolver. As an afterthought, she grabbed a box of bullets. Then she slipped out of the room and across the hall, ducking into the guest room she'd begun to think of as her own. Well, hers and Ethan's. She tucked the gun and bullets into her purse before turning to the cradle. She stood staring down at the sleeping angel inside. Her fingers stroked his satiny dark hair, and a single tear dropped from her cheek to dampen Ethan's. "I love you, baby," she whispered. "And I'm gonna make this world safe for you. I promise. You're never gonna go through what your Mamma and I did. You'll be raised with love. You'll have a real family just like I promised you, Ethan. Right here."

She bent low and gently kissed his pudgy cheek. Then she turned back to the bed and sat down, pulled out a notepad and pencil from the stand beside it and began her note to Garrett.

"I have to leave," she wrote, struggling because her hands were shaking and because she couldn't say the things she was longing to tell him. If she did, he'd come after her. He'd never stop until he found her.

"I have a life to get back to. And I know Ethan will be better off here with you than he could ever be with me. Don't try to find me. I'm going to change my name and start over somewhere fresh, where de Lorean can never find me. Thanks for the laughs. Chelsea."

She'd like to add a warning about Lash because she'd finally remembered why the name de Lorean had sounded familiar to her when Garrett had first mentioned it. But that might give too much away. She'd just handle Lash the way she did everything else. Alone.

She dug out the slip of paper he'd dropped, unfolded it again, staring at the name and address, memorizing it. Vincent de Lorean. 705 Fairview. Ellis, Texas. She hadn't known this name when she'd found the note. And then she'd tucked it away and forgotten about it. But now...

She sat very still and quiet, waiting for the sound of Garrett's tired footfalls on the stairs. His steps paused outside her door...briefly. And then moved on, over to his own room. Hinges creaked. The door closed. Bedsprings squeaked. Two boots thudded to the hardwood floor. She waited longer. And still longer. And then, carrying her shoes and her bag, she slipped down the stairs.

Lash answered the door wearing a pair of white boxers and a frown. Bleary, pale blue eyes and tousled brown hair completed the look, and he stared at her, shaking his head. "What do you want?"

"I want you to get out of town," Chelsea said, thinking that she sounded like an old spaghetti Western.

"Huh?"

"I know about your connection to de Lorean," she went on. For emphasis she handed him the slip of paper. "You dropped this the other day."

He took it from her, blinked down at it and came more fully awake. His eyes sharpened as they scanned her face. "Why didn't you just hand it over to the Brand brothers?"

"Because they'd have probably killed you. They'd probably assume...as I do...that you were behind that stampede. And the fire in the stable. My guess is that you're just hanging around, doing de Lorean's bidding and waiting for the chance to kidnap a helpless baby. Hell, I oughtta kill you myself."

"Now wait a minute. You don't know—"

"I know plenty. I know if I tell Garrett about you, your hide will end up nailed to the barn wall. Or at least sitting in the town jail. So you get out of town. Tonight. If I see you again, I'll tell him everything."

His blue eyes narrowed, and he glanced past her at the car that sat alongside the curb. "How come you're out at this time of night alone?"

"None of your business."

"Where are you going, Chelsea?"

"I told you—"

His hand shot up fast, gripping her arm as if to haul her inside. Panic gripped her, especially since she knew this creep worked for a killer. She brought her knee up hard and fast into his groin, and he grunted at the impact, stumbled away from her and doubled over. His face turned six shades of purple as he gasped and swore. But still he forced himself to straighten up and take an unsteady step toward her.

Until he saw the gun in her wavering hand, pointing dead center at his leanly muscled chest.

"Damn it straight to hell, what are you—"

"Shut up!"

He shut up.

"Now just step back in there and stay there. I mean it. If you so much as poke your head out the door, I'll—"

"I get the idea."

"And you be gone from Quinn by morning, Lash. You be gone or I'll be back."

"How am I s'posed to leave town if I can't poke my head out the—"

"Shut up!"

He lifted his hands and shoulders in compliance and stepped away from the door. Chelsea backed all the way to the car, got inside and shot away into the night.

There. Safe. She'd done it. She didn't think Lash whatever-his-name-was would dare show his pretty face on the Texas Brand again. Once she accomplished her mission, Chelsea would call or send a note telling Garrett of Lash's duplicity, just in case. But if she'd told Garrett now, he'd have known she was leaving and tried to stop her.

* * *

Garrett lay on his bed feeling sorry for himself for a very short time. Then he gave himself a mental kick in the seat of the pants. Because the whole time he'd been lying there, he'd been remembering every single second of his time with Chelsea tonight, and one instant kept coming back to him. That second he'd held her to him and pushed himself inside her. That incredible feeling of completion, of union, of rightness.

But gradually, he realized those feelings were only his own—she'd reacted a little differently. She'd been real enthusiastic before he entered her. And seconds afterward, she'd been as into it as he had. But at that moment in between, there'd been the slightest hint of resistance. She'd stiffened a little. Her fingernails had dug into his skin, and she'd bit her lip. And he'd felt something.

Something...

Garrett sat up in bed, blinking. Couldn't have been that, though. Couldn't have been...

Frowning, he got up and trotted down the stairs again. He'd tossed the saddlebags into the corner after unpacking them earlier and dumping the leftover food into ol' Blue's dish. The tablecloth lay atop the garbage pail, where Garrett had thrown it in an act of sheer, foolish pride. He reached for it now, held it up by two corners and let it fall open.

He saw the small red stain that told him all he needed to know. He'd been Chelsea Brennan's first lover. She'd trusted him that much. And there was no way in hell she felt as casual about what had happened tonight as she was pretending to feel.

Garrett dropped the tablecloth again and started up the stairs. But when he got to Chelsea's room, she wasn't there. His heart slowly broke, and the only thing that kept it from shattering completely was the happy gurgle coming from the cradle beside her bed.

"Bubba?"

"Dadadadadadadada," the little squirt sang, and his arms began to flail in time with his music.

The relief that surged through Garrett was tinged with bitter sadness. Thank the good Lord Chelsea hadn't taken this child away from him. But God, what it must have done to her to leave him behind.

Garrett went to the cradle and bent over it, reaching down to check the diaper and stroke the silky fuzz that passed for Bubba's hair. Ethan blinked slowly, his eyes still sleepy, but he smiled a little bit all the same. Gently, Garrett turned him over so he lay on his tummy, and then he ran his hand in the slow, clockwise circles that he knew the boy loved. His palm skimmed the baby's small back over and over, and those heavy eyes fell closed more often between peeks at Garrett.

Without stopping, Garrett reached for the sheet of paper Chelsea had left on her pillow. Then he sank onto the edge of the bed, still rubbing that little back and wondering now why the action was as soothing to him as it seemed to be for Bubba. He leaned back against the headboard, reading her callous goodbye. A note that said nothing. Not one damn thing he needed to hear. Like how she felt about what had happened between them. Like why she'd so willingly given him something as precious as her virginity, and why she hadn't told him, and whether she had ever really felt a damned thing for him at all.

A soft sigh from Bubba, and Garrett looked at the sleeping child.

Must have felt something for you, Garrett. She left Bubba with you. That's two priceless gifts in under a day.

He scowled, swinging his head back to the note. He was indulging in wishful thinking. She didn't feel a thing for him. Or for Bubba. If she had, she'd have stuck around and fought for them.

That's right, she would. Chelsea Brennan isn't the kind of woman to give anything up without a fight.

Which kind of added to the theory that she didn't give a rat's—

His head snapped around when he heard tires rolling over the well-worn driveway. Headlights moved across the window, and Garrett was halfway down the stairs before he gave himself a chance to wonder if it were really her. Dammit, he hadn't ought to be sitting around feeling sorry for himself. He ought to be worried. He'd let her out of his sight. Out there alone, she'd be a walking target for Vincent de Lorean and his squadron of goons. Thank God she'd changed her mind and come back. Thank—

Garrett skidded to a stop in the kitchen. The face peering through the window at him was not Chelsea's. Lash. And damned if his normally full load of calm didn't look a brick or two shy.

Fighting to keep the utter disappointment from showing on his face, Garrett opened the door. "What the hell brings you clear out here this time of night?"

Lash licked his lips. "Trouble, Garrett. And I'm sore afraid it's trouble with a capital *C*."

"A capital..." Garrett's brows came down fast. "Chelsea?"

Lash nodded slowly. "Do me a favor and listen to the whole thing before you break my face, okay, big fella?"

Light footsteps on the stairs. A soft voice. "Garrett, you down here? I thought I heard—"

"What whole thing?" Garrett asked, ignoring Jessi.

"That for the past few months, I've been—technically speaking, at least—employed by Vincent de Lorean. But it isn't what it—"

Garrett's big fist connected soundly with most of the front portion of Lash's face. Bone crunched. Blood spurted. Jessi screamed. Lash sort of bounced off the door behind him into Garrett's chest, then slumped to the floor.

Stampeding feet crashed down the stairs at Jessi's scream. Wes bounded to her side, his bowie in his hand and fire in his onyx eyes, while Elliot stood at the bottom of the stairs looking around and blinking in confusion.

Jessi lunged into the kitchen and fell to her knees beside the incapacitated Lash, though with all that blood, Garrett wondered if she even knew who he was. She was crying and swearing, using words Garrett didn't know she even knew. And most of them were aimed at him. She stomped away, but he knew she'd be back.

Lash didn't so much as wiggle.

"You kill him?" Wes asked, looking down at the mess at Garrett's feet as he slid the bowie back into his boot.

"Nah."

Wes frowned hard and poked Lash in the ribs with the toe of one boot. No response. He looked up at Garrett again. "You sure?"

"I'm sure. Look, he's breathin'."

Wes stared for a minute. "How can you tell with all that blood?"

"I can tell."

"Get the hell away from him, the both of you!" Jessi shouted, shoving through them and dropping down beside Lash again. You'd have thought he was one of her brothers the way she was acting. She started dabbing the blood away from his nose and lips with a wet cloth. She'd brought bandages and various ointments back with her, too. Looked like she intended to doctor him up thoroughly.

Garrett glanced at the inert man once more, shook his head and stepped toward the table and out of Jessi's way.

Wes joined him, fixing a pot of coffee to brew as Garrett sat down. "So what happened to your infamous, endless, unshakable temper, big brother?"

"I lost it."

Wes set the carafe under the basket and flipped the On button. "Why?"

"He said he'd been working for de Lorean."

Wes nodded, sending a glance toward the stranger when he moaned softly. "You suspected that all along, though. Shouldn't have come as such a surprise."

"Chelsea's missing, Wes. She just took off tonight. Left a note. I got no idea where the hell she is—"

"So you took it out on Lash, hmm?"

Garrett watched as Jessi cleaned the blood away, revealing a split lip and a nose that was probably broken, judging from the odd angle of it.

"I shouldn't have hit him that hard."

"'Cause he didn't deserve it?"

"Hell, no. 'Cause I have a feeling he might know where Chelsea is. Now I can't even ask him until he comes around."

"Oh." Wes pulled the half-filled pot out from under the drip and shoved a cup under there to catch the still-brewing coffee while he filled two others. Then he yanked the third cup away and shoved the pot back underneath, all without spilling a drop. "We gotta get one of those new ones that stops dripping when you move the pot," he muttered, handing Garrett a cup. He took a seat and joined Garrett in watching their little sister work her veterinary wonders on a horse's backside.

"You think she's sweet on him, Wes?" Garrett asked.

"Who, Jessi? Nah. No way in hell." Wes watched her hand stroke Lash's hair away from his forehead. "Besides, if he ever laid a finger on her..."

"Yeah," Garrett agreed, rubbing his slightly sore knuckles absently. "Me, too."

Elliot stood in the doorway, looking from Jessi and Lash to Garrett and Wes, and shaking his head.

"You mind going back up and guarding little Bubba?" Garrett asked him. "I don't like him being alone, under the circumstances."

Elliot swallowed audibly and nodded toward the man on the floor. "What about him?"

"I want to talk to him. Soon as he comes around."

"You...uh..." Elliot shifted his feet. "You aren't gonna hit him again, are you?"

"I'll make sure he doesn't hit him again, Elliot," Wes assured his younger brother.

"Hell, Wes, your temper is ten times worse than Garrett's!"

"Yeah, but it isn't my ladylove who's run off. So I'm not as likely to lose it with Lash."

Elliot looked around slowly, taking it all in. Finally, he nodded and turned to head upstairs to the baby's room.

Chapter 13

Chelsea drove out of town, pulled the car off the road and opened the map that was still in her glove compartment—the one she'd bought at that convenience store before she'd come to this dusty little Tex-Mex town. It seemed like a lifetime ago now.

Still, with a little help from the overhead light, she was able to make out the town called Ellis—which looked like a crossroad right on the border. Less than twenty miles away, using her fingers to measure by. She took a moment to check out her rental car, making sure there was still plenty of gas and double-checking the water level in the radiator. Everything was fine, just as she'd left it the night she'd arrived on the Texas Brand. No one had touched the car except to move it out of the middle of the driveway.

She started the car again, heading directly along the route she'd already plotted out in her mind. She was going to find this Vincent de Lorean. And she was going to kill him.

Lash was lying on the couch, Jessi hovering over him like Florence Nightingale or something, when he opened his eyes. He met Garrett's, and they narrowed dangerously.

"I'll get you back for that, Brand. You gorilla."

Garrett only shrugged. "Tell me something, Lash. You the one who spooked those cattle after all? Hmm? Was it de Lorean who gave the order to burn down the stable or was that on your own initiative?"

"You're dumber than you look if you think I came all the way out here to tell a damned giant that I burned down his stable."

"I told you so, Garrett," Jessi snapped, closing her hands around one of Lash's. Lash looked at her and frowned as if he was seeing in her eyes something he hadn't noticed before. The look of discovery and surprise on his face made Garrett even more uneasy than he already was.

Wes reached over and gently tugged Jessi's hands away. "Go on upstairs and check on Elliot and Bubba, hon."

"But I—"

"Go."

Jessi stood reluctantly and eyed her two brothers. "If you hurt him—"

"We won't lay a finger on him. Promise," Wes said.

She glared at Garrett until he nodded agreement. Then she sent a tender gaze down at Lash. "If you need me, just call."

"I...er..." He sent wary glances at the two other men and squirmed a little. "Thanks."

As soon as she was gone, Wes knelt beside the couch. "Just for the record, Lash, regardless of the outcome of this conversation, I don't ever wanna see any part of your person make contact with any part of my little sister ever again. If I do, the part in question is gonna get cut off. Got it?"

Lash swallowed hard, but nodded. "She's a kid. I got no interest in kids."

"Exceptin' for Bubba, right?"

Lash shot a defiant glare at Garrett. "If you'd let me finish what I started to say before, you'd have your answers by now. I was working for de Lorean so I could gather enough evidence against him to bring him down."

Garrett's mouth suddenly went dry. "You're a cop?"

"No. I'm an ex-fire fighter from Chicago, just like I told you."

"Then why—"

"Why doesn't matter. It's my private business and I have no intention of discussing it with the likes of you. Now do you want to hear what I have to tell you or not?"

Garrett's knees bent, and he fell into a chair. Wes stood to one side, shaking his head slowly.

"De Lorean was getting suspicious of me. I still didn't have enough on him. But I knew he was after Chelsea and the baby, so I stuck around. Kept trying to feed him false leads and throw him off track. I knew from the beginning where she was. I was the one assigned to tail her from the morgue. But I told de Lorean I'd lost her."

"You..." Garrett whispered. "It was you who called me that night."

Lash nodded. "De Lorean found out where she was just as I'd figured he would, with or without my help. Chelsea called her apartment manager and left an address where she could have her mail forwarded. That was one of the bases de Lorean had covered. He had the address within a few hours after Chelsea hung up. I called to warn you as soon as I realized it. Well, since the jerk was already suspicious of me, it seemed there was no more I could do on that end, short of maybe getting myself shot once between the eyes. So I headed out here. Thought I could help protect her and the kid from that bastard."

"The stampede?"

Lash shook his head. "When I arrived in town, I spotted a vehicle belonging to one of de Lorean's goons heading from this direction. So I made a beeline out here and came up with the first excuse I could think of to ride out and catch up to you and Chelsea."

"And you saved our butts."

"I'm *sure* you'd have done the same for me," Lash said, lightly touching his broken nose.

"And the fire?"

"When I saw the trucks heading out here, I knew damn well..." He shrugged. "I followed to try and help. Hell, it was half-instinctive. It's what I did for a good portion of my life."

Garrett shook his head in disbelief.

"No need to thank me," Lash quipped.

Garrett looked him square in the eye. "What do you know about Chelsea?"

"She came to see me tonight. Seems I got careless that day in the stampede. I dropped..." He lifted himself into a sitting position with a grunt and shoved a hand into his blood-smattered T-shirt's pocket. Pulling out a slip of paper, he handed it to Garrett. "This. She found it and must've thought I was really one of the bad guys. What I can't figure is why she didn't tell you in the beginning."

"She didn't even know de Lorean's name until yesterday," Garrett muttered, cussing himself for keeping it from her.

Lash nodded. "Anyway, she told me to get out of town tonight. Told me if I set foot near you or the baby again, she'd tell you I was working for de Lorean and let you toss me in jail…or worse." He pressed a finger to his split lip, drew it away and checked it for fresh blood.

Garrett nodded. "Before she left us, she wanted to be sure you didn't pose a threat."

"She *is* gone, then?" Lash asked.

"Yeah. Said she wanted to start over someplace fresh. Said she thought little Bubba would be better off here with us."

"She lied through her teeth, Brand. She's gone after de Lorean."

Garrett's head snapped up. "What the hell makes you think she'd do that?"

Lash rolled his eyes. "Wake up, big fella. One, she knows where he lives." He ticked the points off on his fingers as he went on. "Two, she threatened me to be sure you and the baby would be safe, so it stands to reason she'd want to protect you all from him, as well. Three, she was heading that way when she left. And four, she was brandishing a handgun the size of a damn cannon. I seriously doubt she brought it along because it went so nicely with her shoes."

Wes swore, slamming a fist against the wall.

Garrett felt the bottom fall out of his stomach. He glanced at the slip of paper again. "Ellis. Lord, she could be there already."

"We have to go after her, Garrett," Lash said. "De Lorean is a snake. He'll hurt her, dammit. He wants her out of the way so there'll never be a challenge to his keeping custody of the kid.''

Garrett swore. But ran upstairs to grab a shirt and fill Elliot and Jessi in on what was going on.

The place was like something straight out of "Lifestyles of the Rich and Famous," Chelsea thought. Chelsea parked the car, lifted the gun and headed up the brick path to the front door of de Lorean's home—a Spanish-style mansion, with adobe-brick arches and stucco everywhere. A tall wrought-iron fence surrounded the place, but the gate between the towering center columns stood open. Almost as if de Lorean was expecting someone.

Chelsea walked softly, eyes wide and alert. Around her, night birds chattered and chirped. Other than that, though, there wasn't a sound. No movement. Not even a breeze. She tiptoed up the front steps, and peered at the stained-glass panels in the door, but couldn't see through them. Her hand was slick with sweat when she closed it on the ornate door handle. She started in surprise when she turned the thing and found no resistance.

Pushing the door slightly, she peered inside. The entry hall towered and glittered. Her glance took in chandeliers and arched ceilings and marble tiles on the floor. On the far side of the room, she saw a silvery-haired man, reclining in a chaise, his back to her as he lifted a crystal glass to his lips.

She glanced to either side but saw no one else. She listened and heard only the soft strains of a Spanish guitar floating from a hidden speaker.

Swallowing hard, Chelsea stepped inside. She lifted the gun, leveled its barrel at the back of the man's head and moved closer. He still showed no sign he was aware of her presence. She curled her forefinger around the trigger, drew a deep breath.

"Vincent de Lorean?" she asked to be sure.

"That's correct." His voice was deep and smooth. He didn't seem surprised or even unnerved. "Come in, Chelsea. The least you can do is look me in the eye when you kill me." He rose in one smooth movement and turned to flash a brilliant white smile from beneath a thin, salt-and-pepper mustache. His deeply tanned skin didn't sport a single wrinkle or flaw. "May I offer you a drink first? From the way that gun barrel is wavering, I think you could use one."

She glanced down at her shaking hands, fought to steady them. "How do you know who I am?"

"I know," he said softly. "I have ways of knowing everything." And without batting an eye, he sipped his drink again. One hand remained casually in the pocket of his satin robe. He didn't seem the least bit nervous.

"You killed my sister." Her voice was trembling now.

He only shrugged. "A drink would really bolster you, Chelsea. They don't call it liquid courage for nothing, you know."

"I don't want any damned drink."

Again, that careless shrug, accompanied by a tilt of his head. "I suppose you should get on with it, then. You came here to kill me, I assume?"

She blinked the moisture from her eyes. She hadn't expected it to be this hard. Again, she steadied the gun, sighting the barrel at the center of his chest.

"It's going to make a terrible mess, you know. That's a rather large caliber weapon you're holding. A forty-four, I believe. You shouldn't have to fire it more than once." He took a step closer, downed the last of his drink and set the glass on a marble table. Then, with one hand, he pulled the robe open, exposing his bare chest to her. "Go ahead. Pull the hammer back. And lift the barrel just a little. Your aim seems a bit low. I'd really prefer to die right away rather than lie around with a bullet in me and suffer untold agony... wouldn't you?"

Chelsea stared at his exposed skin and imagined the bloody hole she was about to put in it. The bullet would rip right through the man's body. There would be blood. There would be a lot of blood.

She lifted the barrel.

Her hands shook even harder. Why was this so difficult? Why couldn't she just pull the trigger and end this? It was for Ethan, for Garrett and his family. She had to kill this man. She'd be doing the world a favor.

"Some would say, Chelsea, that you have a lot of your father in you. It surprises me, really. I didn't expect it. But here you are, ready to kill like a vengeful god. You've decided I'm not worthy of living, so—"

"Shut up!" She gave her head a shake, blinked again. The damned tears were blurring her vision.

"You have a killer's genes in you, Chelsea. We're a lot alike, you and I. We do what needs doing, with no—"

"I said shut up!"

She lifted the gun higher, and her finger tightened a little on the trigger. Kill him, she screamed at herself. Just do it!

"Don't act so surprised, Chelsea. You've always known there was a lot of your father in you, haven't you? Isn't that the fear that's been haunting you all your life, the fear that deep inside, you might be just like him? Isn't that what made you believe you could come here tonight and execute me for my sins?"

She bit her lip, refusing to listen to his words, refusing to consider them. She steadied the gun, put a little more pressure on the trigger . . .

She couldn't do it. There was *nothing* of her father in her, and Chelsea knew that now. She'd been afraid of the anger inside her, of the rage. She'd always had this horrible feeling she could be just as cruel, just as violent.

But she simply wasn't. And taking a life, any life, was beyond her power. Even now, with so much at stake. There had to be another way. There had to. She'd seen too much violence, too much death. She couldn't bear to be the instrument of still more.

Slowly, she lowered the gun. De Lorean's smile grew wider. "A wise decision, Chelsea," he purred. And before she'd even seen him move, he'd pulled his own gun from the deep pocket of his robe. She realized it had been aimed at her the whole time. No wonder he hadn't been afraid. "Don't lift that Magnum again, *chica*. If you do anything other than drop it on the floor, you'll find yourself in excruciating pain. I know how to inflict it. Believe me."

She swallowed hard, closed her eyes, and let the heavy weapon fall from her hands to the floor. It didn't matter now. He'd kill her anyway.

"Very good. I believe I have finally figured out how to get my son back, Chelsea. And you've helped me. I thank you for that." He grabbed her arm, bruising it with the force of his grip. He pulled her forward and shoved her down into the chaise where he'd been sitting before. "Now, if you'll just be still for a moment, I have an important call to make."

Garrett's earlier ascent upstairs had been stopped cold by the ringing of the phone. Now, he stood at the foot of the stairs, feeling sick to his stomach just from the look in Wes's eyes as his brother swore into the receiver and finally slammed it down. "What is it, Wes? Who was on the phone?"

"De Lorean."

Garrett closed his eyes.

"He has Chelsea, Garrett," Wes went on. "Says he's gonna kill her unless we hand little Ethan over to him."

Garrett's legs wouldn't hold him. He sank down onto the bottom step feeling as if all the bones in his body had just dissolved. The air rushed from his lungs.

"What else?"

"We're supposed to keep quiet. No police. No Feds, or he'll kill her anyway."

"And he'll know about it if you do report this, Garrett," Lash added. "He has enough turncoats on his payroll that he'll know. We have to handle this ourselves."

A sob from the top of the stairs drew Garrett's gaze upward. Jessi was standing there, her face colorless and damp. "Dammit, Garrett, what are we gonna do?"

"I don't know." Garrett turned back to Wes. "When is this supposed to happen?"

"He said he'd contact us in twenty-four hours to tell us where to meet him for the exchange."

That brought Garrett to his feet. "He expects me to wait that long? To leave Chelsea alone with that bastard for—"

"You have to, Garrett. You try to go after him now, you'll be signing Chelsea's death warrant." Lash paced the living room, shaking his head. "He won't kill her. Not yet, not when he sees her as the key to getting his son back."

"You sure about that?" Wes asked.

"As sure as I can be."

"I can't just wait," Garrett said tightly. "I can't just sit here and wait."

"Don't wait, Garrett." Jessi came down the stairs and slid her arms around her brother's waist from behind, hugging him hard. "Use the time to plan. We have to be ready. We have to get Chelsea out of this alive, and we all know we can't hand our sweet little Ethan over to that animal." She released him and he turned to face her. "We need help, Garrett."

"No." He answered her before she said what he knew she was going to say. "Jessi, I don't want any more people I love risking their lives over this."

"Adam and Ben will never forgive you if you don't let them help. And you'll never forgive yourself if something goes wrong. They'd be here in a heartbeat if they knew what was going on. We have to tell them, Garrett."

He shook his head.

"She's right," Wes said. "This involves all of us now, Garrett. Not just you and Chelsea. We're family. We stick together."

Garrett met Wes's eyes, and again his heart damn near burst with pride at the way his brothers and his baby sister had turned out.

"That's true," Lash said. "Even if de Lorean gets what he wants, he's going to have to get rid of everyone who knows what went down. And I'm afraid that includes all of you."

"Which is why I'm going to send them all away."

Jessi gasped. Elliot had joined them in the middle of the conversation, and as Jessi quickly brought him up to date, he stared at Garrett with accusing eyes.

"Don't argue, Elliot. You have to go. You, Wes, Jessi and little Bubba, as well. I want you all to get as far away from Texas as you can until this is over one way or another. Lash, if you had half a brain, you'd take off, as well. This is my fight. I don't want anyone else getting caught in the crossfire."

"Garrett—" Jessi began to protest.

Elliot silenced her with one hand on her arm. "Come on, sis. There's no sense talking to him when he gets like this. Let's go check on the little one."

Garrett watched them go, his heart twisting. Then he turned to Wes. "I'll book a flight for you in the morning. You can all go visit Adam in New York for a few days."

"They can go, you mean," Wes said, his voice level and deadly. "If you think you can bully me the way you can the kids, you'd better think again, brother. I'm staying. You want me on some flight out, you're gonna have to knock me out cold to get me on the plane. And we both know that won't be easy."

Lash's eyes widened a little at that.

Garrett saw it and shook his head. "What I have in size, Wes has twice in speed and pure meanness," he explained. "I'd hate like hell to have to find out who'd still be standing if we ever went at it."

"So don't force me to show you," Wes said. "I'm staying."

Garrett nodded once. He'd known Wes would argue, just hadn't been sure how hard. "It might get ugly."

"You're my brother, Garrett."

And with those four words, Garrett knew the tension between him and Wes was over. Buried. A thing of the past. One of the burdens weighing on his shoulders floated away. Too bad the remaining ones were threatening to break his back.

* * *

It was the longest night of Chelsea's life. She spent it in
a locked room with no windows and nothing on the walls
but a yellowish brown paint. The only piece of furniture
was a small, twin-size bed with a bare, striped mattress
and no pillows or blankets. An ugly room, out of place in
an opulent mansion. She guessed de Lorean used the
room especially for guests like her. Prisoners. She knew
instinctively she wasn't the first to be held here. She
cringed at the thought that Michele might have spent
endless hours in this cell-like room.

She'd heard other voices shortly after de Lorean had
dumped her here, so she knew he had brought in rein-
forcements. She'd been present when he'd placed his
threatening phone call and realized that Garrett now knew
what a fool she'd been. He knew—and he'd try to rescue
her. He would never turn Ethan over; Garrett loved that
child as if it were his own. But, God, he wouldn't stand by
and let de Lorean murder her, either. Maybe he'd call the
police. Maybe they'd bring in a SWAT team or something and storm this place. Maybe...

Chelsea closed her eyes and sank onto the bed. She
couldn't just sit here. She had to do something. She'd put
Garrett right in the middle of this, when all she'd wanted
to do was protect him. She couldn't just wait around for
him to get himself killed trying to save her.

She couldn't live through that again.

Because she loved him.

At dawn, as planned, Marisella's battered old pickup
truck pulled in close to the front porch. Garrett paced
nervously, hoping this damned plan of Lash's wouldn't
backfire. Still, he couldn't have come up with a better one.
Lash figured de Lorean probably had some men watch-

ing the place. They'd have to be doing so from a distance or they'd be obvious. So in order to send Jessi, Elliot and little Ethan to safety, they'd have to be sneaky about it. If de Lorean knew they'd moved the baby, he'd also know they were up to something. And that would put Chelsea in even greater danger.

Blue whined at the door but stayed put at Garrett's sharp command. Wes led two horses up just behind the pickup and made a big show of rubbing them down. Their true purpose was to block anyone's view. Elliot carried two suitcases and slung them into the back of the pickup before climbing in himself. He was none too happy about his forced vacation and he let Garrett know it every time he glanced his way. Jessi came out next, carrying the baby. She handed Ethan over to Elliot, then climbed in herself. They lay down in the pickup bed. Garrett spread the tarp over them. Then, as planned, Wes led the horses back to the corral and turned them loose. Garrett stood on the porch, talking to Marisella as if he'd been right there all along, doing just that. In a few minutes, Marisella climbed back into her truck and left. She would drive carefully home, pull the truck into her garage, close the door and get the kids out. They'd wait an hour, then drive to the airport and take a flight to New York. It was all arranged.

As the pickup rolled out of sight, Garrett breathed a sigh of relief. At least three of his charges were safe. Thank God. Now all he had to do was come up with a way he could single-handedly confront Vincent de Lorean and a horde of his thugs and still manage to get Chelsea out alive.

He shook his head at the enormity of the task.

Chapter 14

Garrett had never been so torn in his life. He'd always been the responsible one. The one who looked out for his family. Made sure they were all right. To let Wes come along when he pitted himself against Vincent de Lorean was going against everything he'd been practicing his whole life. To drag a stranger like Lash in on it and maybe risk his life, as well, was not something he would have considered.

But Chelsea was at risk. Dammit, if he took them along, he risked their lives, and if he didn't…if he didn't, he might just be risking Chelsea's.

The choice had been taken firmly from his hands when Wes and Lash had steadfastly insisted they were coming with him, no matter what he said or did. But he still worried.

And then, unexpectedly, the choice was dropped right back into his lap again. Wes and Lash had gone into Quinn—Wes to call Adam in New York just to be sure the kids arrived there safely. They didn't dare use the phone at the ranch because Lash had suggested it might be tapped. Lash wanted to pick up a few things from his place. Weapons, Garrett figured. Most men were more comfortable using their own guns when push came to shove. Lash was probably no different.

So Garrett was left alone in the house. He had the niggling suspicion it was fate that had arranged things this way. Garrett never had been one to argue with fate.

He sat in the rocker in the living room, holding his big denim shirt. It was the one he'd used to cover Chelsea's body with last night when they'd fallen asleep under the stars. Her scent remained on the shirt, its very softness making him think of her. He sat there, running it through his hands, pressing it to his face to inhale her fragrance.

Chelsea. She'd been hurt and he'd made a vow to himself that he'd never let that woman be hurt again. But maybe she was being hurt right now. Maybe de Lorean...

He'd kill the bastard.

Images of her frightened eyes haunted Garrett. He hoped to God this episode didn't scar her injured heart still further. Damn, it wasn't fair for one woman to have to go through so much! The crap she'd been fed all her life had left her incapable of trusting him, of loving him. Men like her father and de Lorean had robbed her, and in doing so, they'd robbed Garrett, as well. He'd been denied something more precious than life—Chelsea Brennan's heart. Garrett realized then that it wasn't her fault she couldn't feel anything for him. It was selfish of him to have let himself get so angry over it.

Didn't matter that she was incapable of loving him. Didn't matter at all. All that mattered was getting her out of this mess alive and unharmed. If de Lorean hurt her, he'd—

The telephone snapped Garrett out of the chair like a shot. He snatched up the receiver before it even finished ringing.

"Garrett Brand?"

"De Lorean," Garrett growled. "Where is Chelsea? I want to speak to her."

"Do you have my son?" de Lorean asked, that calm, smooth voice flowing through the phone lines like honey. "Are you ready to return him to me?"

"Whatever it takes." A bald-faced lie, yes. Garrett had no compunction about lying to a killer.

"Good. Now, I want you to meet me—"

"No way, de Lorean. Not until I talk to her."

There was a long pause. A ripple in the bastard's unshakable calm? "All right."

Another pause, this one brief. "Garrett?"

Every cell in his body came to life at the sound of her voice. "Chelsea, are you all right? Has he—"

"I'm sorry, Garrett. This is all my fault. I was so—"

"It's not your fault," he told her quickly. "I'm coming for you, Chelsea. It's gonna be—"

"No! Don't do this, Garrett. Don't risk your life for me. I'm not worth—"

Her words were suddenly cut off. De Lorean's voice came back on the line. "I wouldn't advise you to take the lady's advice, Brand. It could prove very unhealthy for her."

"If you hurt her, de Lorean, I swear to God—"

"You'll come alone," the man continued as if Garrett hadn't spoken. "If I get even an inkling you haven't followed my instructions to the letter, I'll put a bullet in Miss

Brennan's pretty face. The only person with you will be my son. Is that understood?''

"Perfectly."

"Good. You'll meet me in one hour at Thompson Gorge. Alone. When I have my son in my arms, I'll release Miss Brennan. Then we can all go our separate ways. Agreed?"

The creep was lying through his teeth. There was no way in hell he intended to let Garrett leave Thompson Gorge alive. The very fact he'd chosen a box canyon with only one way in and out, a place only accessible on horseback, was proof enough of that. Garrett swallowed his rage. "Agreed."

There was a click, and then the silence of a dead phone line. Garrett held the receiver in his hand for a long time. He had one chance, and one chance only. He had to get there first, find himself some cover and hope to God he could get Chelsea behind a rock before the shooting started. And he was going in alone. Leaving before Wes and Lash returned. They'd have no way of knowing where he'd headed. By the time they figured out where he'd gone, if they ever did, it would all be over.

Garrett put the phone down and crossed the room to unlock the gun cabinet.

Lash knew something was up the second he and Wes walked into the empty house. Garrett had refused to leave the house with them in case Chelsea or de Lorean called. He wouldn't have left now. Not unless...

Wes cussed, and Lash turned to see his black eyes narrow as he scanned the gun cabinet in the corner.

"What is it?"

Wes took off his Stetson and slammed it onto the back of the couch. "Some of the guns are missing. Two forty-fives and the Winchester. Dammit, de Lorean must have called early.''

"But Garrett's pickup is still out front." Lash parted the curtains to look again, just to verify he'd seen the big truck the first time.

"Come on." Wes snatched his hat and strode out of the room. Lash followed. He had an inkling, but it was confirmed when Wes stomped out the door, crossed the front lawn and stopped at the corral where the horses grazed. The scowl on Wes's face was all the confirmation Lash needed. "Garrett's horse and saddle are gone. Damn him, he's taken off on his own. I should have known better than to leave him for a second. The oversize, overprotective, damned—''

"Who the hell...?'' Lash interrupted Wes's tirade when he saw the old pickup bounding into the driveway, passengers in both the front and back.

Wes followed Lash's gaze and started swearing all over again as the pickup came to a halt and people started piling out. Two men Lash didn't recognize—one so big and blond that Lash thought he must be some out-of-time Viking, and the other smaller, but powerfully built and dark like Garrett. Then came Elliot. And Jessi.

Pretty, stubborn, long-legged Jessi, with her jaw set and her chin up high. Looked like she was ready for a fight and more than willing.

Wes continued swearing, but shut up when the two men approached, grim-faced.

Jessi made a beeline for Lash. Her hand closed on his forearm, and she stood too damned close for comfort. The last thing he needed was hot-tempered Wes thinking Lash had eyes for his little sister.

"Lash, these are my brothers, Adam and Ben," Jessi said. "Guys, this is Lash. The one I told you about.''

Oh, great, Lash thought. *More* Brand brothers. Just what he needed.

"Where's Garrett?" She turned her big brown eyes on Lash, and he thought he'd rather take on all her brothers than tell her.

"Took off on his own," Wes said, not too tactfully elbowing his way between them and taking Jessi's arm. "I'm afraid he's gone to meet de Lorean."

Her eyes widened, and the others muttered. "He'll get himself killed, Wes! Why did you let him—"

"I didn't *let* him, Jessi. He gave us the slip the second we turned our backs. You know how he is."

"What the hell are we gonna do?"

"Watch your mouth, Jessi," the Viking told her. Ben, Lash reminded himself.

"Look, we only know he didn't go too far away. He took Duke," Wes explained.

"Duke can cover a lot of ground." Jessi gnawed her lower lip…her very full and rather sensual-looking lower lip, Lash noticed, then kicked himself for noticing. She nodded twice, firmly. "Okay, we'll have to track him. Wes, you and Ben go on inside and grab some weapons. Adam and Elliot, saddle up six horses. Lash and I will take a look and see if we can spot Duke's tracks."

Adam and Ben exchanged surprised glances, maybe because of their baby sister's take-charge attitude and no-nonsense tone.

"Five horses," Wes said, not moving a muscle. "Jessi, you're staying here."

"The hell I am."

"The hell you aren't."

The two faced each other, almost nose-to-nose. "Dammit, Wes, there's not one of you who's a better shot than I am and you all know it. Not to mention that I'm the best tracker. You gonna risk Garrett's life just so you can keep your image of your innocent, helpless baby sister intact?''

"Damn straight I am."

"Fine." She crossed her arms over her chest and stared at him. "You all just saddle up and go on without me. Two minutes after you leave, I'll be heading out on my own. And the way you guys read sign, I'll probably find Garrett and this de Lorean jerk before you do. But I'm sure my big brother and I can handle it on our own. Don't you worry about us."

Damn, but she was something else, this girl. Er, woman, Lash reminded himself. But she couldn't be very old. What, twenty-two or twenty-three at the most? Really just a kid.

She sure as hell wasn't acting like a kid, though.

Wes was looking scared he might just lose this battle. "What about little Ethan?" he asked, and Lash recognized it as a last-ditch effort.

"Safe and sound with Marisella. Now are you gonna stand here arguing while Garrett gets himself killed, or are we going after him?"

"We're going after him." It wasn't Wes who spoke, but Ben—the blond one. He came forward and put an arm around Jessi's shoulders. "You've grown up, little sister."

"I'm glad *somebody* noticed," she snapped. "Now let's move. Come on, Lash. Let's go look for those tracks."

"Help the boys saddle those horses, Lash," Wes ordered. "I'll help Jes look for the trail." At his sister's killing glance, he added, "It's in my blood, sis. Don't forget I'm half-Comanche."

He sent a sideways glance at Lash that said plainly he would also be willing to scalp his enemies should the need arise. Lash swallowed hard, walked to the corral and grabbed a saddle.

Garrett crouched behind a boulder about five yards in from the canyon's entrance. A steep, rocky wall rose at his back. There was another one just like it fifty yards to his right and another one across from him. On his left was the opening—the only way in. And the only way out. That was the direction he watched. De Lorean would have to enter from there.

A couple of times, as he crouched there, Garrett heard the telltale clatter of pebbles and dirt tumbling down the canyon walls. Someone was on the ledge above, no doubt about that. Probably several someones. De Lorean's men. The back of Garrett's neck prickled, and his back felt sorely exposed. He didn't think they'd seen him yet. But if they did, he would be an easy shot. And once they saw he didn't have the baby, they wouldn't hesitate.

No breeze stirred in the canyon. It was darker here, Garrett thought, than any place on earth. No moon tonight. And though he could see a rectangle of star-dotted sky above him, its light didn't make the place any brighter. Every sound echoed endlessly. The Comanche believed the place to be bad medicine. And no wonder. Many an ambush had occurred within these towering stone walls. A lot of blood had soaked the ground here.

He looked up again, eyes scanning the rim. But it was too dark. Even if they were up there, he wouldn't be able to see them. He crouched until his thigh muscles screamed, checked his watch time and again.

Finally, ten minutes early, the headlights of a Jeep bounced into view. Garrett grimaced in surprise. De Lorean must have had the thing customized for rough terrain. No normal vehicle, even a four-wheel-drive one, could handle the trek out here. The vehicle came to a stop at the canyon's entrance. The lights remained on, effectively blinding Garrett to the people beyond them. He only knew they got out when he heard the doors slam. And then he heard de Lorean's voice.

"Brand. Are you here?"

"Turn off the lights," Garrett replied. "Or you'll never see your son."

De Lorean's laugh was low and ominous, and it bounced from the stone and rolled through the canyon. "You're in no position to be giving orders. Step out where I can see you."

Garrett drew a breath. "We can argue about it all night. I don't move until the lights go out."

"I don't think we'll argue about it at all, Brand. You see, I have Miss Brennan, and I have a very short temper. Oh, but you can't see me, can you? Well, then, listen."

Chelsea cried out. Not loudly. It was obvious she was struggling not to make a sound. But the bastard hurt her enough so the cry was torn from her throat, and Garrett's stomach clenched so hard and fast he thought he'd vomit.

If he stepped out from behind this rock, he was a dead man. The men on the rim above would pick him off so quick he'd never know what hit him. But if he remained hidden and safe, the bastard would torture Chelsea. Damn, if only he'd shut those headlights off.

Garrett eyed a group of boulders closer to the canyon's entrance and the wide stretch of coverless ground in between. If he could make it there, the lights wouldn't be in his eyes. He might be able to get a shot. But he might not

be fast enough. And for the first few yards, those headlights would make him a sitting duck. Still, he had to try.

Grating his teeth, he pushed off and ran.

True to her claim, Jessi Brand turned out to be one hell
of a tracker. They picked up the trail right away and rode
for all they were worth, only stopping when Wes held up
a hand.

The horses stopped in a cloud of dust as Wes tilted his
head in a listening posture.

"What is it?" Lash whispered.

"I heard a vehicle."

"Thompson Gorge is up ahead," Jessi said softly.
"God, Wes, Garrett wouldn't have gone in there, would
he? He'd have to know it was a trap."

"He'd go," Wes replied, his tone grim. "If it was for
Chelsea, he'd go. Dammit, de Lorean will have snipers
lining the rim of that godforsaken canyon."

"Not for long, he won't," Adam said. His eyes met
each of his brothers in turn, making his meaning clear.

Ben nodded his blond head in agreement. "We take
them out. At least give Garrett a fighting chance."

"Leave the horses here," Wes said. "We'll go in on
foot."

Elliot lifted the neatly looped rope from his saddle and
ran his hands over it. He dismounted and the others followed suit.

Lash got down, too, but his throat was suddenly very
dry. "You . . . uh . . . we aren't going to just kill them, are
we?"

Wes grinned at him. "Only if we have to. What's a
matter, Lash, you got a weak stomach?"

"Shut up, Wes," Jessi snapped. "Lash, we aren't going to kill anyone. Contrary to first impressions, the Brands are not barbarians."

"Speak for yourself, Jes," Wes returned sharply. But then his voice softened. "I don't suppose I could convince you to stay here with the horses, could I?"

Jessi shook her head firmly and poked a bullet into the chamber of her rifle to emphasize the point.

Wes sighed hard, but started off at a quick, silent pace. When they could make out the shapes of horses in the darkness ahead, Wes whispered, "Fan out. Adam and Ben, work around to the far side of the canyon. Elliot and Lash, you take the end. Jes, you and I will work in from this side. Move in and take them out fast and quiet, then move on to see if you're needed elsewhere."

"Seven horses," Jessi whispered from her crouching position on the ground. "One of us will have to handle two men. Be ready for that."

They broke up and slowly worked their way around the canyon. Lash kept one eye on young Jessi. He was worried about her, and if he'd been her brother, he thought he'd have argued harder against her coming along. Not that it would have done much good. He could still make out her form in the darkness as she crept from boulder to bush, working her way closer and closer to the canyon's edge. And when he looked off in the direction she moved, he saw a man standing there, his back to her, a rifle cradled in his arms. He shivered.

Elliot's elbow dug into Lash's rib cage. "Pay attention to your own problems, Lash. Jessi can handle herself."

Lash followed Elliot's pointed gaze and spotted two more armed men standing at the lip, about ten yards apart.

Lash swallowed hard and started off after the closest man. He only turned once when he heard a soft, whirring sound. Then he saw Elliot's rope sail through the night, settle around the second man, and jerk sharply backward. The man was yanked off his feet, landing hard on his back with a low grunt. Before he could utter a cry, Elliot had pounced on him. Lash heard the thud of knuckles connecting with flesh just once. The guy didn't move again.

Lash wanted to check on Jessi, but there was no time. He moved forward rapidly, and grabbed the man hard, one hand covering his mouth, the other pressing the gun barrel into his spine. "Not a sound, pal, or you'll be singing with the angels."

The man nodded. Lash liberated the man from his weapon, then snatched the duct tape from his belt and managed to tear a strip off with his teeth. He sealed the man's lips, then bound him hand and foot and left him on the ground. He quickly made his way back to where Jessi was just moving up on her target. He wasn't close enough to intervene, though he tried to hurry.

She moved like a panther, he thought as he watched her in awe. Those long limbs stretched out to bring her closer and closer to her prey, soundless and deadly. Not a hint of hesitation or fear. But damn, he couldn't stand to see it and not try to help. He moved still faster and stepped on a twig. The snap seemed as loud as cannon fire. The man whirled on Lash, gun raised. Jessi launched herself at him. She landed on his back, knocking him facedown in the dirt, and his gun skidded away from him. She gave him one sharp crack on the head with the butt end of her rifle.

Voices floated up from below. De Lorean's. Garrett's. Then Chelsea cried out in pain.

Jessi ran to the edge, and Lash followed just in time to see Garrett's fully illuminated form rush out from behind some rocks right into the open. From the corner of his eye, Lash spotted movement and turned to see another sniper raising his rifle, sighting in on Garrett. Lash took a single step, but it was unnecessary. A huge knife sailed out of nowhere, flying end over end and sinking deep between the sniper's shoulder blades. The man groaned and sank to his knees. The rifle fell at his feet. Wes stepped out from behind some brush, came forward, bent down and yanked the bowie knife from the dead man's back. Then he calmly wiped the bloody blade clean on a patch of crabgrass before replacing it in his boot.

Below, in the canyon, Garrett dived behind another group of boulders.

"You're trying my patience, Brand!" De Lorean's voice rang clearly from below, and then Chelsea screamed again.

"Come on," Wes whispered. "Let's get over to the other side. That bastard keeps hurting her, Garrett's gonna lose it and probably get himself killed."

The four of them ran around the back of the canyon, then crept up the other side. They only halted when they spotted Adam and Ben surrounded by four, not three, of de Lorean's goons.

"Damn, I must have missed a horse! I only counted seven sets of tracks!" Jessi shouldered her rifle. Lash saw her. Everyone else was too busy watching the fight. Seemed he was the only one whose eyes were constantly on Jessi. He covered her hands with his and pushed the gun down. "If de Lorean hears a shot, he might kill Chelsea then and there, Jes."

Wes's head snapped around. "He's right. The only way we can help Adam and Ben is if we can get close enough to jump the bastards."

"Help Ben, you mean," Elliot whispered as they all moved closer. "Look."

A meaty fist had connected with Adam's jaw, and he'd fallen backward, his head hitting a boulder. He didn't move again.

"I'll kill that oversize son of a—"

Jessi's threat was cut off then, because Ben seemed to launch himself into the air, kicking high with one leg, snapping one man's head back so hard Lash thought he'd broken the guy's neck. When he landed, Ben ducked another blow, rolled, sprang to his feet and grabbed another man. The man flew through the air and landed with a heavy thud. Ben never stopped moving. He whirled like a maddened dervish, and with his foot, *his foot,* he delivered so many rapid-fire, hard blows to the face that his lumberjack-size opponents were left teetering and blinking and dazed. And then, one by one they collapsed.

Ben lowered his hands to his sides, turned and bent over his brother. The others joined him there.

"Just what in the Sam Hill was *that?*" Wes demanded. But he, too, bent over the unconscious Adam, examining the cut on his head. "I've never seen a guy as big as you move like that!"

"Just something I picked up," Ben said. "Never thought I'd have to use it in a fight, though."

"What the hell else would you use it for?"

Ben lifted his pain-filled eyes to meet Wes's. "Peace," he said softly.

Lash knew, because Jessi had told him, about Ben's short marriage to the woman he'd known was dying from the day he'd met her. And he knew Ben had taken off right after he'd buried his young wife. Gone into seclusion in the wilds of Tennessee.

"Did it work?" Wes asked, his voice soft, husky.

Ben lowered his eyes. "Not yet."

Adam groaned a little, and his eyes fluttered open.

"You'd best not spend too much more time in New York City," Wes said, gripping his hand and pulling him to his feet. "It's making you soft."

"He caught me by surprise," Adam argued, but he looked rather sheepish as he dusted himself off.

From below in the canyon, Chelsea cried out again, and every eye turned in that direction.

"We'd better get down there," Jessi said. "And we'd better make it fast."

Chapter 15

De Lorean held Chelsea to his chest in a crushing grip, his head bent close to her ear. "He's surrounded, you know. But you'd already guessed that, hadn't you? That's why you're trying so hard to keep quiet. Isn't it, Chelsea Brennan? That's why you've bitten your lip until it bleeds, because you know the second he steps into the open he's a dead man. He's going to join all the others who've died here in this canyon down through the ages. The Comanches say it's haunted, you know. They say the spirits of the murdered still linger here."

He'd twisted her arm behind her back, trying to make her cry out. Trying to make her scream, so Garrett would step out of the sheltering rocks. And she'd grated her teeth, refusing to make a sound. Until she'd felt the popping of her shoulder, and her cry had been wrenched from her unwilling lips.

Garrett lunged from the cover of the boulders and dashed across an open expanse, and she would have shouted a warning if de Lorean's hand hadn't been clamped firmly over her mouth. His paw covered her nose, as well, and she couldn't draw a breath. But the panic of not being able to breathe paled beside her fear for Garrett. She kept her gaze on him as he ran, fully expecting to see him cut down at any second. But somehow... somehow he made it. He dived behind another cluster of boulders, this one not bathed in white light as the other had been.

De Lorean's hand on her mouth eased its pressure, and she dragged a gulp of air into her lungs, then released it slowly in relief. She felt de Lorean's head moving as he scanned the ledge above, and he cursed in hot whispers that made her skin crawl. Why hadn't his men fired at Garrett? It was obvious he'd expected them to.

Her shoulder screamed, though the pressure on it had eased. Her eyes watered, making it even harder to see through the inky darkness to where Garrett now crouched.

De Lorean seemed to compose himself. He straightened a little, turning slightly so her body still remained directly between him and the boulders sheltering Garrett. A human shield, she thought, and hoped that wouldn't stop Garrett from shooting. He ought to shoot right through her to get this bastard.

But Garrett wouldn't. He was no more like her father than she was. She accepted that knowledge slowly, with dawning wonder, though she guessed she'd known it all along. Garrett was nothing like her father. Nothing like de Lorean. Nothing like any other man she'd ever known. She'd thought she could never love a man because of all she'd witnessed of that gender. But she'd been wrong.

"Very impressive, Brand," De Lorean called, not so loudly as before since Garrett was closer. "But I didn't see my son cradled in your arms as you sprinted past. And unless I see him soon, Miss Brennan is going to join her sister in heaven.''

Garrett said nothing, didn't make a sound. Chelsea was glad. No use in his giving those killers above anything to shoot at—not even the sound of his voice.

Then de Lorean wrenched her already-throbbing arm still higher behind her back. She hadn't been expecting that, and she cried out again, but quickly bit down on the scream. Damn! The fingers of her right hand were within reach of her left ear, and they were tingling and slowly going numb. Sweat popped out on her face, trickling into her eyes, and pain made her breathing quick and shallow. It hurt! The entire right-half of her torso was on fire. Even drawing too deep a breath brought more intense pain.

De Lorean gave one more tug, and dizziness swamped her. Her stomach convulsed, and her inability to move with the spasm only resulted in more agony. She thought she was going to vomit soon.

"You'll never see your son unless you let her go. Now, de Lorean! Let her go!"

So he could see her now. She realized that, and as she did, she lifted her head and straightened up as much as her captor would allow and tried to force her facial muscles to relax. She didn't want to look as if she were suffering. She didn't want to do anything to help the lowlife who held her.

"You didn't bring him, did you, Brand?" de Lorean observed flatly. "I should have known better than to trust you."

"De Lorean—"

"Pity. Now I'll have to kill you both. I, you see, *am* a man of my word." He lifted his gun to the side of Chelsea's head. She felt the cold steel, the circular shape of the barrel pressing tight to her scalp.

"No!" Garrett leaped out of his hiding place and ran forward.

In slow motion, it seemed, de Lorean's gun swung toward him, away from Chelsea, and his other arm fell away from her, as well. Leaving her free to sink to her knees in agony, or to run for her life. And in the split second she had to decide which to do, she knew that had been Garrett's intention all along. To distract de Lorean and give her the chance to escape. To take the violence that was directed at her, to take it himself in her place.

Just the way her mother had done.

Rage filled her and escaped in the form of a tortured cry that sounded only half-human as it split the night and echoed from the canyon walls.

Chelsea hurled herself at de Lorean while her battle cry still floated skyward, and at the instant she hit him, the gun he held spit fire and death. An earsplitting explosion was followed by the acrid scent of sulfur. Garrett jerked backward, his eyes wide, then closing as he staggered, teetered and fell like a giant redwood. Chelsea screamed, clinging to de Lorean's back, kicking and clawing him with renewed vigor. De Lorean wrenched her free and slammed her to the ground. She landed on her wounded shoulder, the wind knocked out of her, and fought for breath even as she scrambled to her feet again. De Lorean walked forward slowly until he stood right over Garrett's big, prostrate form.

"Where is my son, you bastard!"

But Garrett didn't answer.

"Die, then," the monster said, and he pointed the barrel downward.

She couldn't get there in time. She couldn't...

Two things happened at once. A knife came flipping through the dark, and a lasso sailed into view. The blade embedded itself in de Lorean's right arm, and he screamed aloud even as the lasso settled around him and was pulled tight. His gun fell and landed on Garrett's chest, and Chelsea wondered for a moment if the spirits said to haunt this place had come to Garrett's aid.

Then with a jerk of that spectral rope, the criminal was yanked right off his feet. He landed with a thud and a grunt. And as Chelsea looked on, shocked, forms took shape in the darkness. She only realized they were actual human beings when she heard a voice she recognized.

And then it didn't matter. She ran forward to where Garrett had fallen, and flung herself on him, heedless of the raw pain slicing her shoulder to ribbons. The tears she cried dampened his face. But there was more on his face than just her tears. Blood. Lots of blood. So much she couldn't even see his features. God, he'd been shot in the head. Chelsea went cold all over as nightmarish memories swamped her. For an instant she was a frightened little girl again, clinging to the lifeless body of her mother. That same sickening horror engulfed her now as she realized that her worst fears had come true. Garrett had stepped in to protect her, just as her mother had. And just as her mother had, he'd . . .

"No," she whispered. She gripped his shoulders, shaking him. "No, Garrett. Not this time. Not you, too!"

A warm hand closed on her shoulder. "Easy, Chelsea," Wes said softly, bending over her, touching his brother with his other hand. "He's still alive."

Chelsea collapsed on Garrett's chest, sliding her arms beneath him and holding him to her as she sobbed in a terrifying mixture of relief and fear. "Please, Garrett.

Please be all right. Just open your eyes and tell me you're all right."

But he didn't. And it took several pairs of hands to pull her away from his still body so his brothers could get close enough to inspect the damage, stanch the blood flow, then lift him into de Lorean's Jeep.

Jessi was there, climbing into the back with Garrett. And Lash, who told her he could help. Wes firmly guided Chelsea to the passenger seat, though she'd wanted to climb into the back with Garrett. Then Wes went to the driver's side and started the vehicle.

He shouted at his brothers through the open window. "Hog-tie that bastard and get him into town. Lock him up and notify the Rangers. If I stick around here, I'm liable to kill him. Leave the others. One's dead, and the rest will keep. They aren't going anywhere."

"Don't worry, Wes, we can handle them. Take care of Garrett," Elliot replied, sounding older than he ever had.

And then the Jeep was bounding over the trackless ground.

"...hospital," Jessi was whispering in the back.

"Moving him any more than we have to is liable to kill him, Jes," Lash argued gently. "We can't even see how bad the damage is! Let's get him to the house and call for help."

Chelsea turned in her seat, reaching over it to lay a hand on Garrett's face. She had to touch him, to cling to him, as if doing so could somehow keep him from leaving her. She closed her eyes, a feeling of dread such as she'd never known settling in the pit of her stomach. She couldn't live with another death on her conscience. She simply couldn't. And she found she didn't really want to. Not without Garrett.

Something was pressed into her free hand, and she glanced down to see a cellular phone. De Lorean's.

"Call for help, Chelsea," Wes instructed. "Tell them to meet us at the ranch."

She blinked up at the hoarse tone of Wes's voice and saw unashamed tears glistening on his dark lashes.

"I'm sorry," she whispered.

"Sorry?" He shook his head and reached for her, stroking the hair away from her face with a gentleness that surprised her. "Hell, Chelsea, he'd have been dead for sure if it hadn't been for you. De Lorean had him point-blank when you jumped on him. You saved my brother's life. I'm not gonna forget that any time soon. None of us are."

"B-but...if it wasn't for me, he wouldn't be...he *shouldn't*. Why didn't he just..." Her throat closed then, making it impossible to speak.

"Because it isn't in him, that's why."

Wes's hand touched her good shoulder, squeezed a little. It reminded her of the way she might have touched her own sister once upon a time. A reassuring shoulder squeeze—sometimes it worked wonders.

"Now stop your blubbering and make the call, okay?" He sniffed and took his hand away to knuckle his own eyes dry.

Garrett's head seemed to be engulfed in a cloud of pain. The waves of throbbing encompassed his skull and even reached down into the base of his neck. He couldn't pin-point the epicenter from which the waves emanated. It hurt *everywhere*. And his brain didn't seem to be functioning on all eight cylinders. Because it was a full minute before he heard the soft crying, and he still wasn't sure where it was coming from. And it was still longer before he smelled the combination antiseptic-and-mothball aroma that seemed to cling to Doc wherever he went, or felt a pair of old, leathery hands pressing against his head and causing even more pain.

It took even longer for him to think to open his eyes, and when he did, it took a while for his eyes to get the message.

"He was lucky," Doc was saying in his thick Spanish accent. "The bullet, it only grazed him. Lots of blood, but little damage."

"Guess we can call off the medevac chopper," said a voice that sounded an awful lot like his brother Ben.

"Hell, I can still use it. I think that jerk broke my jaw," said another, that sounded an awful lot like his brother Adam.

"So maybe you'll learn to duck when some Neanderthal takes a swing at you." Ah, now that voice made more sense. Wes.

"Now, Señorita Brennan," Doc said, "you will let me take a look at that shoulder of yours. And I will not take no for an answer this time."

"But, Doctor, he's still unconscious." Ah, that was Chelsea's voice. The one he'd been waiting to hear. He sighed inwardly in relief. "Surely if it's only a graze and not serious, he should be awake by now."

Gee, she sounded awfully worried about him. He tried to smile at the thought, but wasn't sure if his facial muscles responded or not.

"That bullet hit him like a hammer, Chelsea," Jessi said softly. "He probably has a concussion, but—"

"But nothing. I want him in a hospital! I want him x-rayed and CAT scanned and—"

"Garrett, he will be fine," Doc said. "His head is harder than the brick."

"You're hurt, Chelsea," Jessi coaxed. "Let Doc have a look at you."

That was Jessi, all right. Always... Wait a minute. Hurt? Chelsea was hurt?

Garrett's eyes opened wide, and he found it wasn't quite the struggle it had been before. He fought to bring the room into focus. Not his room. The living room. He was at home at the ranch, sprawled on the couch like a sack of feed.

Wetness coated his palm, and he shifted his focus to see ol' Blue licking his hand. The dog looked back at him and whined.

"Garrett?" Chelsea dropped to her knees right in front of him. He was relieved. Shifting his eyes around looking for her was making him dizzy. "Garrett, you're awake."

Tear tracks marred her beautiful face, and her hair was even wilder than usual. Her swollen, puffy eyes searched his face, and she lifted one hand to his cheek. Her other arm hung oddly. She sort of clutched it against her side. And her shoulder looked funny.

"You..." He licked his lips, swallowed hard and tried again. "You hurt?"

"No. I wrenched my arm a little, but it's fine. No big deal."

He didn't think he believed her. But he had to know everything. "Bubba?" he asked when his painful scan of the room didn't produce any signs of the child.

"Marisella just arrived with him, Garrett. He's upstairs napping. She's watching over him. He's fine. Just fine."

"De Lorean?" Garrett asked, angry that it took so much work to make his lips move.

"In jail where he belongs," Wes said. "And you can have all the time you want with your girlfriend here, big brother, but not until Doc takes a look at that shoulder of hers. And that's an order!"

Garrett frowned at her, gave her a nod, or tried to. "Go." Reluctantly, Chelsea took her hand away from Garrett's face and rose. Doc led her away, and Garrett tried to focus on Wes again, but found it difficult. Things were blurry and tough to look at for long. "Thought I heard the boys. Adam and Ben..."

"That's because we're here," Adam said, and took Chelsea's former position beside the couch. "You didn't really think Jessi and Elliot would follow orders, did you?"

"And lucky for you they didn't, you big lug," Ben added, leaning over the couch from behind so that his shaggy blond hair hung forward. "Don't tell me you didn't know there were snipers lining that ridge."

Garrett smiled, but it felt as if only one side of his mouth was working. "Wondered...why they didn't...pick me off."

"'Cause we picked them off first," Ben told him. "And don't think baby sis didn't get in on the act. She made at least one guy sorry he messed with this family."

"Yeah," Jessi said from somewhere beyond Garrett's range of vision. "Might say I Branded him."

Laughter surrounded him. Garrett relaxed a little because that sound—his sister and his brothers laughing in this living room—told him more than anything else ever could that everything was really all right. Finally all right.

"That's it, Garrett," Ben said, his voice softening. "You go on back to sleep. Just don't expect me to carry you up to your room. A hernia, I don't need."

Another round of laughter. This punctuated by a happy whine from Blue and the sound of Ethan's gurgles as Marisella brought him down the stairs. He heard Chelsea speaking softly with Doc in the background. The kitchen, maybe. She sounded just fine.

And he fell into a contented sleep.

"Good," she said. "You're awake."

He blinked, noting first that Chelsea wore a sling on her arm, and then that she was freshly showered and dressed, and that her hair was tamed down a bit. He slanted his gaze toward the window. Late morning at the earliest. Gosh, how long had he slept?

"Chelsea..." He stopped himself, noticing as he sat up that there was a suitcase on the floor beside her chair. His heart hurt worse than his head. And *that* was saying something.

"I wanted to talk to you before I left. I've been waiting for hours."

She'd been crying. Not violently or hysterically like yesterday. But the signs were there. Her eyes started swimming again, even as he watched her.

"That's good, because I want to talk to you, too. I want to tell you—"

"Wait." She held up her good hand, and he fell silent. She bit her lip, looked ceilingward, took a deep breath. "Just let me get this out, okay?"

"Okay." He leaned back on his pillows.

"I need..." She cleared her throat and met his eyes again. "I need to thank you, Garrett."

"I'm the sheriff, Chelsea. It's my job to rescue—"

"No, not for that."

He frowned, but waited.

"Garrett, before I met you I thought...I thought every man I ever met would turn out to be just like my father. You showed me...how wrong I was about that."

"That's good to know."

"I was angry at first that all that... that courting you did was only an act. Just a ploy to keep me and Ethan here where we were safe. But even so—"

"Now hold on a minute! I—"

"Please, will you just let me finish?"

He stared at her, jaw gaping, and decided it could wait. Maybe. At least until she'd let him get a word in edgewise. He lifted his hand, palm up, to tell her to go on.

She sighed, pushing her good hand through her hair. She rose from her chair and paced the room. "There's more. I also never thought I could trust a man enough to... enough to be with him... the way we were the other night. But you showed me that I could."

Silence wouldn't cut it anymore. "Chelsea, you tried to make me believe it didn't mean anything. But I was your first, wasn't I?"

She nodded. "I lied. It meant something. But you really have to be quiet, Garrett, or I'm never going to get to the point here."

"I'm trying." He smiled at her, and she closed her eyes as if in pain. "Is it your arm?" he asked, suddenly concerned.

"No. The arm is fine, just a dislocated shoulder. Doc gave me something for the pain."

"Then why do you look like you're still hurting?"

She opened her eyes, licked her lips. "Quiet."

"I'm quiet. Go on."

She cleared her throat, then turned her back to him, pretending to look out the window. "I didn't think I could ever love a man," she said softly.

"Dammit, Chelsea, it doesn't matter." He flung back the covers and swung his feet to the floor and, gripping the arm of the couch, stood up. "It's selfish of me to ask you to. I don't care, Chelsea Brennan." He went up behind her, gripped her good shoulder and bent his head low, speaking soft and close to her ear. "I don't care if you can't love me the way I love you. I'll take whatever you can give and count myself lucky to have it, honey. If only you'll stay."

Chelsea went utterly still. It was as if she'd frozen in place. "I thought," she whispered, still not turning to face him, "that I asked you to keep quiet and let me finish." Her voice wavered, and Garrett figured it was damned near time to give up hope. She was gonna shoot him down here and now.

"Sorry," he told her, giving her shoulder one last squeeze. "I had to get it said."

"I was trying to tell you, Garrett, that I never thought I could love a man." She turned very slowly, and when she looked up into his eyes, hers were brimming with tears. A shaky smile toyed with her lips. "But you proved me wrong once again. Because I do. I love you, Garrett Ethan Brand."

The grin that split his face must have been a mile wide. Sure as hell felt like it was.

"Hot damn! You do?"

She nodded.

And Garrett kissed her like he'd never stop. But he did stop. Because he wasn't finished talking yet. There was one more thing that needed to be said.

He lifted his head, clasped her hand in his and lowered himself down on one knee. "You belong here, Chelsea. Do you know that yet? You're good for this family, and I think the Brands are good for you, too. I want... I want you to marry me, Chelsea. I want you to stay right here on the Texas Brand as my wife, and I want Bubba to be my boy. I'll love the two of you like nobody else ever could. I'll make you happy. I promise you that."

She smiled down at him as her tears spilled over. "I'm gonna hold you to that promise, Garrett. Forever."

"Forever," he echoed, and then he pulled her into his arms.

* * * * *

INTIMATE MOMENTS®
Silhouette®

COMING NEXT MONTH

Assignment:
R♥MANCE

by
Cathryn Clare

The Cotter brothers—two private detectives and an
FBI agent—go wherever danger leads them...except
in matters of the heart!

But now they've just gotten the toughest assignments of
their lives....

Wiley Cotter has...
THE WEDDING ASSIGNMENT: March 1996
Intimate Moments #702

Sam Cotter takes on...
THE HONEYMOON ASSIGNMENT: May 1996
Intimate Moments #714

Jack Cotter is surprised by...
THE BABY ASSIGNMENT: July 1996
Intimate Moments #726

Assignment:
R♥MANCE

From Cathryn Clare—and only where
Silhouette Books are sold!

INTIMATE MOMENTS®
Silhouette®

CCAR1

Silhouette's recipe for a sizzling summer:

* Take the best-looking cowboy in South Dakota
* Mix in a brilliant bachelor
* Add a sexy, mysterious sheikh
* Combine their stories into one collection and you've got one sensational super-hot read!

Summer Sizzlers

MEN OF Summer

Three short stories by these favorite authors:

Kathleen Eagle
Joan Hohl
Barbara Faith

Available this July wherever
Silhouette books are sold.

Look us up on-line at: http://www.romance.net

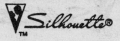

**The wedding celebration was so nice...
too bad the bride wasn't there!**

Runaway Brides

Find out what happens when three brides have a change of heart.

Three complete stories by some of your favorite authors—all in one special collection!

YESTERDAY ONCE MORE
by Debbie Macomber

FULL CIRCLE
by Paula Detmer Riggs

THAT'S WHAT FRIENDS ARE FOR
by Annette Broadrick

Available this June wherever books are sold.

Silhouette®
™

SREQ696